Playing

Playing

Melanie Abrams

Black Cat
New York
a paperback original imprint of Grove/Atlantic, Inc.

Published simultaneously in Canada
Printed in the United States of America

FIRST EDITION

ISBN-10: 0-8021-7047-1
ISBN-13: 978-0-8021-7047-7

Black Cat
a paperback original imprint of Grove/Atlantic, Inc.
841 Broadway
New York, NY 10003

Distributed by Publishers Group West

www.groveatlantic.com

08 09 10 11 12   10 9 8 7 6 5 4 3 2 1

For Vikram

Playing

CHAPTER ONE

WHEN THE TWO O'CLOCK BELL RANG, KIDS SWARMED THE ELEMENTARY school pickup zone, their backpacks dragging on the warm asphalt or slung upside down on their tummies. Tyler was usually one of the last children to arrive, but today he ran to the car and waved an orange construction-paper leaf in Josie's face. "We made leaves," he said. "There are deciduous trees and evergreen trees." He held it out to her. "This is from a deciduous tree."

"That's great, Ty," she said, and took it. He had drawn brown spidery veins down the middle, and on each point of the leaf was carefully printed the letters of his name. "Did you write this by yourself?"

"Of course," he said, and snatched the leaf back. "And I cut it with left-handed scissors." He climbed in the backseat and buckled himself beside the baby. "Twelve more days of first grade," he said. "Where's Mommy?"

"Home getting ready for the party tonight." Josie looked in the rearview mirror and watched Tyler scowl.

"It's Friday," he said.

"I know, but today we had to make an exception to the rule," she said.

"But it's Friday."

She looked back again and tried to change the subject. "How big is Australia again?"

"Australia is two point nine six million square miles and is located on the Indo-Australian Plate," he said.

"Wow, that's a lot of space."

"China is over three point four seven million square miles and has one point two eight four billion people as inhabitants," he said, and kicked the back of her seat in time with the syllables.

"Tell me more," she said. It wasn't the best way to avoid a tantrum, but it was one way, and she was too tired from reading about the burial rituals of the Konkomba all night to try any of the recommended "positive coping skills."

Josie hadn't wanted to be a nanny. She had moved from Santa Barbara to North Carolina and into the graduate dorms—small, cramped spaces with a shared kitchen and antiseptic-smelling bathrooms—and holed up with her books. She liked her classmates, went running every weekend with a girl from Boston, ate breakfast once a week with the head graduate TA, and she had met guys—slept with a graduate student in library science who could compare every part of her body to food (her hair was like honey, her eyes like the inside of a kiwi)—but she felt temporary and untethered. Then in October of her second year, she had been assigned Tyler's first-grade class for her Ethnographic Research Methods seminar and everything had changed.

She was ill the day sites were chosen, and later tried to convince the professor to change her topic. But the professor told her it was only one small paper and it would be good for her to branch out early in her career. Perhaps, he said, she would find out her interests lay beyond corpses and coffins. She had gritted her teeth and said nothing. She was a second-year graduate student but had been researching for years— books on the burial rituals of the Ewe of the Volta Region and the Ga of Accra—and she had spent the previous summer at the University of Ghana at Legon, studying and doing preliminary research alongside the program director. She was twenty-seven, not one of these fresh-out-of-college kids with notions of discovering the missing link. But she accepted the assignment and told herself to think of it as a kind of test; if she could put up with fifteen hours of the alphabet song, she would prove herself worthy of higher pursuits. So she sat in the corner with the coats and the lunchboxes thinking Tyler just one of the many towheaded boys who kicked their sneakers against the table legs and peeled the paper wrappers from his crayons. But on her second day, Tyler approached her after lunch and said, "This classroom is twenty-four feet by twenty-five feet and three inches." He stood so close, he was almost on top of her shoes, and he looked at the ground and fumbled with the measuring tape in his hands.

"And the ceiling has seventy-four tiles on it," she said. He froze and then looked up and at her right shoulder.

"How do you know that?" he asked.

"I counted," she said. He didn't say anything else, just stood there pursing his lips and pulling on his zipper until Mrs. Grayson told him to take his seat. But after that, he began seeking her out. The bell would ring for recess and he would hurry to her chair and spout distances as if they were observations on the weather. Mrs. Grayson would try to talk him into going to the playground and, when that didn't work, try to physically pull him away, but the truth was, Josie didn't mind. "It's okay," she finally said. "Let him stay." There was something calming about the emotionless hum of his numbers. She would sit in her chair and go through her notes and listen to fact after fact play reliably in the background.

This went on for a week until one morning Tyler dragged his mother into the classroom. Mary was pale and dark-eyed with a halo of black curls, and although she looked nothing like her own mother, Josie was struck by their similarity—the vast amount of space they seemed to occupy despite their small frames.

"So you're the infamous Josie," Mary said. "I'm Tyler's mother . . ."

"She's a doctor," Tyler said. "And that's my sister Madeline," he said, pointing to the baby in Mary's arms.

". . . and we need a nanny."

"Oh . . . no," Josie had said. "I'm a graduate student." But Mary persisted, said that their last nanny had been a graduate student and couldn't she at least take Josie out for coffee to discuss it? She grabbed Josie's hand and pleaded, and Josie felt all Mary's confidence pressing into her palm like a warm penny.

So they walked down to the coffee shop on the corner, Tyler scuffing his shoes against the curb, Josie awkwardly holding the baby's diaper bag, and Mary charming Josie with stories about her stint as an encyclopedia salesgirl in college.

She was just like Josie's mother, who could hold an entire room's attention just by clearing her throat, could get even the tightest-lipped strangers to share their secrets. People adored her, adjusted their schedule around her elaborate themed parties—A White Christmas in December (complete with manufactured snow and sleigh rides), the Black and White Ball in April, and Josie's favorite, because of the snow-cone machine and petting zoo, the Morgan Backyard Carnival in August. At the fancier events, Josie was allowed to come for appetizers and then put to bed. Often her cousin Natalie would also stay the night, and the two of them would sneak out to the stair landing and sit with their nightgowns pulled over their knees and watch the festivities. "Let's count the drunk people," Natalie would say, but Josie would shake her head. "Let's send down a paper airplane with a message," Natalie would try, but Josie would ignore her and, if that didn't work, elbow her quickly in the ribs and send her sulking back to bed. Josie wanted to watch her mother, watch her enchant her many admirers with just the turn of her head, a hand on a lapel. Josie's father was always close by, ready to refill her wineglass or light her cigarette—the perpetual suitor. It was spectacular, her mother's magnetism—all that power so effortlessly exposed. "Your mother should have been born a French princess," her mother's sister, Aunt Steffi, would say, and Josie would nod solemnly, a bit terrified at the vision of her mother in her tennis whites shouting "Off with their heads!"

But unlike her mother, who even her father admitted was sometimes too "self-possessed," Mary's self-assurance seemed to radiate to those around her. At the coffee shop, Mary bought Josie a coffee and a cinnamon roll. They sat at a cramped table and Mary told Josie how she was researching the human immune response to tuberculosis, how most Americans weren't even aware that TB was making a comeback. Her hands fluttered when she spoke, and once she gripped Josie's knee for emphasis, and there was something about the way she placed her hand on Josie, the way she dipped her chin and looked intently, that created an unexplainable swell of softness in Josie's stomach. So after the second coffee date, Josie relented and came and looked at the sunny room with a bay window that she could have for only twenty-five hours of work a week. And after their third date, a late dinner with too many glasses of wine, Mary told Josie the story of her divorce—the cheating husband, the unexpected second pregnancy, her ex's complete disappearance after he was served with the child support order—and Josie handed over her references and soon found herself packing her things and moving into the extra bedroom.

At first it was strictly twenty-five hours a week and no weekends—a perfect part-time job, especially in preparation for June when she would have no classes and only be reading for exams for a year. Mary was in the lab more than fifty hours, but the baby could go to the university day care, and Tyler had school. Soon, though, Mary was asking for just a few more hours, just one extra errand, and Josie was glad to concede. After all, Mary was generous with Josie. She gave her books on West African art, picked her up an extra lipstick at the department store, brought home grocery store tabloids because Josie confessed they were her guilty pleasure. So even when the requests increased, Josie reasoned, it was really a partnership. Mary liked doing things for Josie, and Josie liked doing things for Mary, but perhaps even more true was that Josie liked the velvety blanket of Mary's attention. Mary smoothed Josie's hair and Josie wanted to pick up Mary's dry cleaning, make her tea, organize her office.

And there was Tyler. He had crept into her affections. He was a peculiar little kid, and he had fallen for Josie. Her third week at the house, Josie had cut a basket of strawberries into inch-long pieces and let Tyler carefully dip each into chocolate. It made him deliriously happy—all that dipping and placing, dipping and placing—and after, he had snuggled up to Josie on the couch and astounded Mary. Tyler did not take to people, and he certainly did not cuddle them; he rarely let his mother that close to him. For whatever reason, Mary said, Tyler had chosen Josie. And the way Mary said it—like she was bestowing a blessing—and the way Tyler felt against Josie's side—firm and unwavering—made Josie believe that perhaps she had found something good and solid.

Now Josie pulled into the driveway and honked the horn, and Mary came out to help with the groceries for tonight—a dinner party for nine people. Nine people and a man named Devesh Khanna. Devesh, who the dinner party was really for. Devesh, for whom Mary had composed ten different e-mails before impulsively picking up the phone and calling. He was a trauma surgeon at the teaching hospital where Mary worked and had first called Mary to consult on a case. "The patient was febrile and not responding to first-line treatment," Mary told Josie excitedly. "He wanted to know what drug regimen to give!"

Josie had finally met him last Thursday when she and the children had gone to pick up Mary from the hospital. He had been waiting with Mary on the quad, and when Josie pulled up, Mary made Josie get out of the car to meet him. He was dark-skinned and stood close enough to Mary to graze her briefcase with his stiff white shirt cuff. Josie looked at him, looked at Mary, and felt a prick of apprehension at the base of her spine. "You're the children's nanny?" he had asked. "Josie's more than a nanny," Mary answered, but Devesh had fastened onto the idea. "More than a nanny," he smiled. "Is that what it said in the job description?" Josie tried to laugh politely but was grateful when Tyler interrupted. "Africa is more than eleven point five million square miles, that's twenty percent of the earth's surface," he said. "Its highest point is Uhuru Point at nineteen thousand three hundred and forty feet." Mary quickly got in the car and rolled up the window.

Later that night, Mary had sat on Josie's bed and peppered her with questions: wasn't he cute, didn't he have the darkest eyes, wasn't his accent sexy? "Yeah," Josie had said indifferently and tried to change the subject. "You're just jealous," Mary said, and Josie, incredulous, had asked, "Of him?" "No, of me," Mary said and looked at Josie coyly. Josie rolled her eyes, but she could feel the blush spreading upward from her neck.

Now, Mary opened the backseat door, and Josie took a deep breath and tried to sound convincing. "Damn, I forgot the coffee." She'd been shopping all afternoon, found the organic basil and Chilean wine, the two dozen white tulips and filigreed place cards Mary had insisted upon, but she had purposefully forgotten the coffee. She wanted to go to the coffee shop and just sit by herself, an hour free of sticky juice boxes and *The Wheels on the Bus* CD.

"Don't worry about it, we'll use the grocery store stuff," Mary said.

"No, it's okay, I'll go."

"That's silly. No one can tell the difference." Mary unbuckled Madeline from her car seat and hoisted her onto her hip.

"Ow," Mary said, and grabbed for the baby's hand. "Not the hair."

"I know, it's her new thing. If you make her laugh, she lets go." Josie blew into Maddy's face and she broke into a wave of giggles and batted her hands at Josie.

"Smart girl," Mary said and kissed Maddy on the head.

"Twelve more days of first grade, Mommy!" Tyler said.

"That's great, Ty," Mary said.

Josie grabbed two bags and followed Mary into the house. "Do you . . . mind if I go to the coffee shop?"

Mary looked at her and readjusted the baby on her hip.

"I won't if you don't want me to," Josie said.

"No, you go." Mary dug in her purse and pulled out a twenty.

"I have money," Josie said.

"Take it," Mary said.

Josie hesitated, and Mary pushed the bill into her hand. "Get a smoothie or something."

Josie looked at her feet but took the money. "All right . . . well, thanks," she said.

"Be back by four, okay?"

Josie nodded and walked down the block toward the coffee shop.

Every time Mary insisted on giving her extra money, Josie felt guilty and uncomfortable. Because the truth was, she had money. Lots of it.

Her father had made his fortune in real estate when Josie was still a baby. He had started with a parking lot in Canoga Park, old grazing land that no one wanted; then came an office building on Ventura Boulevard; some warehouses in downtown

L.A.; and then the malls—mammoth retail and entertainment centers that spanned Southern California. Now he was dealing in luxury hotel properties all over the West Coast.

The day before she drove east, her father had put one hundred thousand dollars in an account and handed her the checkbook. And there was more if she wanted. Plenty more. "Sweetie, please use the money. It's a gift from me; your mother doesn't even have to know," he had said. It made Josie sick, nauseated by both her own spite and the way her father allowed it, her father who still gave her mother gifts and effusive cards on the anniversary of their first date, their first kiss, the day of their engagement. "No," Josie had said, "I want to do it on my own," and although this wasn't exactly a lie—she did want to find her own way—it was about spite. "I refuse to tell people my daughter studies corpses," her mother would say. "I don't study corpses, Mother. I study rituals, Ghanaian rituals." "It's morbid, Josie. It's just perverse," her mother said, and Josie would feel the adrenaline pump from her heart to her fists—that overwhelming frenetic feeling—and before she knew it, she was storming out of restaurants, slamming doors, throwing glasses against floors. Her mother would stare at her, calm and collected, and tell her her anger was more suited to a four-year-old. "But then again," she murmured, "you seem somehow stuck at four." It was this comment that finally made Josie back off, go inside herself. Her mother could win any game with this. Because at four Josie's world had turned upside down, and at four Josie seemed to slip from her mother in a matter of moments. No, Josie refused to be beholden to her mother any longer, and if she took the money, she would be beholden. Despite Josie's efforts, even secrets had a way of revealing themselves to her mother.

The coffee shop was one of her usual study places—with bad coffee and pay-as-you-go Internet, it was usually empty and quiet, and Josie would often let Maddy nap in her stroller while she struggled with her Twi translation exercises or tried to get through whatever book she was reading. She had set herself the goal of a book a day, giving herself a break from the heap of social theory every three days with an ethnography. Today she had brought a book her advisor had already nixed from her Orals list. It was almost all photographs, but spectacular ones, and she thumbed through pictures of Ga customized coffins—giant tunas, colossal onions, body-sized airplanes. Only in Ghana could you be buried in a gigantic wooden Mercedes-Benz. Josie brought the book close to her face to make out the grillwork on the hand-painted car.

"You'll strain your eyes doing that."

Josie looked up and saw Devesh standing above her. He held a cup of coffee in one hand and a newspaper in the other.

"Do you mind?" he asked, and gestured to the empty chair beside her. There were plenty of empty seats around her, and Josie wished she could tell him to find another seat. She would need to be pleasant, though, could hear Mary's brusque "Josie!" just thinking about what she would like to say, so she shook her head.

"Thank you," he said, and placed his paper on the table. "Just need to get some sugar."

She watched him wind his way around the empty tables and chairs to the coffee bar. Once there, he poured four packets of sugar into his coffee. He emptied one, then stirred, emptied another, then stirred again. His actions were polished and slow, as if the world were waiting for him to perfect his latte.

She watched him until he finally turned, and then looked quickly down at her book.

"There we go," he said, and sat down.

She nodded and picked up her book. She didn't want to talk to him, but she thought he would try, and she supposed she would have to be cordial. Instead, he leaned back in his chair and opened the paper on his lap. It was a foreign paper— she could tell by the size and the brightly colored pictures on the front—and she tried to peek at the headings beneath his large dark hands without being noticed.

"*Indian Express*," he said.

She looked quickly back at her book. "Ah, right."

"And you're reading?" he asked.

"Oh." She faltered. "I'm just looking at pictures right now." She hoped he wouldn't ask more. She definitely didn't want to discuss her work.

"Pictures?" He looked at her and waited for her to go on.

"Of coffins."

He waited for more.

"Ghanaian coffins, but they're not really coffins." She paused. "I mean, they don't look like coffins."

"Some light afternoon reading?" He grinned.

"Ha-ha," she said.

"May I see?" he asked.

She handed him the book, and he flipped slowly through the pages. It seemed to take an interminable amount of time, and Josie had to bite the tip of her tongue to keep from demanding it back.

"People do all kinds of strange things with death," he said, and finally handed her the book. "In Madagascar the Sakalava decorated their tombs with carvings of men and women engaged in compromising positions." He kept hold of the book for a moment and grinned at her. It was a wicked grin, and she felt her heart contract.

"Quite something," he said, and released the book.

She looked at it in her hands. She could feel his steady gaze, and although she wanted to look up, to meet his stare, she knew her face was bright red, and she refused to give him the satisfaction of knowing he had affected her. She kept her head down and put the book back in her bag. "I need to go," she said. She stuffed her notes and the other books in her bag and swung it over her shoulder.

"I'll see you tonight, then," he said.

"Yes." She stood from her chair and walked toward the door. She knew he was staring at her, could feel his gaze warm and heavy on her back, and it made her muscles itch inside her skin. She stopped and walked back to him. "You can keep it," she said. "If you're so interested." She dropped the book on the table, turned, and swung the door open so the bells jangled loudly on the door.

Stupid, she thought. It was a library book. And what kind of retort was that anyway? She shook her head and gritted her teeth. She did not like him. She stopped on the sidewalk, thought about going back to get the book, then ran her fingers through her hair and rested her forehead in one palm. "Josie, you idiot," she said aloud, then took a deep breath. She didn't know why she was so bothered, but she was, and she tried to think about Tyler's calculations: the capital of Nigeria is Abuja, five thousand two hundred and forty-four miles from New York City. The capital of Kenya is Nairobi, seven thousand three hundred and sixty miles from New York City. She would think about all fifty-four African countries, have the numbers weave in and out of each other, an imaginary wrap, distances twisting tightly around her until all that held her were numbers.

At seven, the guests began arriving—the dean of the medical school and his wife, a handful of other faculty members, two of Mary's friends from Boston, and "Dr. Bob," a resident at the hospital that Mary had invited for Josie. Dr. Bob was charmingly boyish—lanky and slightly disheveled—and he had worked in a clinic in Ghana for a year. Josie sat with a glass of wine balanced on her knee, listening to him talk about malaria medicines, but alert for Maddy's cries. The baby had been fussy all evening, and Mary and Josie had debated for an hour over whether a tablespoon of children's cough syrup would put a one-year-old to sleep. They finally decided against it when Maddy fell asleep on Tyler's bed. Josie piled pillows around her and let Tyler watch TV in Mary's room, and now, every so often, Josie could hear a cartoon explosion followed by Tyler's high-pitched laugh.

"So you're a graduate student?" Dr. Bob asked.

"Just finished my second year, anthropology," she said.

Dr. Bob was cute, in a geeky way. He wore glasses and had a crooked nose and sandy stubble across his chin.

"And Mary says you study burial rituals; that's fascinating."

Josie smiled and sipped her wine.

Devesh had not yet arrived, and Josie could sense Mary's apprehension. Before the party, Mary had spent almost two hours getting ready: putting her hair up, then down; trying on different outfits. Finally, she had held a long red dress up to her body. "Too much?" she asked Josie. Josie shook her head and watched Mary slip her shorts, tank top, and then bra to the floor. With the red dress on her arm, she was strikingly beautiful. Her skin was pale and her breasts heavy, and Josie followed her curves to her belly. It was small and round and Josie had a sudden urge to press her lips softly and slowly against it. "When you have a baby, you'll have a belly too," Mary kidded. Josie blushed. "No," she said. "I wasn't thinking that," but she didn't know exactly what she was thinking, and she suddenly felt young and ashamed. She had often watched her mother dress for an evening out, wishing she could touch the skin that was normally covered, wondering if it felt somehow different from the papery smoothness of her arms.

"I've never seen a Ghanaian funeral," Dr. Bob said.

"Neither have I." Josie smiled. "Not yet, at least." She finished her wine and set the glass on the table.

"Can I get you some more?" he asked.

She could already feel the first glass swirling its way around her head, but she hadn't been drunk in a long time, and it felt good to have someone wait on her. "Sure," she said.

Dr. Bob walked to the kitchen, and Josie scanned the room. Mary was still talking to the dean of the medical school, looking serious and nodding, when her expression suddenly changed. Her eyes widened and her lips parted slightly, and Josie followed her gaze to the front door.

His hair was still wet from a shower—brushed back tight against his head—and he looked smaller framed by the doorjamb. He was dressed in cream linen slacks and a white

button-down shirt that made his skin all the darker. Her heart
quickened, and she shrank down into the couch, but he had
seen her, and he smiled. She blushed and then blushed harder.
What was this adolescent embarrassment? She didn't know why
he was so fiercely affecting, but he made her feel surprisingly
exposed. Josie gritted her teeth and looked away.

"Here's your drink," Dr. Bob said, and handed her the
glass.

"Thank you." She tried to take a sip, but the wine sat in
her mouth like medicine.

Behind Dr. Bob, Josie could see that Mary had led Devesh
into the kitchen. She poured him a drink, and Josie watched
the glass fill. She watched Mary brush his palm as she handed
it to him, watched it nestle firmly between his fingers, and felt
the blood rush to her head.

"Can you excuse me for a minute?" she said to Dr. Bob.

"Sure, no problem."

She stood quickly and her head spun. To get to the bathroom, she would have to walk through the kitchen, and to get
to her room she would have to walk directly in front of them.
She wished Maddy would cry so she would have an excuse to
go upstairs, but all she could hear was the clinking of glasses
and the hum of conversation.

"Do you need something?" Dr. Bob asked.

"Oh, no, sorry. I just have to check something outside."
Her head was still spinning, but she willed herself through the
living room, to the sunroom and then to the backyard.

The air was cool and it felt good on her skin, and she
slipped off her shoes and walked barefoot across the grass

to the redwood bench under the trellis. She sat down, put her wine on the ground, and rested her forehead in her hands.

She did not like this surgeon. She played the moment with the book in her head a number of times, trying to figure out what it was that had her so undone. If anything, he irritated her, she decided. He would probably do the same to Mary—scratch at her until she couldn't bear it.

She heard the backdoor open and looked up. He stepped onto the patio and she stood.

"No," he said. He pointed his finger at her and grinned. "This time you're going to stay." He walked slowly to her. "Running from coffee shops, dinner parties . . ." he said. "Where exactly are you going in such a hurry?"

She opened her mouth, but could think of nothing to say.

"And without any shoes," he continued.

She looked down at her bare feet. She had knocked her wineglass over when she stood, and it had splashed her ankles red. "I live here," she said.

"I know. You're the 'more than a nanny.'"

She swallowed. "I take care of Tyler and Madeline." His confidence was maddening, and she wished he would just leave her alone.

"And you study the more than eleven point five million square miles that is Africa, that's twenty percent of the earth's surface," he said.

She looked up.

"I have a useless ability to remember conversations," he said. "Thanks to Tyler, I'll forever remember that 'Africa's highest point is Uhuru Point at nineteen thousand three hundred and forty feet.'" He sounded so surprisingly like Tyler that Josie's mouth curled into a small smile.

"I know, I know. I can tell you what you said the last time we met, as well."

She raised her eyebrows at him.

"I'm looking at 'Ghanaian coffins, but they're not really coffins. I mean, they don't look like coffins.'"

She laughed and then covered her mouth.

"Useless, really. My overly male brain systemizing everyday interactions. I suppose some neurologists would say I received too much prenatal testosterone."

"Or too much adult testosterone," she mumbled.

"Hmm?" he asked.

"Nothing," she said, and turned slightly away.

"Oh, don't be cruel," he said. "I'm just a bungling surgeon. Take pity. How about we start again. I'm Devesh, and you are?"

She turned to look at him, and he extended his hand. He looked earnest. If Mary had her way, Devesh would be spending a lot of time with them. She supposed she should try and be nice. "You have my book," she said.

"Ah, Josie. A pleasure to meet you."

She folded her arms and set her chin.

"Josie who studies Africa," he continued.

"Ghanaian burial rituals, but Tyler doesn't know about the burial part."

"Six-year-olds and death, not a good combination, I suppose. Although my grandfather died when I was six and the thought of him coming back as a superhero was quite pleasing."

She smiled despite herself. She rubbed her ankle with the sole of her foot and looked at him. Maybe not smug, but something. Something that tickled at the base of her spine, part painful, part pleasurable.

"And you're a surgeon," she said.

"Yes; I try and keep the bodies alive, or at least teach medical students how to do that. But as of the summer, I'm just in the lab doing very boring research on wound repair."

"And you're from India."

"And I'm from India. And you're from?"

"California."

"Ahh . . . California. I can see that."

Normally, she felt comfortable around men. She would tilt her head, turn one corner of her mouth into a smile, and feel confident that she could at least charm the last bagel or only newspaper out of a man, but now she felt hyper-aware of her bare knees and sunburnt shoulders. She took a deep breath and determined to settle herself. "Santa Barbara, actually," she said.

They talked about Santa Barbara—he had been there once for a conference—and he asked her questions—about burial rituals and Ghanaian politics; about her favorite books and movies; about her family and friends; and her thoughts on talk shows, and fashion, and ice creams, and toenail polish. He listened intently and smiled at her shyness, and pulled Tic Tacs from his pocket when she ran out of answers.

"We should go inside," she said.

"Running off again." He sighed.

"No . . . I just thought . . ." She was afraid Mary would find them here, alone.

"Don't worry. She told me to find you."

She looked at him, surprised.

"So you could introduce me to the people I don't know."
He smiled. "But this is much more pleasant."

Josie looked down and then bent to pick up her wineglass. "I should help Mary."

"Then you have to promise to meet me later."

The statement took her off guard, and she had to put both
hands on the ground to steady herself.

"All right?" He wrapped his hand gently around her arm
and pulled her to stand. "After the party."

"I don't know," she said. Meeting him was a bad idea, a
very bad idea. He was Mary's guy, Mary's big chance, but she
could feel her resolve like a loose thread being unraveled. She
looked at the ground.

"Nothing formal. We'll just take a turn around the block."

She laughed and then bit her lip.

"What?"

"Nothing, nothing."

He tilted his head and crossed his arms in play anger.

"Just what you said . . ."

"What?"

"'Take a turn. . . .'" She giggled. "Who says that anymore?"
She tried not to, but the laughs came.

"Laughing at me," he teased. "Shameless."

She was giggling now, laughing at him just like he said.

"Acting like a little kid," he said. He was trying not to, but
she could see his mouth threatening to break into a smile. "Making fun of your elders."

At this, she broke into a new wave of giggles.

"Brat," he said. "You deserve a spanking."

Her heart seized. The laughs caught tightly in her throat and a bullet of heat shot from her head to between her legs. It was hot and fierce and it expanded until there was no room for breath, and she gasped. She looked at him, saw his smile fade and then a flicker of recognition, and then he was still. He said nothing, and she felt his stillness settle heavily within her until she thought she might suffocate.

"I need to go," she said.

He was quiet, and then spoke suddenly. "Maybe later then." He walked slowly toward the house, then stopped and turned back to her. "Maybe later when we take a turn around the block." He grinned, and she knew she was transparent.

At dinner, Mary sat herself and Devesh at one end of the large table and Josie and Dr. Bob at the other. Devesh seemed a continent away, but still, every time Josie reached for the salt or answered a polite question, he would catch her eye, and she would lose all composure. She had acted—as he said—just like a little kid, and here she was doing it again. And with Mary only feet away.

She tried to focus on her plate, tried to find something interesting in the eggplant parmigiana. There were conversations and cross-conversations. She heard fragments—debates over how many ethics courses med students should take, whether the new campus grocery sold organic produce—and every now and then Devesh's low voice—he had bought a house on the corner of Juniper and Second, he had found a great Thai restaurant near campus. Josie was afraid to look up, and when Mary asked her with help clearing the dishes, Josie almost jumped.

She picked up a stack of plates and followed Mary into the kitchen.

"Isn't he charming?" Mary asked.

"Sh, he'll hear you."

"There's a wall between us. Now isn't he?"

Josie put the dishes in the sink. If she didn't look at Mary, she might be able to handle the conversation. "Yeah," she said.

"And sexy," Mary continued.

"Uh-huh." Josie ran the water over the dirty dishes.

"Oh, don't do that right now. Bring the dessert plates out, but you're not getting off that easy. Later I want you to tell me exactly what you think of him."

Josie closed her eyes. If she didn't talk to him the rest of the evening, she could tell Mary she didn't have enough information to really give feedback. Or she could pretend she wasn't feeling well, go to bed, and deal with this in the morning when she was more collected and the wine hadn't made her think strange men could read her thoughts.

The rest of the evening, Josie focused on the meal—making sure everyone had enough cheesecake, that the coffee didn't run out, that dirty plates were cleared and clean utensils provided. Even when Mary insisted she sit down, she couldn't keep still. She was sure he would corner her again, and she drank two cups of coffee while standing in the kitchen, trying to sober up enough to shake his hand goodbye and mean it.

At ten-thirty, the guests began to leave and Josie steadied herself—she would say a quick goodbye and then excuse herself to check on Tyler and Maddy; by the time she came back downstairs, he would be gone. Instead, Mary grabbed Josie's hand and made her stay.

"Josie made the eggplant and the salad *and* the cheese-cake," Mary said. "I just did the appetizers and boiled water for the pasta." She was tipsy, and she held Josie's hand tightly.

Josie tried to smile, and Dr. Bob grabbed her other hand.

"It was a great dinner," he said. "And I really enjoyed talking to you."

"Yeah; great." She knew she was bordering on rude, but she could feel her heart accelerating, and she wanted her hands to herself.

"Maybe I'll see you again?" he asked.

"Yeah, maybe."

He smiled and let go of her hand, and Josie ran it through her hair and pressed her temples. The wine and the caffeine had made her head pound, and she wished she could sink to the ground and be absorbed into the carpet.

"Midnight then?" Devesh leaned in close, and Josie could feel his breath tickle the hairs on her neck. She shivered, and he laughed softly. "It's only a walk."

She opened her mouth to protest, but he stayed his ground. "Don't make me ring the doorbell."

And then it was done. He said his goodbyes, walked slowly toward the door, and any resilience Josie clung to dissolved with that final threat.

At eleven fifty-five, Josie crept from her room. She carried her shoes in one hand and opened the front door with the other.

It was colder than earlier, and she wished she had brought a sweater, but she was afraid to go back. She sat on the porch step and slipped on her shoes.

If Mary looked out the window, she was sure to see them. The thought pinched at Josie, and she wrapped her arms around herself and wished he would hurry. Who did he think he was, anyway? She had heard Mary and her friends joking about surgeons and their arrogance, and now Josie understood why. But here she was, still waiting. She would go on this one walk, and then no more. No one would ever find out, and Mary could have him if she wanted. She looked down at her watch and followed the second hand circle after circle.

Finally, at twelve-ten she heard his steps on the concrete. She stood, and he smiled at her. "Ready for your evening constitutional?" he asked.

"Sh," she said. "We have to be quiet."

"Well, come on then."

He had his hands in his pockets, and she wished she had changed into jeans, that she had somewhere to put her hands or something to do with them. She walked along next to him, determined to stay quiet. He could talk if he wanted. She would stay focused on all the reasons this was a very bad idea. They walked to the end of the block, then down on Grove Street, and when they reached Elm, she couldn't stand it any longer. "Where are we going?"

"It's a surprise," he said, and smiled at her.

She looked at him, saw the soft lines around his eyes, the thin scar above his eyebrow, and for the first time felt at ease, and yet behind this feeling was the sting of something else. She looked down, and he took her hand in his. It was warm and broad, and she focused on his thumb, the way it stroked her fingers slowly and firmly, back and forth, back and forth, and felt safe.

"Okay?" he asked.

She took a breath. "Okay," she said.

They walked until they reached the park on Walker. It was small—only two swings and a slide—but she often took the children there. It was bordered by oak trees, and Tyler liked to collect the acorns and line them up on the perimeter of the sandbox.

"I know this park," she said.

"You do?"

"Tyler likes the acorns."

"You know what's on the other side of the stream?"

"There's a house back there," she said.

"Not just a house," he said. "Let me show you."

He held her hand tighter, and she followed him over the boulders and onto the bank on the other side. She scrambled behind him, up the steep incline until the ground leveled off. It was densely wooded, but the moonlight streamed through the trees revealing a small clearing a few yards in front of them. He led her to it and then stopped. Inside, were rock pillars, large sculptures made up of hundreds of flat rocks placed atop each other, each at opposing horizontal angles and each growing progressively smaller so that the result was ten symmetrically balanced towers.

"What is it?" Josie asked.

"Some college kids built it years ago. There are different theories on why. Some people say it was a physics experiment, some say it was an alien hoax."

"And they don't fall?"

"A few must in heavy rainstorms, but someone always seems to rebuild them. Come on." He led her close to one. "It's all sandstone, which means whoever built them hauled these rocks in here."

Josie looked closely at a pillar. It towered a few feet above her head, and when she looked up it seemed to sway. She took a step back.

"They won't fall. Don't worry."

This time she took his hand. He led her between the pillars, and it reminded her of how her parents had once taken her and her cousin Natalie to a park filled not with swings and slides and jungle gyms but enormous fiber-glass toys—dolls the size of grown-ups, a cradle too high to see inside, a tea set with a cup big enough to bathe in. "Go ahead, Jojo," her father had said. "You can pretend you're the size of a mouse," but she clung to his hand and pressed herself close against his waist, and when he questioned her, she was only able to tell him that everything was too big.

Now, she pressed herself a little closer to Devesh. In the back corner of the clearing was a platform of sorts. "What's that?" she asked.

"A bench, but you can tell it was built by someone else. The stone they used is from down by the stream."

She walked toward it, and he let go of her hand. The bench was a series of boulders, almost waist high and about six feet long. She traced her fingers along the rough stone, and then sensed him behind her. He placed his hands gently on her shoulders. She froze, and he ran his palms down her arms, back up to her elbows, and then down to her hands. He twined his fingers with hers and moved in closer. She shivered, and he let out the same gentle laugh as when he had said goodbye. "You're lovely," he said.

She felt the blood drain through her feet, and when he turned her gently to face him, she had to close her eyes to keep from losing her balance.

"I'm going to kiss you," he said.

Okay, she thought. Okay. He pressed his lips gently against hers, a soft gentle kiss. His curls brushed her forehead, and she imagined him holding her arms behind her back, imagined him running a hand up her thigh and—but before she could finish the thought, he pulled away, and she opened her eyes. He was smiling, and she felt the crush of shame in her chest. Just a kiss, she thought, but the moonlight illuminated his lashes casting long shadows on his cheeks, and she couldn't help but wish that dark something still there.

"We should head home, no?"

No, she wanted to say. But that was wrong—there was Mary to think about, and a million other things. Nevertheless, she couldn't force herself to agree, couldn't say, Yes; it's late. Take me home, and they stood in silence until he finally reached for her. He took her wrists in his hands, his thumb and forefinger encircling each, and pulled her toward him.

"You don't want to go home?" he asked, and spun her gently around, his hands still holding her so she was bound and close to him. She closed her eyes and felt his lips on her neck. "You'd like something else? Something more than a kiss?" he asked.

She drew a quick breath, felt it shiver through her body. His hands seemed enormous, her wrists like twigs, and she was suddenly aware of the intensity with which she had ached for this moment, how simultaneously terrifying and familiar it was. She swallowed hard, opened her mouth.

"Is that what you'd like?" he asked again. "Something more?"

Yes, she wanted to say, yes; but she could barely take a breath. Her head began to spin, large loping circles. She knew the answer, but even the thought of saying it aloud was enough to make her pull away. Sure she had thought it, but now, with him here asking for her permission, she couldn't even open her mouth.

"Tell me," he said. He tightened his grasp slightly, and the pressure of his grip seemed to squeeze the answer from her belly.

"Yes," she said.

He laughed gently. "Then we'll just have to do something about that, won't we?" He kissed her softly on the neck and then turned her to face him. "Dinner, tomorrow?" he asked.

She swallowed hard and nodded.

"Good," he said, and slipped his hand in hers, squeezed gently, and led her back across the stream, through the park, and home again.

CHAPTER TWO

THE NEXT MORNING, JOSIE SCRAMBLED EGGS AND THOUGHT ABOUT the night before. What was she doing, and what about Mary? Mary who had bought Josie her first sweet tea, showed Josie her first firefly, made Josie her first bowl of grits. Mary who absent-mindedly stroked her hair, and called her Jojo like her father, and was brave enough to cuddle up with her on the couch. Part of her wished Mary had just looked out the window last night, seen Josie sitting there, and ordered her back inside.

"Hung over?" Mary entered the kitchen and Josie stiffened. She should do it now, admit her mistake and beg forgiveness.

"Not much," Josie said, and spooned some egg onto Madeline's high-chair tray. "You?"

"I'm pretending I'm not," she said, and poured some coffee. She was dressed unusually nicely for a Saturday morning—a blue summer dress that Josie had picked out for her on a recent shopping trip. "I have to go to the lab this morning, but this afternoon I'm going out," she said. She smiled, and Josie felt a wave of panic.

"With who?"

"Dr. Khanna."

Josie's heart seized.

"Devesh," Mary continued. "The surgeon from last night?"

Josie stared blankly.

"Hello? Earth to Josie." She laughed and put a piece of bread in the toaster.

"When," Josie stammered. "When did you arrange that?"

"Last night. I would have told you if you hadn't been in such a hurry to rush off to bed."

Josie still had the spatula in her hand. She turned, dropped it in the sink, and gripped the counter.

"He's great, isn't he?" Mary asked

"Uh-huh." Josie heard the toast pop, the refrigerator open.

"You okay?"

"Yeah, just tired."

"Well, Jenna, next door, owes me a babysitting exchange, so the kids are going there for the night. You'll have the house to yourself for a change." She walked over to Josie and handed her a glass of orange juice. "Drink plenty of fluids and I'll see you tomorrow morning," she paused. "Hopefully." She winked.

Josie felt the color drain from her face.

"Go for a walk," Mary said. "Get some fresh air, get the alcohol out of your system."

"Okay," Josie said. She put the juice down, made her way to the front hallway, shoved her feet into her flip-flops.

"Take deep breaths!" Mary called after her.

"Okay," Josie said, and walked out the front door without her keys and without any idea where she was going or what she was going to do.

It was already quite warm, but Josie could see the dark, soupy rain clouds building on the horizon. She stood frozen in the driveway. Last night he had stood here, in this very spot,

and almost seduced her into betrayal. She had known he was
trouble, could feel it the first time she met him, and confirmed
it last night. She threw her hands to her sides. "Bastard," she
said. So why had she allowed herself to be herded down this
predictable path? Like a dumb cow, she thought. "Moo," she
said aloud. "Moo." She laughed, then sighed.

She had done this, swapped allegiance like a trading card,
and now she was angry—angry at herself, but also angry at him.
How dare he seduce her at his date's own party? How *dare* he?
But it was more than his poor form she was angry about. It was
the "something more" he had promised. He had tweezed her desire to the surface and made her admit it. But no, she had misunderstood. He was just flirting—a silly courting ritual. But what
if he wasn't? What if he could see all those thoughts that edged
their way into her mind at night, creeping their way down into
her fingers, inching her hands under the covers? She did want
what he offered, just as she had since she was seven, and six,
and younger. He saw this, and she hated him for it.

She walked down the driveway. She would call him, or
better yet go find him. She could be vicious when she wanted,
and sometimes when she didn't—and now it was justified. She
would find him, and he would be sorry he had ever messed
with her or Mary. She knew she was thinking like one of Tyler's
Saturday morning cartoon characters, but she didn't care. She
could feel the muscles in her fingers expand, readying for a
fight.

His house was only a fifteen-minute walk. She could show
up and tell him off, throw things at him, tear his beautiful hair
out. She walked quickly down the street, turned left, then right,
then right again, and then it began to rain. A summer storm that

came down fiercely, making her wet and cold, and she wished she had on more than shorts and a T-shirt, but she was determined, and she hugged her arms around herself and walked down Terrace, over on Walker, and finally to Juniper.

There were four corner houses. One had an upended pink bicycle in the driveway, and in the front yard of another, a tire swing hung from a tree. She looked at the remaining two houses— one boxy and yellow with a large white porch and two giant maple trees, and the other a two-storied Colonial with boxes full of geraniums in the windows. It had to be the yellow one. She stood on the sidewalk and felt her anger begin to drain. Even if she did spew some kind of tirade, so what? It wouldn't change anything. She would still have betrayed Mary, and he would still have hurt them both. She felt her heart begin to race, and she stretched her hands hard, trying to regain some of that intense anger, but all she could think of were bus routes. If she walked down Juniper she could catch a bus to Wedgewood, and then it was only a two-block walk to the Griffins'. But she had come all this way, and she didn't have her house keys, and Mary was probably gone by now. He probably wasn't even home, and before she could decide one way or another, he stepped onto the porch. He was wearing a deep blue shirt and tan shorts, and he held a black umbrella in his hand.

"Josie," he said.

"Oh, God," she mumbled.

"What are you doing? It's pouring rain."

She couldn't think of a single thing to say, and when he told her to come inside, she felt stuck to the sidewalk, and he had to walk all the way over to her, place his hand on her back, and usher her into the house.

"What are you doing? You're soaked," he said. "Stay here."

She stood dripping in the entryway and looked at the dark living room. There was a couch and two armchairs and a blue area rug and an abstract painting above the fireplace. She had expected his house to be full of dark, muted colors—rugs and pillows draping over each other, incense and spices filling the rooms, all ancient romance. He brought her an oversized towel and wrapped her in it, and she felt so small, she thought she might disappear under his hands.

"What in the world were you doing?" he asked.

She wanted to be angry, to be the "hateful thing" her mother often called her when she lost her temper and turned violent, but all she could manage was something about a walk and rain and an unexpected turn of events.

"Well, you're soaked," he said and put his hands to her cheeks and lifted her face, "and freezing." His palms felt warm on her skin, and she wanted to close her eyes and give in to his hands, but she steadied herself and turned her face away.

"I'm fine," she said. He took a step back, and she felt a small pull in her chest.

"Why don't you take a hot shower; I'll bring you some dry clothes."

"I'm fine."

"You'll catch your death."

She felt the laugh catch at the back of her throat, and she put her hand to her mouth and turned away.

"What?"

She raised her eyebrows and shook her head.

"What?" he asked again.

Now she looked at him, fixing herself against his stare. "Again with the quaint sayings—'catch your death'—what are you, one of the town elders?"

"Older than you." He narrowed his eyes, and she felt as if she had been struck. "And I'm not the one who showed up looking like a drowned kitten on my doorstep," he continued. "Now just go take a shower." He put his hand on her back and led her into the bathroom and closed the door.

She stood and stared at the sunny yellow walls and blue flowered tiles.

Twenty-two tiles. Twenty-two tiles, no doubt chosen by someone else. Twenty-two tiles and one missing at the corner. Oh, God, this was wrong. She should protest, tell him a sweatshirt would do just fine and that *Mary* could return it later, but she was shaky and light-headed, all her determination gone, and she peeled off her clothes and stepped into the shower. The knobs were old and unlabeled, and the water came out first in a blast of cold before slowly warming. She would take a shower, borrow some clothes, and leave immediately. Forget the tirade. Forget revenge. She would accept defeat. She would suffer this failure.

Finally, the water was hot, and it pounded rhythmically on her back. There was a bar of green soap and some generic grocery store shampoo and conditioner—normal guy stuff, she told herself—but he wasn't normal. Guys didn't *do* this to her. There was something not right with this one. There were probably hidden cabinets in this house, secret drawers. He probably advertised on the Internet. She had scanned the personal ads once: Good Looking SWM Seeks Naughty Girl; SWM Looking for SWF in Need of a Sound Spanking, but the pretense of it overwhelmed her and she had never responded to any of them. It was just pretend for those people, just play. What she wanted was real, and not, and she just didn't know. She didn't want any of it. No. She just wanted to leave.

She turned the water off, and as she did, the door opened, and she jolted.

"Sh, sh, sh," he said. "Just me. Just leaving the clothes." He snuck an arm in and placed them on the counter.

"Close the door," she said.

"Yes, yes," he said, and pulled it shut.

She stood there for a moment, and then he knocked.

"What?"

"Forgot the towel."

She sighed loudly, and he tossed it in.

"Now go away," she said.

"I am."

"No you're not; you're standing there."

He laughed.

She grabbed the towel from the floor and dried herself quickly. "I can hear you out there," she said.

"You didn't say how *far* away."

She reached for the sweatshirt, and a pair of boxers fell to the floor.

"I'm not wearing your boxers," she said.

"Suit yourself."

"Don't you have any sweatpants?"

"No."

It was quiet, and she held up the blue plaid boxer shorts.

"I wasn't expecting a wet little girl, you know."

She blushed, then banged her palm against the door.

"All right, all right, I'll make some tea."

She heard him walk down the hallway, and she put his clothes on and slowly opened the door.

"Sit down," he called from the kitchen. "I'll be right there."

She made her way to the living room and sat on the over-sized couch. Next to her, on an end table, was a pile of books, a dusty lamp, and a black sketchbook. She pulled the sketchbook to her lap and opened it. On the first page was an inked circle enclosing a number of smooth lines that intersected to make dozens of triangles pointing up and down and across each other. It was precisely drawn, and the whirling smoothness of it all made her feel as if it were somehow moving, rolling toward the center, and then out again from it.

"You like that?" He walked to her and took the book. "You should ask permission before you look at people's things," he said.

She could tell he was both teasing and serious, and it made her feel young and uncomfortable.

He handed her a cup of tea and stood in front of her. "Drink."

She held the mug in both hands, wanting to both drink and not drink. Her heart beat faster with his proximity, and she thought she might scream if her brain didn't stop all this flip-flopping. She forced herself to take a tiny sip. It was hot and milky and sweet, and she wanted to take another mouthful, but she set her jaw and looked at him.

He sighed, and then took the mug and placed it on the floor. "You are a handful," he said.

Her chest ached, and she felt the sting of tears threatening behind her eyes. "You're supposed to see Mary today," she blurted.

He looked at her. "Yes?"

She didn't know what to say next. The tears were in her eyes now, and she looked down at her hands. There was a long silence, and she could hear the tick of a clock coming from another room.

Finally he spoke. "Ohh," he said.

She didn't say anything, just stared at her hands.

"Mary told me she wanted some help with an NIH grant. Is that what she thought? That it was a date?"

She recoiled at the word, then shrugged.

"Oh, Josie." He bent down and took her hands in his. "It is not a date." He laughed.

Josie stared at his hands and felt foolish. It hadn't been a date; of course not. One does not say the things he'd said to her one night, and then take someone else out for dinner the next, but this was, of course, not true. Josie had known plenty of men who did this kind of thing. And Mary had *said*.

"Forget it. I won't meet her," Devesh said.

"No," she said weakly.

"Yes," he said.

She was still staring at her hands, not wanting him to see her wet eyes, but he tilted her chin up and kissed her softly.

"Warm now?" he asked.

She nodded and wiped at her eyes.

"Come," he said, and laid her down next to him on the couch. She rested her head on his chest and listened to the rain. It was coming down fiercely now, and she tried to hear each drop slap against the rooftop.

"In India, monsoon season is very romantic. Lots of films with torrential rains and young girls running around in wet saris."

She giggled.

"Lots of songs about rain and love and love and rain," he said, and ran his fingers along the back of her neck. "*Ek baar tumko jab baraste paaniyon ke paar dekha thha,*" he sang softly.

She closed her eyes and listened to the words, felt them warm on her cheek.

"*Yoon laga thha jaise gungunaata ek abshaar dekha thha.*" His fingers massaged down her spine, each vertebra vibrating under his touch, and he pushed gently at the small of her back.

"What does it mean?" she asked.

"Once I saw you through a downpour"—he paused—"and it was as if I had seen a humming waterfall."

And as he said this, she could feel her heart swell, could feel him like a splinter trying to pinch under her skin. The room began to pulse, and she pushed hard against him and ducked her head into his chest. He pulled her close, held her hands in his, and then slipped his fingers firmly around her wrists. She inhaled quickly, and he laughed.

She looked up at him.

"Yes, *baba*. I know," he said.

She closed her eyes, and his hair tickled her eyelids and lips, and she opened her mouth and let a strand fall on her tongue. It tasted salty and coarse as rope, and she imagined she was naked, her wrists in one of his hands, head empty of thought, body electric and planted in only the moment.

CHAPTER THREE

WHEN JOSIE WENT HOME THE NEXT MORNING, SHE FOUND MARY sitting on the front porch, reading the paper.

"Where were *you*?" Mary asked.

Josie felt her heart contract, and she wanted to put her arms around Mary and smother her in apologies. "Out." She looked at the ground and focused on the thin line of ants making their way through the cracks in the walkway.

"Out? What's that supposed to mean? In case you didn't notice, you didn't come home last night." She was pretending to tease her, but Josie could hear the edge in Mary's voice.

"I noticed."

"So? Who was it?"

Josie wanted to tell her, to unload this sandbag of a secret, but she couldn't, and she stared at her toes and tried to figure out what was worse: hurting Mary or not seeing Devesh. The first was terrible, but the second was inconceivable.

"It was Dr. Bob, wasn't it?"

Josie scuffed her flip-flop against the first step of the porch.

"It was, it was! I knew you'd like him. He's a good guy; unlike some people," she muttered.

"I'm going inside," Josie said.

"What's the matter with you?" It was the same voice she used with Tyler, and Josie felt it in the whole of her stomach.

"Nothing, I'm just tired."

"Well, you don't have to be rude. I had a bad day yesterday, and I don't need another one today."

Josie took the steps slowly. "Okay," she mumbled, waiting for her mother's "Just watch yourself," but Mary said nothing, and Josie walked to her bedroom and sat down on the bed. This was ridiculous, she thought. Mary was a rational woman, she would understand. But Josie knew this wasn't true. If Josie told, the invisible tether she felt between her and Mary would snap like a dry rubber band.

She lay down on the bed and put her arms over her face. She could still smell his aftershave from when he kissed her goodbye, and it made her heart quicken. Oh, God, he was beautiful. She had walked home feeling as if the air were suddenly infused with nitrous oxide. She could spin all day on this feeling, and he had asked her to come over again that night. They would watch a Bollywood movie and drink Fanta and eat egg rolls and pretend they were Samosas, and later maybe he would do that thing to her. She pressed her hands against her chest. This was bad; it was bad, but it was also good, it was very, very good.

For weeks, Josie would sneak out after the children were asleep and meet Devesh at his house. They watched movies, and read supermarket tabloids, and drove all the way to Charlotte for *mithai* and *bhel puri*. They took night walks, and he told her about India and his childhood and the schoolmaster who smacked him nearly every day for reading *Phantom* comics in the classroom; and about his work, and how he was researching the role of gene therapy in wound repair. And he gave her a house key that he strung on a red ribbon and hung around her neck.

Almost nightly, she would nestle into his bed, ignore her own reading, and work her way through his vast collection of books. She was slowly falling behind on her promise of an anthro book a day, but she had a whole year, she told herself, and his books were so enticing—unusual books on Roman and Greek medicine, each full of intricate and confused drawings of the inner body; large volumes of Eastern art filled with page after page of blushing brides, bathing courtesans, slave girls at auction; travel guides to destinations like Mt. Kailas, Bhaktapur, and Polonnaruwa, places she had never heard of and could barely locate on a map; books on psycho-semantics and evolutionary theory and theoretical biology; but the most entrancing of all were the shelves of Indian books—novels and histories, books on gods and goddesses, mandalas and chakras, tantrikas and sadhus, caste and class, storybooks, comic books, erotic books, books in Hindi and English and French, hardcovers and paperbacks, shelf after shelf after shelf. Often she would stand in front of them, force her fingers over their worn covers, and guess at what they contained. She wanted to heap them around her, peek into this world, but she couldn't seem to get past the covers. It was ridiculous. India was no more foreign than Africa, she would reason with herself, but each time she pulled one from the shelf and held it in her hands, she felt nine years old and terrified of slumber-party ghosts.

Once he caught her holding a thick volume of Indian short stories. "Careful there," he teased. "Those books are full of bad Indian men. You sure you want to get involved with a bad Indian man?"

She laughed, but he grew serious.

"Some Indian men are bad," he said.

She looked at him and felt a second of apprehension. "But you're not like that."

"No. I'm not."

She put the book back and put her arms around him. "You're all good."

"I wouldn't go that far." He laughed and kissed her head.

Josie felt pitched into a new reality. It was wonderful, even if they hadn't yet done that thing he promised. Still, she could feel it building, something terrifying and splendid layering between them.

Everything seemed perfect. Everything except Mary. A few days after the dinner party, Mary had pulled Josie into her bedroom and closed the door.

"I'm sorry," Mary had said. "I didn't mean to yell at you." Josie looked at the floor and nodded. "Will you tell me what's going on? Please?" Josie felt her heart stretch taut in her chest, and she gritted her teeth. "I can tell you're happy," Mary continued. "I'm so glad. Really. So . . . tell me. Come on." Mary paused and Josie stared at her hands.

"This is ridiculous," Mary continued. "Please."

Josie counted the lines on her palms, and they sat there in painful silence until Tyler knocked on the door asking for raisins. After that, Mary didn't ask again, but the question hung over the house like a wrecking ball.

*   *   *

Three weeks into the affair, Josie and Tyler were sitting in the
driveway drawing on the pavement with sidewalk chalk when
Mary came home from the lab early. Tyler had drawn concen-
tric blue circles around himself and was now retracing them
yellow.

"What's that?" Mary asked him.

"Circles," Tyler said. "They're just circles."

Josie dusted her palms on her jeans and stood. "Maddy's
asleep on a blanket under the tree."

Mary nodded and looked down at the drawing. "Looks
like a giant breast," she said.

Josie laughed and then covered her mouth.

"Doesn't it?" she asked Josie.

"Yeah." Josie smiled. She looked at Mary and her chest
tightened.

Last night, Josie had stood in the hallway, rocking Maddy,
who had a slight fever, and watching Mary play some game
with Tyler. Everything was opposite: night was day, Tyler was
Maddy, dinner was breakfast. "Time to get up," Mary had said.
"Time for school clothes," Tyler responded. Pajamas went on
backward and Tyler, who normally fought whenever clothes
came on or off, stripped down quickly and shoved his arms
in his backward top. "Time to make your bed," Mary chirped
and Tyler jumped under the covers and pulled out his animal encyclopedia. Mary smiled brightly and kissed Tyler on
the head. "I love you, Boo Boo Bear." Josie had breathed in
sharply. It was what her mother had called her. And her
younger brother, Matthew, had been Baby Bear. Often, her
mother would put the two of them to sleep together in Josie's

wide canopy bed, and Josie would curl like a shell around Matthew while he sucked his bottle and stared transfixed into her eyes. "Say it," Josie would whisper, and her mother would—a simple statement, over and over, but enough to put them both to sleep, two bears in their bed—"He is your only brother; you are his only sister."

She looked at Tyler drawing circles, then at Mary. "You're home early."

"What a day." Mary sighed. "The power went out at the university, and when the generator didn't go on, there were a dozen crazy academics running around like chickens with their heads cut off. Of course it went on five minutes later." She dropped her briefcase and leaned against the garage door. "Then I locked myself out of my office, had to go all the way to maintenance to get the key, and of course on the way I ran into that stupid surgeon."

The ground shifted beneath Josie's feet. She looked down and concentrated on Tyler's smooth yellow circles.

"But I got butterscotch ice cream," Mary said and held up the bag.

It was Josie's favorite, and she suddenly felt sick with guilt.

"I never told you what happened with him," Mary continued.

Josie could hear her heart beating, and she crossed her arms to try and quiet it.

"He stood me up."

Oh, God, she thought. If only he had called, but they had completely forgotten, and then it was noon and when he did call, Mary had already left for the restaurant. Now Josie wondered if she had forgotten on purpose, a small dig at Mary's mantle of influence.

"And then today he wanted to chitchat as if nothing had happened."

Josie's head jerked up. "What did he say?"

"Nothing. Some stupid pleasantries. I told him I'd prefer if he left me alone, and he said he was sorry for what had happened, sorry if he had *offended* me." She laughed. "I told him I doubted it was possible for him to offend me, but just in case, I would make sure not to give him an opportunity." Mary paused, and Josie realized her mouth was hanging open. "What?"

"Nothing," she mumbled.

"What do you mean 'nothing'? You look like someone just died."

"Nothing . . . I . . . nothing . . . nothing." She ran her hands through her hair and realized how dumb she sounded. She had never been able to lie to her mother either, had always confessed in one heaping, bawling mess, and now she could feel the tears threatening. "Nothing . . . I . . . ." She swallowed and looked at the ground. She could feel herself shrink, and as much as she dreaded what was about to come, she couldn't help but feel an overwhelming sense of relief. You asked for this, she told herself.

"What?" Mary asked, then again more insistently, "What?"

Josie could feel the pressure in her throat, nonexistent words scrambling in her mouth. Her nose stung, and she pressed her knuckles firmly against her eyes and then held them over her mouth.

Mary stared at her, and then Josie saw the grimace—a quick contraction spread painfully across her face "Oh my God," Mary said. "He's the guy."

Josie shut her eyes to keep the tears back. "I'm sorry," she said.

"Oh my God," Mary repeated. "I can't believe this. I can't believe you would do this."

"I didn't mean to."

"Jesus, Josie, can you at least come up with something more original?"

She knew Mary could be cruel, had heard the stabbing sarcasm in Mary's conversations with her mother and sister, even felt it herself—when Josie couldn't convince Tyler to put on his shoes ("It's not brain surgery," Mary would say) or get Maddy's car seat buckled ("You've gone through sixteen years of schooling, figure it out")—but this was only when Mary was cranky and tired, and later she always apologized. But now, Josie knew, this stab was just the beginning.

"I'm sorry." Josie tried again.

"You're sorry." Mary crossed her arms and shook her head. "I can't believe you would do this to me, and that he would stand me up for *you*."

Josie felt the words crack through her. They burned and then settled in her palms, and she squeezed her hands into fists and pressed them tight against her sides. "Don't," she said.

"Don't what? You're a fucking student. You understand that, don't you?"

"I'm not his student."

Mary laughed. "Very good, Josie." She narrowed her eyes. "Fine, go ahead and fuck your surgeon. I'll make sure to avoid the both of you." She turned, snatched her briefcase, and stormed into the house.

Josie could feel the blood pulsing in her hands, and she dragged her nails against her thighs and let out a muffled cry. Below her, Tyler was still drawing, tracing yellow against blue, absorbed and oblivious. She tried to focus on the circles, tried to calm herself, but she felt as if she were caught in the drawing—pinned at the heart.

That night Devesh was in the lab and Mary refused to talk to her, and the pain and guilt of it all curled heavy like a cat on Josie's chest. She picked up her cell phone and called her mother. Josie hadn't spoken to her in weeks, and when she answered, Josie could hear the chill in her mother's voice.

"How's school?" her mother asked.

"Good," Josie said.

"And work?"

"Fine."

There was an uncomfortable silence, and Josie knew she should say something, but she wasn't sure what, wasn't even sure exactly why she had called.

"Did you want to talk to your dad?" her mother asked.

"No." She answered too quickly and then took a deep breath. "I . . . talked to him yesterday." She always returned her father's calls when she knew her mother was at her biweekly tennis game. "I just wanted to say hi."

"Hmm," her mother muttered.

"I can't call just to say hello?" Josie could feel the familiar spur of anger pang in her chest.

"Of course you can."

"Good."

There was another uncomfortable silence before her mother chimed in. "Oh," she said. "I ran into Dorothy Winters yesterday. Dana just got married to a fellow she met at Columbia. They're living in Palos Verdes now, both investment bankers, both working at Smith Barney."

"Oh," Josie said.

"And remember Mark Sandburg? Your dad just got him a job, so we took him and his girlfriend out for dinner last night. She's getting her masters in urban design, which is what your cousin Darren did. It's a very lucrative field, you know."

"Yes; you told me." She knew what would come next— the supposed concern for her job prospects, the commentary on how she was getting too old to be "babysitting."

"Have you seen any good movies lately?" Josie tried.

"Our movie group meets next week. I don't know what they have planned."

"I'm taking Tyler to see the new Disney movie on Monday."

"Can he sit through it?"

"Yes, Mother."

Tyler's "affliction," as her mother called it, had been a source of contention since Josie began. "A boy like that needs someone with professional experience," her mom had said. "What if something happens?"

Now Josie took a deep breath and tried to steady her tone. "He's six, Mom."

"Yes, but . . . Josie, you need to seriously think about whether you should be involved in this whole thing."

"What whole thing?"

"Taking care of a boy like that. You don't know what he could say or do. You know I've heard of cases where the babysitter was accused of hurting the children when it was really the parents' doing."

"What are you talking about?"

"I'm just saying, children like that should be under specialized care, which you don't have. Who knows if you're unintentionally making him even worse?"

"I'm not making him worse!"

"I'm just asking you to think about what you're doing." It was a line she used repeatedly and indiscriminately—for vacation plans and sweater purchases, university decisions and boyfriend choices—and the use of it now, in reference to Tyler, made Josie furious.

"There's nothing to think about," she said. "I have to go."

"Well, fine then, Josie, but don't blame me because this conversation didn't go the way you wanted it to. It's your temper that gets you into trouble."

"It's not my temper," she yelled.

"Oh, really?"

It's you, she wanted to scream, but she knew better than to prove her mother right. "I'm going."

"Of course you are, darling. 'Bye," her mother singsonged.

"Damn it," Josie yelled, and threw the phone on her pillow. It was always like this. Always.

She lay down on the bed, looked out the bedroom window, and began to count the leaves on the trees.

CHAPTER FOUR

THE NEXT DAY WAS SATURDAY, AND ALTHOUGH JOSIE HAD NEVER officially worked weekends, she normally took Tyler for breakfast—just the two of them. They would both ask for separate plates for their syrup and count the number of wells in their waffles. But last Saturday she had met Devesh for brunch, and today they were going on a hike. Tyler had said nothing when Josie explained the night before, but on her way out this morning, she found the front doorknob messily tied with red yarn and knotted to the entry table and coat rack.

"Guess who did that," Mary said. She was sitting on the couch drinking her coffee.

"Hey," Josie said. She hadn't been able to sleep last night, and neither had Mary. Josie's bedroom was below Mary's, and Josie had heard the upstairs floorboards creaking every half hour, the TV turned on, then off, the groan of the stairs and the refrigerator door opening.

"Look," Mary said. "I'm sorry I yelled at you."

"No," Josie said. "*I'm* sorry. I . . . ." She stumbled and tried to find something to say, but Mary waved dismissively.

"You're young. Hormones. Whatever. At least you have good taste."

Josie tried a smile, and Mary nodded. "I'll be fine. Maybe Dr. Bob is still available."

Josie laughed, then paused. "Thank you."

"Go out the back door. I'll deal with the little locksmith."

Josie smiled. "Next weekend I'll take you both for waffles."

"And pancakes."

"And French toast," Josie said. She made her way to the back door and Mary called after her.

"You'll be back in time to take the kids to school Monday morning, right?"

"Of course."

"And croissants!" she yelled.

"And croissants," Josie said, and wheeled her bike to the street.

When she arrived at Devesh's, he was sitting on the front porch reading the paper.

"Well, I told her," Josie said.

"And?"

"This morning she seemed okay."

"And last night?"

"Let's talk about it later," she said, and pulled him to her.

He kissed her, then paused. "Do you have to go home tonight?" he asked.

"No," she said.

"Good; we're going to play this evening."

It was what she had been waiting for, what she'd held her breath for every time he ran his hand down her back, every time he unbuttoned her jeans. Now she said the word in her mind and felt her cheeks burn, and then that dizzying intoxication, what a first surge of the needle must feel like to a heroin addict, an instant of wild anticipation and then the rush. "Okay," she said.

That night they went to dinner and perhaps because she was tired or perhaps because she was slightly afraid of what would follow, she was irritable. She ordered a full dinner and then ate only bread and butter, complained that the restaurant was too hot, that the waiter was inattentive, that she had a headache. On the way home, she maneuvered her hand into his. He pressed it tightly and then let go, running his fingers up her arm and to the back of her neck. He squeezed gently but firmly, and she felt her body go awkward, her legs too long and her tongue too big. The blood pumped loud in her ears and she let him lead her. She was scared, and yet charged, unsure of what to do or even how one foot was supposed to place itself in front of the other.

When they reached his front door, he held it open for her and walked her into the bedroom. It was dark, but the moon was almost full and the light streamed in through the window. He led her to the wall and stood her in front of a tall iron sculpture. It was attached firmly to the wall and grew like a black vine, creepers shooting out and up, ends curled in like buds. She had always considered it decoration, but now, on a jutting limb, hung two small leather cuffs and a thick black rope.

"Everything off," he said.

Josie's heart quickened. She had seen cuffs like these once, when a boyfriend of hers had taken her to the Pleasure Palace in Los Angeles. They had scanned the aisles, looking and laughing at the apparatus some people needed just to have sex. "I would just laugh," he had said, and she had agreed, but wondered—with the right person, if he really believed? But no, no one did that in real life, no one was bound with black leather cuffs. And who was punished anyway? Little kids? Yes. Naughty adults? No. Sometimes yes? She *had* been naughty tonight. But naughty? Even the word seemed full of pretense.

She shook her head and tried to focus on her clothes. She fumbled with her shirt, her jeans, folding each article of clothing before moving onto the next, and soon she was naked except for her panties.

"Those can stay for now," he said. He turned her so she was facing the wall, cradled her chin in his palm, kissed her cheek, and then ran his hand down her neck to her breasts to her belly. She felt shaky and clumsy, and when he slipped her wrists through the cuffs, she realized she had been holding her breath. She watched him fasten the small buckles, watched him thread the rope first through the steel rings and then over an iron rod above her head. He tied the knot quickly.

"Pull," he said.

She could hear him, but the word seemed to take forever to get to her brain, and before she could obey, he brought his hand down quickly on her behind. "I said, pull."

She startled and tugged at the ropes. The knot was solid, and the iron securely attached to the wall, and she knew she would not be able to get out on her own.

"Good," he said. He stepped away from her, and without him close, she was suddenly afraid. She heard him open the trunk at the end of his bed, and she tried to turn around, to see what he was doing.

"Face forward," he said, and she did.

Her mind was a tumbling mess, and she focused on the cold iron against her fingertips until she felt something soft graze the backs of her knees.

"This is a cat-o'-nine-tails," he said. "Do you know what it's used for?"

She debated what the right answer was, or if there was one, and before she could come to a conclusion, she felt the hot leather high on one thigh like an explosion of tiny stars.

"A cat-o'-nine-tails," he said, and there were a thousand more stars, "is used," and more, "to discipline little girls. Do you think you need to be disciplined?" he asked.

Her mouth steamed with saliva and her heart started to race. A million times she had played this in her head, and now it was real. Each explosion on her skin insisted it was.

"Hmm?" he said, and brought the whip down again.

"Yes," she said, and it spilled out as if there were someone else speaking for her.

"Yes, what?"

"Yes . . . I," she stuttered and tried to force the words out, "need to be disciplined."

There was a pause, and she could feel him tighten his grip on the whip, feel him take a slow breath in and then out again. He stepped behind her and tapped the thin leather tassels against her thighs. "Yes, Sir," he said.

The words snaked through her ears and into her brain, and she felt tickled harshly from the inside out.

"Yes what?" he asked.

She could feel the leather tapping insistently against her thigh, and she opened her mouth, then closed it, then opened it again.

"Yes what?" he asked again, but this time it was not a question, and she felt suddenly safe in the command.

"Yes, Sir," she whispered.

"Good girl." He ran his fingers through her hair, brushed his lips against her neck. "Do you like this?"

"Yes," she breathed.

He stood still, his fingers fixed in her hair, and waited. His other hand had found her breast, and soon he pulled his hand away and placed it firmly on the back of her neck. "I thought we had just gone over this," he said. "I thought we had just talked about how you were to answer me." He squeezed her gently. "Am I wrong?"

The blood drained to her feet, and she shook her head.

"How are you to answer?"

"Yes, Sir."

"Did you forget?"

"No, Sir."

"So you disobeyed me on purpose?"

"No . . . Sir," she said.

"Then you forgot?"

She spun in circles, wonderful, maddening circles, charged with the game and the unspoken rules, and how easily they had found themselves here. If it was a game, it didn't matter, all that mattered was the force of his commands and the insistent flick of the whip.

"Would you like to know what I think?" He circled behind her. "I think you want to be disciplined. I think that you like getting your ass whipped, that it turns you on."

Yes, Josie thought, I do, I do.

"Slut," he said, and brought the whip down harder.

"Turned on by being tied and beaten." He whipped her with even, steady strokes, a thousand pinpricks caressing her, a million razor-sharp kisses, and she arched her back and was ashamed of how wet it made her.

He stopped, stepped toward her, and placed his hand between her legs. "You *do* like this."

She whimpered and felt she would explode if he moved his hand.

"Not yet," he said, "but I think these can come off now." He pulled her panties down to her knees. "Spread your legs," he said, and she did. "You're to keep these at your knees; don't let them drop. Do you understand?"

She nodded.

He took a step back, and she could hear him sit on the bed.

"You look lovely tied up, your legs spread and your ass red."

There was a long moment of silence, and then he sighed.

"You're going to require much discipline, I see."

She could hear him get up, then the trunk again. "Discipline and deportment."

She ground the balls of her feet into the rug and tried to slow her breathing.

"What does one normally say when one is given a compliment?" he asked

"Thank you . . . Sir," she mumbled.

He stepped toward her. "Yes; one says thank you." He pressed something harder than the soft leather of the whip into her back and ran it over her behind and down to her panties, which she realized she had let drop to the floor.

"I thought I told you to keep these where they were." He tickled her ankle with the object. "We're going to have to do something about that."

She shifted her weight from one foot to the other and whimpered. She knew whatever he had in his hand was going to hurt more than the whip.

"Don't be afraid," he said, "it's just a crop." He held it on her naked skin. "A different sensation." He put his hand on the small of her back and whispered in her ear, "I'm going to give you five strokes; do you think you can take five strokes?"

"Yes, Sir," she said.

"Good girl." He ran his hand through her hair, pressed his thumb into her mouth, and before she could kiss or suck or taste, he brought the crop down in quick succession, five searing strokes that made her cry out. The pain after was almost worse than the strokes. It burned and pulsed, and she stood up on her tiptoes and gripped the iron. Still, she could feel her body craving more, could feel the almost instant rush of need.

"Good girl," he said and stroked her hair, "good, good girl."

She pushed her head into his chest and half wished it was over and half wished he would never stop.

He kissed her forehead. "You took those so nicely for me." He brought his hand softly down to her behind, and she wished she could feel what he did, could touch the searing heat of those five stripes.

He breathed into her hair, and she softened under him. He held her close, and she realized how utterly natural this all felt. All these thoughts, all these fantasies—she had kept them so sequestered that even when she allowed them to creep outside the black box she kept secreted in her head, they felt somehow removed, as if she were watching a movie from the last row—the images sharp, and focused, but far, far away. But now, he seemed to have floated her down, and she stood, not watching, not performing, just herself with him.

She pressed hard against him and felt washed in shame and love, and she sighed into his chest and was closing her eyes when the next swat came. It hurt more than the others, and she jumped and tried to pull away.

"What was that for?" she said, and glared at him.

"Because I wanted to." He grinned, and his eyes were so radiant, she had to look away.

The unfairness of it pricked her, and she tried to turn her back to him, but he held her still. He ran his fingers through her hair and held her tightly. "Now," he whispered. "I'm going to give you five more, and you're to count each of them, nice and loud. Do you understand?"

It was unfair, but she felt her head expand, her body yield, and she nodded.

"Good." He stepped away and brought the crop down, a hot fiery snap.

"One," she said.

Quickly, he did it again, and she cried. "Two." It was electric, and she could feel the welts rise, the heat emanating from the crop to her flesh to her very center. "Three." The top of her head seemed to open up, and with the next molten snap of the crop, she felt sucked into the ether. It was a familiar feeling, this going outside herself, but this time, her consciousness disintegrated, leaving her body below and counting. "Four." Just bones and flesh planted firmly. "Five," and then he was telling her to beg to be fucked, and she was begging, over and over until he was cupping one of her breasts in his hand, and then pushing inside her, his mouth tight on her ear, telling her all the nasty things she'd only thought to herself for years and years and years, and her head was pushing into the cold iron, full of nothing but space and air, her insides alive and present, her outsides his completely.

CHAPTER FIVE

FOR WEEKS AFTER THE FIRST TIME THEY PLAYED, JOSIE FELT AS IF a magic wand had touched each of her nerve endings and made them vibrate. Sometimes in the middle of the night, she would reach below the bed where she had hidden one of the wrist restraints and finger the leather, stroke the silver loops and buckles, and feel the world grow brighter, louder, overstimulating.

And yet, she was also aware that these toys might not have been purchased for her. She wondered how many girls there were before her, how many he had tied to the wall, how many had felt the same leather explosion on their backsides. A lot, she thought, probably a lot, but she was too afraid to ask. It made her stomach churn, and she tried to tell herself that everyone had a past, but the idea didn't make her feel better, and instead she decided that perhaps what came before didn't matter now, that the world had begun that night at the dinner party.

After all, the world even looked like a different place. She would see couples in the grocery store, in restaurants, waiting for the bus, and immediately she would work to categorize them. She would search for clues—the woman signaled the waiter, the man pushed the shopping cart. She would flash on images of them naked, see the blonde woman with the pink handbag on top of the man at the coffee shop. You were either one or the other, and it reminded her of how, after she had lost her virginity, she had wandered around school and saw only virgins and non-virgins. Back then, the possibility that anyone else would think these violent thoughts, let alone act on them, was inconceivable, and she tried to keep focused on whatever bare-chested teenage boy was kissing her neck or caressing her belly. But even her first time, this had been difficult. She had been fifteen and at her mother's holiday party, and had come out of the bathroom to find the high school senior that her mother paid to drive her to school waiting for her. He was a tall, blond boy, a basketball player who only grunted at her to get in or out of the car, but here he was—Scotch in one hand, cigarette in the other—and waiting for her. "You're hot," he said. She felt flattered and scared, and she tried to look cool, flipped her long hair and asked where he got the drink. He tilted it to her mouth until she felt it burn its way down her throat, and then set it on the carpet, ground the cigarette into the glass, and pushed her into the bathroom. She could feel her adrenaline spike, and when he thrust his tongue into her mouth and his hand between her legs, she startled and pushed him away, but he came back quickly. "Come on, baby," he said. "I promise I'll be gentle." He was drunk and clearly incapable of being gentle, and the thought both excited and scared her. "No," she said and went for the door, but he grabbed her, ran his fingers through her hair, and told her to just do it, and the more forceful he became, the more she softened, until it was she who maneuvered herself onto the sink, stripped off her panties, and pulled him to her. She watched the whole thing in the mirror above the toilet, ignoring the slicing pain she felt between her legs, trying to keep her head empty, trying to focus on his hands on her ass, but soon she felt her mind drifting to the dark box in her mind, and the harder she tried to pull it back, the harder it pried at the lid, until eventually the images came rushing out—thick leather belts and hard wood paddles, swift slaps on bare skin, legs bound and spread—this is what bad girls got, this is what they deserved. The thoughts forced themselves on her. They were invading little gremlins, but she was the willing victim.

But now, everyone seemed to fall on one side or the other—friends haggling over a check, strangers sharing the same elevator, and children. She even saw it in Tyler. Lately, he had become more obstinate—refusing to obey and then throwing tantrums that lasted hours. She would print maps from the Internet for him to examine, spill dried macaroni on the floor for him to count, read him entire recipe books—nothing seemed to satisfy him. He had become the Tyler she had only heard of.

A few months after Josie had moved in, Mary confessed that their three previous nannies had quit. "Tyler was too much for them," she said. "But you two are peas in a pod." Josie beamed and, after this, shared every one of her and Tyler's achievements with Mary—Josie taught Tyler to tie his shoes, convinced him to wear jeans, encouraged him to go up to his neck in the swimming pool. Then one day Josie told Mary how she had finally persuaded Tyler to try a bite of broccoli. "It was only a tiny bite," Josie said, "but it was a bite." "Yes, well, you can do everything, can't you?" Mary shot back.

Later, Mary had apologized, but after that, Josie kept their successes to herself.

And there had also been that one drunken night last year. After the kids had gone to bed, they had opened a bottle of wine and told stories about their own mothers. "Mine made me wear skirts until I graduated high school," Mary said. "Mine told an entire dinner party I had gotten my period," Josie said. They laughed and then Mary was quiet. "Sometimes I wish Tyler was normal," she said, and when Josie tried to console her, tell her that those feelings had to be expected, Mary interrupted her. "He knows," she said. "I think he knows I love Maddy more." She paused, looked at Josie, and said, "But he has you now. Little Miss Perfect." Josie did not know what to say, and they stared at each other through the thick glaze of drunkenness until Mary laughed and Josie tried to, but she could feel the steely accusation beneath the confession.

But now even Josie was pulling away from Tyler—Josie who brought his measuring tape to school when he forgot it, who carried toothpicks in her purse for him to count when he felt anxious, who never forced hugs or kisses on him. And his mother was no better. Mary had been working more and more—attending at the hospital, researching in the lab, and trying to get a grant proposal in by Thanksgiving. She was tired and irritable, and she alternately wanted to be alone with the kids or have them as far away from her as possible, but it was impossible to tell which until she was either snapping at Josie or yelling at Tyler. Josie reasoned that the tension would pass. Mary was under a lot of pressure; Josie was keeping only their agreed-upon hours now. New circumstances took adjusting to. But

Devesh disagreed. "She wants you all for herself," he said. "What nanny do you know that has a glass of wine waiting for her mistress when she comes home?" "I don't do that anymore." Josie scowled, but she had. Still, Josie knew it was more than that, felt Mary's resentment tunneling more often to the surface—each bitter comment pushing Josie a bit farther away from the girl who wanted nothing more than to share a cigarette with Mary.

But it was Tyler she felt most sorry for. So, one hot afternoon when he begged to go to the park, and she wanted nothing more than to sit under the cool blast of the air conditioner and drink iced tea, she buckled his sandals and told him that if Maddy got too hot, they would have to go home. She thought she would push him on the swings for a few minutes, let him make tiny mountains of sand for a while, and then tell him Maddy needed to be inside, but when they got to the park, she found Phillip sprawled under a magnolia tree cutting coupons.

She had met Phillip and his daughter at Tyler's adaptive physical education class. He was young and smoked, and he preferred her company to the mothers who talked church gossip and claimed their children didn't really need to be in the class. He told her his wife had died of a brain aneurysm when Katie was six months old. He leaned back in his chair, and said in his thick southern drawl, "We both cried a lot and sucked down a number of bottles," and she knew he was flirting with her. He was good looking—dirty-blond hair and natural muscles—and so after weeks of listening to him compliment her on the green of her eyes, her perfectly freckled shoulders, she figured the novelty would at least be interesting, and she followed him back to his house. They sent Tyler and Katie outside to play, put Madeline down for a nap on Phillip's bed, and fucked in the bathroom. After that, they saw each other often, but they had an understanding. She didn't want a relationship, and he was moving to Atlanta to run his uncle's restaurant. Long distance was impossible, he said, and she happily agreed. Still, often when he held her, she could sense his loneliness, could feel him try to squeeze her inside of himself, and this was what made her knock softly on his door only when she had less than an hour to spare.

"Hey, Mister Mom," she said, and pushed the stroller beside him. Tyler ran to find Katie, and Phillip looked up and smiled.

"Don't make me get up," he teased.

"When did you get into town?" she asked, and sat down next to him. The last time she had talked to him was on the phone almost a month ago. He was in Atlanta, experimenting with bluefish and polenta, and she had spent the entire conversation trying to decide whether she should tell him about Devesh. She hadn't, and now she wished she had.

"We got in last night," he said. "We're visiting my parents for the weekend."

"How's Atlanta?"

"The restaurant opens in two weeks," he said. "I'd love for you to come down."

She looked at the ground and nodded. "And Katie? She's happy?" she asked.

"Yes; fine. She just started camp. They've now informed me she no longer has poor spatial orientation. Instead, she has delayed motor proficiency, whatever that means."

Josie managed a smile but felt uncomfortable now with Phillip. She didn't know what to do with her body, and she worked on trying to extract strands of grass at the root. There was a long silence, and she listened to the high-pitched squeal of the swings grinding back and forth.

"It's good to see you," he said and placed his hand on her knee. She hadn't felt his hands on her in months, and she tensed.

"Yeah," she said.

Last winter, Phillip and she had gone to dinner. They had drunk too much bourbon, and on the walk home he pushed her against a brick wall and ran his hand up her skirt. She let him, but when he nuzzled her neck and whispered he loved her, she stiffened and pushed her hands against his chest. "No, you don't," she said, and when he insisted, told her he had for months, she twisted out of his arms, told him he was drunk, and took him home. They never spoke of it, and she passed it off as drunk-speak, but she knew he was earnest, had felt his sincerity curl around her like an octopus.

"It's good to see you too," she said. She fingered the pile of grass she had made and shifted uncomfortably. "I'm seeing someone," she blurted. "A guy. A man." She stumbled and couldn't look at him.

"Oh." He paused. "That's great. That's . . . really great."

She was wearing a skirt, and she thought about the eraser-sized bruises high on her right thigh.

"He's a doctor . . . . He's Indian" She tugged at her skirt.

"Dots or feathers?" he asked.

She looked up at him and slapped his knee. "Indian like from India."

He laughed and nodded, and she was thankful.

"You know him through Mary?"

"Kind of."

"That's great." He paused again. "And . . . you're happy?"

She felt oddly protective, and she wanted to change the subject. "Where's Tyler?" she said.

"They're under the slide."

She looked and could see Tyler in the shade doing something with Katie's hair. She heard Katie shriek, and she was glad to get off the subject of Devesh.

"Tyler," she yelled. "What are you doing?"

She waited for Tyler to answer, but he didn't.

"What are they doing?" she said to Phillip.

He shrugged. There was a long pause, and then he said, "Look; it's okay with me. The guy, I mean. I'm happy for you. If you're happy . . ."

Katie shrieked again and then there were giggles.

"I'm gonna see what's going on," she said, and walked across the hot sand. She was surprised at how difficult it was for her to talk about Devesh, and not only with Phillip. The other day, she had simply mentioned Devesh's name to a classmate and immediately tensed, as if discussing him would make whatever was between the two of them dissipate like a spoken birthday wish.

She walked around the jungle gym and heard Tyler's voice. "Lay still," he said. Josie felt her body jolt.

"And don't talk," he said.

Next to the slide was a hollow cement cylinder that had been turned into a hideout, and when she crept beside it, she could see in and under the slide and still be hidden.

"Don't move," Tyler said. His voice was strong, and she almost didn't recognize it.

"I'm not," Katie said. She was lying on her back with her arms and legs spread as if she were making a snow angel.

She could see Tyler burying Katie's feet, piling sand in mounds and then packing it forcefully down.

"Don't move," he said.

"I'm not."

"You moved your hand."

"No, I didn't."

"Yes you did," he said and topped first her left and then her right hand with sand. He pressed down on each with both his palms, and she giggled.

"I'm stuck," she said.

Tyler looked at her.

"I can't move," she said.

He didn't say anything, and Josie could see his brain working like a movie projector, each frame skimming quickly past his eyes. He could pull Katie's hair, tickle her tummy, bury her completely. She saw his mind spin in on itself, and she waited, but instead he started digging, and Josie realized that she had been holding her breath.

"I'm digging a hole," Tyler said.

"Let's dig a tunnel," Katie said, and unearthed herself. "You dig on the other side and we'll make our hands meet."

Josie leaned her head against the warm concrete. She looked at Tyler and Katie on their knees, collecting sand between their thighs, and realized she had wanted to see what Tyler would do but, more so, wanted to see Katie's reaction.

That night, she cuddled into Devesh's chest and told him about Tyler and Katie.

"It was . . . scary," she said. "I could see what he was thinking."

"You could see what *you* were thinking."

She thought about this. When she was six, maybe seven, she had gone to a Fourth of July party at a beach house. She couldn't remember the house or the hosts, but she did remember the little boy who dug a hole big enough to lie down in. She had crawled in and asked him to bury her, and when he said no, she closed her eyes and refused to move until he got bored and went in for ice cream. She lay in the bottom of the cool pit and wished the sand would spill around her. Of course, it hadn't, and she eventually called for her father, who laughed and packed her in. She could feel his hands, the sand a buffer between the two of them, and with each scoop she felt more and more compressed and more and more weightless. It had been blissful, and she had closed her eyes until she heard her mother's laugh, saw her red toenails, and then shot instantly up and out of the hole. Her mother pulled Josie to her, called her her little mummy, and kissed the top of her sandy head, but Josie knew she had been caught doing something very wrong.

"Well," Devesh said. "Freud says all children have a desire to be punished, that it's a normal stage in development." He rested his hands under his head. "Don't you remember wanting to be spanked?"

Of course she remembered, but she never imagined that other children envisioned the same things, soothed themselves to sleep with images of paddles and rulers and hairbrushes. She had thought these things for as long as she could remember and had hated it. What kid thinks these things? What kid *wants* them? Bad kids, she thought. And she had been a bad kid. Her mother could regale her with stories of her horrendous behavior: "You cut your braids off just to spite me," she told her. "You once locked Natalie in the laundry room for *five* hours; your Aunt Steffi had to call a locksmith!" Her mother would laugh and shake her head, and Josie, grown now, would try to manage an amused smile. "Thank God you grew out of that," her mother would say, only sometimes adding "mostly. . . ."

"According to Freud, there are three stages of discipline fixation," Devesh continued. "In the first stage, a child imagines a sibling being beaten by his father. In the second stage, the child himself is being beaten by his father, and in the third stage the child watches a number of unknown children being beaten, this time by a supposed surrogate father . . . a teacher or someone." He ran his fingers through her hair. "The children who get stuck in that third stage are the ones that grow up to be perverts, turn into sadists and masochists." He ran his hand down her neck to her belly and tickled her. "Are you a pervert?"

She squealed and pulled away from him. "You're a pervert."

"Me? Never," he teased and rolled on his side to face her.

She wanted him to tell her more, to explain her fantasies away as nothing but a childhood phase. It was a lovely thought—something small and innocent—and she closed her eyes and let him play with her hair.

"But I don't buy the whole Freudian analysis," he said. "Submission and domination are too primal. Most likely they're an evolutionary adaptation that came down through the apes, who built societies on very explicit negotiations of dominance and submission designed to maximize genetic reproduction."

The scientific terminology was soothing, and she relaxed under his touch.

He grabbed her hands and pinned them over her head. "And what do you think, my little masochist? Do you think you're still part monkey or did you get stuck in your kid head?"

"I don't know." She could hear her voice get girlish, and she tucked her chin into her chest.

"Hmmm?" he said.

She wanted to tell him that either explanation was fine with her—nature, childhood development—however he wanted to rationalize it, the important part was that it just *was*, no reason other than fundamental human nature. Many people had these thoughts, no need to be ashamed, no need to worry about why.

"I think you like the idea of being a little girl."

She shook her head, but it was a feeble attempt.

"I think you wished you were Katie." He ran his finger under the elastic of her panties. "Is that what you wished?"

She could feel the heat of his hand, and she willed his fingers higher.

"Hmm?" He smiled. "You're a naughty little girl for thinking those thoughts, aren't you?"

The blood rushed to her head. Her heart pounded. Her hands shook. Those words: naughty . . . little . . . girl. Her chest tightened, and she thought she might lose all ability to breathe.

He pulled her to him, and in a moment she was over his lap and back to the hazy world where she existed exclusively for him. And then she was on her feet, nose pressed to the corner, panties lowered, and then on the bed—on her knees, her back, her stomach—all real and all for him. She felt so powerless that when he finally lay beside her and asked her to kiss him, she had to remember that she was in charge of her own body.

"Pretty girl," he said.

She snuggled into his chest and gripped him tightly. "How did you know?" she stumbled. "How did you know I would be like this?"

He kissed her head. "How did I know you were a pervert?" he teased.

She pushed away, and he rolled her on top of him.

"Magical powers," he said.

She sat atop him and pushed her palms against his chest. "No; really," she said.

"I didn't. I guessed. Thought there was a high probability."

"Why?" she asked.

"Why?" he mimicked. "Because you whined when I grabbed your wrists."

"I did not."

"You whimpered."

"That's not whining, and I didn't."

"Whimpered, whined, either way, and, yes, you did. You whimpered . . . loudly."

She sighed and pouted. "But that was later. How did you know before, in the backyard?"

"Maybe I didn't know. Maybe I just wanted you to be." He grinned at her.

She sighed again and crossed her arms over her chest.

"I don't know. The way you looked at me, looked down when I stared at you, blushed, tensed. I don't know. And that's enough of this." He pulled her off of him. "I'm going to get some water."

She nodded, but when he got up, she felt such an instant rush of panic that she called him back.

"What?" he said.

"I want to come with you."

He smiled. "All right; come," he said and walked out of the bedroom.

She wished he would carry her, and she padded quickly after him.

"Wait," she said, and wrapped her hands so fiercely around his forearm that when he finally reached the kitchen he had to pry her off to turn on the faucet.

"Josie," he said. "You have to let go for a second."

She did, but she could feel her anxiety spike and wished she could wrap herself around his finger like a ring. If he had seen her so clearly, had read her in only one look, what could other people see? She tried to remember what he had said— those wants, those needs—they were all natural, and the naughty girl stuff—that was just play, but she now felt bandaged in uncertainty. Even if other people did want these things, she was sure they didn't want them for real.

"Did you"—she paused—"did you think those things when you were little?"

"What things?" He put down the water glass and wiped his mouth.

"About being beaten . . . like you said about all children." What she wanted to ask was not only this, but if he had carried—still carried—that constant ache of shame and need in his belly.

"Did I imagine being beaten? No. I imagined being grown and spanking women. I was a precocious child." He smiled.

"How come?"

"How come women? It turned me on. If I had been attracted to men, I would have been beating them, I suppose."

She nodded, but he had misunderstood her. She wanted to know if he really believed what he said, if he was one-hundred-percent sure that there was no reason for a little boy wanting to bring a leather whip violently down on a woman's bare skin, no shameful explanation behind this desire.

"But . . . why?"

"Why what?"

"Why did you think those things?"

"I don't know, bunny. Nature? Must there be a reason for everything?"

She was silent. If he was really so completely unashamed, then why the very expensive wooden toy chest he had commissioned? It was two feet deep with a false bottom that hid his whips, and paddles, and cuffs. "If the house is robbed," she had teased, "they'll take the TV and computer, but they won't find the toys!" But she knew his explanation. He didn't want his father stumbling upon a leather flogger when he visited from India, didn't want his mother discovering the restraints while searching for bedsheets. He couldn't risk *their* embarrassment. Still, wasn't there more? She wondered if it was really possible to be so untroubled by all this. She looked at him. His bare chest was dark and strong with thin black hairs running along his belly, and she wanted to feel small and close to him, wanted him to take away that marble of shame she had carried in her heart for all these years. "Pick me up."

He grabbed her hand and pulled her to him. "You're too big to be picked up." He leaned in to kiss her cheek and, as he did, scooped her into his arms and cradled her against him.

"Like this?" he asked.

She felt the marble throb, and she nodded and wound her arms tightly around his neck.

"Baby girl," he said, and rocked her.

She laid her head on his shoulder and wished she could peel back the years, twenty-seven, twenty-six, twenty-five, until she was six, five, four, and free of everything that came after.

CHAPTER SIX

THE NEXT MORNING, JOSIE LEFT DEVESH'S HOUSE AS THE SUN WAS coming up. Her cell phone rang and she answered it as she quietly closed the front door.

"Hello," she whispered.

"Are you in a movie?" her mother asked.

"No; it's six o'clock in the morning."

"Oh. Sorry. This insomnia is keeping me up again. I figured it had to be daytime somewhere."

"Well . . . almost," Josie said.

"So how's school?"

"Good."

"Work?"

"Didn't we have this conversation last week?" Josie asked. She pulled one of Devesh's sweatshirts over her head and crossed the street.

Her mother sighed. "Yes, well . . ." She paused, then started again. "So I bought this book for you. It's called . . . wait, let me get my glasses."

Josie heard a drawer open, some shuffling, then her father's muffled voice. "Where are you?" Josie asked.

"It's Josie," Josie heard her mother say. "No, nothing. Go

back to sleep." There was a pause; then her mother was talking to her again. "Okay it's called . . ."

"Why don't you go out of the bedroom?" Josie asked.

"Yes; that's a good idea."

Josie heard her mother walking down the hall, probably to one of the spare bedrooms on the second floor.

"Okay; there." Her mother sighed. "Now, let's see. Steffi and I found it together. It's called *The Definitive Guide to Underground Humor: Quaint Quotes About Death, Funny Funeral Home Stories, and Hilarious Headstone Epitaphs.* And some of these quotes, Josie, are just too funny. Listen to this: 'Three days after death, hair and fingernails continue to grow, but phone calls taper off.' That's Johnny Carson."

"Funny," Josie said. She had to admit, it was an offering.

"And here's another one: 'My Uncle Pat, every morning he reads the death column in the paper. And he can't understand how people always die in alphabetical order.' Hah! That's Hal Roach."

Josie crossed the street and headed down Walker. The sun had now risen, and Josie squinted into the light. "Thanks, Mom."

"Well, I just saw it and thought immediately of you."

Josie laughed. "Well, I guess that's a good thing."

"Of course it's a good thing. You're my little Morbid Munchkin."

Josie smiled and rolled her eyes.

"I'll have your dad FedEx it on Monday," her mother said. "Maybe I'll go watch the Food Channel. They have this man who builds cakes that look just like people. Your dad wanted to get one of me for my birthday."

"All right," Josie said. "Talk to you soon."

"'Bye, darling."

Josie closed her phone, smiled, and shook her head. Her mother and her Aunt Steffi were constantly picking up what they thought were hysterical gifts for both Josie and Natalie. Before they went to camp they were both given motorized marshmallow turners; when they graduated from college it was an alarm clock that spun off the bedside table when the snooze button was pushed. Natalie and Josie would roll their eyes, and Natalie always pawned hers off on a friend, but Josie had kept them all. Even now, when she visited her parents, she would often come across some gift at the back of her closet—an egg-laying-chicken key chain, a singing Santa pen—and not be able, still, to discard it. She was just like her father who wore the holey sweater her mother had knitted for him while they were dating. But her mother was entirely unsentimental—gifts were received, used, and then given to charity. She kept nothing except a small lock of Matthew's baby hair from his first haircut. Josie had found it— a lone blond curl unceremoniously tucked in an old envelope— when she was fifteen and rifling through her mother's bedside table looking for stray cigarettes. Her brother had had unusually thick hair for a ten month old—curls that spiraled down his neck and hung in his eyes. "He looks like a girl," Josie had said. "She's right, Carol," her father agreed, "it's got to be cut." Her mother had resisted but finally given in, and all four of them had traipsed down to the salon. Her father had sat Matthew on his lap and they had all held their breath while the barber steadied the scissors. "He's going to scream," four-year-old Josie had said. "He'll move, John," her mother said; "he'll be cut." But Matthew had done neither. To everyone's surprise, he had laughed— hiccupy giggles every time the barber snipped. And then they were all laughing, the curls spiraling to the ground, Josie scooping up the fallen locks from the floor and bringing her mother a pillow of silky ringlets to choose from.

Josie realized she had stopped walking. She was suddenly very tired, and she wondered if she might be able to get another hour of sleep before Mary needed her. She walked quickly home, but when she arrived and opened the door, she could hear Tyler screaming. She closed her eyes, took a deep breath, and went upstairs.

Tyler was sitting on the floor, fully dressed.

"What's the problem?" she asked.

"They're biting me," he howled.

"*What* is biting you?"

"The shoes!"

"Well, take them off then." She bent down to untie them, but Mary walked in and stopped her.

"Leave them on," Mary said.

"I'll take them to be stretched."

"No." They had argued about this before—Mary insisting Tyler do something, Josie trying to soften her. Usually Josie could get Tyler to do what she wanted. She was a master of distraction, and Mary often wondered aloud how she had ever gotten Tyler out of the house before Josie. But in the last few weeks, as Josie spent less and less of her free time with Tyler, he had become more stubborn, as had Mary—insisting her son be obedient, compliant, normal. It was ridiculous, but Josie quietly conceded.

"Mary . . ." Josie tried.

"He has to learn. People aren't going to be coddling him forever."

"I'm not coddling him," Josie said. This seemed a point-less struggle, a power game Mary was unfairly playing, and with Tyler nonetheless. Josie felt a swell of indignation burn through her chest. You couldn't play games with an unwilling participant.

"If they hurt Maddy, you'd take them off her."

"He's not Maddy."

"No kidding," Josie muttered. She bent to pull the shoes from his feet.

"Leave them on!" Mary yelled.

Tyler cried louder and Josie didn't move. She wanted to be angry, to turn and spit out something horrible—he does know, she could say, he knows you love Maddy more—but what did it matter? Mary was right, and Josie felt like she often did under her mother's gaze, that weighted feeling, as if Mary had draped her with a leaded X-ray gown. "Fine," Josie said.

"Good," Mary said, and Josie knew that the tiny space they had wedged between them had just widened.

Josie waited until she heard the slam of the front door and then pulled the shoes from Tyler's feet.

"You can wear your sandals until Mommy gets home," she told him. "Now go play in the backyard for a bit." She got him a juice box, sent him outside, and sat down to read, but she couldn't concentrate. Last week Mary had taken Tyler to the library. "Just the two of us," she had told him, but within half an hour they were home again—Tyler sobbing, Mary storming out of the house to her office. Josie hadn't said anything, but Mary had scoffed at her on the way out. Josie took a deep breath and read the same page again.

"Josie," Tyler called.

"I'm in my room!" she yelled.

"There's a bird outside." He stood in the doorway with a long stick in his hand.

"That's good," she said absentmindedly. "What kind of bird?"

"A red bird," he said.

"Uh-huh."

He stood there, not moving.

"Why don't you go look up what kind of bird it is," she said and shut the book to check her e-mail.

He ran to his room and then back with his bird almanac. "It's a Northern Cardinal," he read. "Size: eight to nine inches. Range: eastern half of United States and west to the great plains. Food: seeds and fruit. And it's a male because it's red."

"Hmm," Josie muttered. "What other animals are out there?"

"I'll go look," he said, and dashed out the door.

He was only gone a minute when he ran back, breathless. "There are no other animals. Just ants. Ants are insects."

"I see," Josie said. "Why don't you go count them?"

"I tried," he said. "There are too many, and they're crawling too fast on the bird."

"What?" She turned and looked at him. "They're on the bird?"

He nodded.

"Where's the bird?"

"On the ground."

Josie sighed. "Why didn't you tell me?" She stood and walked outside. It was bright and she squinted in the sunlight. "You didn't touch it, did you?"

"No."

"Where is it?"

Tyler led her to the cardinal. It was lying on its side beneath the oak tree, its bright red wings tucked close to its body, its bill wide open. It hadn't been dead long, but the ants had already begun to swarm in and around its chest.

"Oh, God," Josie said, and turned her head.

"What's wrong with it?" Tyler asked.

"It's dead," she said.

"Oh." He was staring intently at the bird.

"Do you know what dead means?"

"It means it's not alive," he said.

Once they had gone to the park with Phillip and Katie and seen a dead squirrel on the sidewalk, but Phillip had said it was only sleeping and Josie had just added "for a long, long time." Now, she placed her hand on Tyler's shoulder. He stiffened, and she removed it. "Do you know what alive means?"

"It means it's not dead."

Josie smiled. "Yes." She looked at the bird, its bright red chest puffed unnaturally out. "I think we should bury it. We can find an old shoebox and dig a hole under the tree."

"Why?" he said. He was still staring at the bird, and Josie took a deep breath and tried to figure out how to explain this.

"Dead means not here anymore," she said and realized this was obviously untrue. "The body is here, but it doesn't work anymore, so we bury the body."

"Why doesn't it work anymore?"

"Well. . . ." She took a deep breath. "When things get old, they sometimes stop working. Like cars." She closed her eyes and grimaced. "And animals." She paused.

"People are animals," Tyler said.

"That's true." She wondered how she could possibly be this bad at explaining what death meant when she could speak for hours on what the living did with the dead.

"When do animals stop working?" he asked.

"When they're old, Tyler. When they're very, very old."

"But when?"

Josie sighed. "When . . . when . . . when their bodies stop working. When their hearts stop working."

"Blood makes the heart work," he said.

"Yes. Yes, that's exactly right. People's bodies stop working when there's not enough blood going to the heart." She realized this was what he was asking all along. He was unconcerned with the philosophical reasons. He just wanted the science.

"Oh," he said, and was quiet a minute. "But where does the bird go?"

"He goes in the ground. We need to put him in the ground."

"No, where does the *bird* go?"

And then she understood. He meant its consciousness. He meant its self. "You mean the bird's . . . the bird's . . ." She didn't know which word to use, and she knew less about how to explain. "The bird's soul?"

He didn't answer, but she knew he understood.

"That's a good question."

He stood quietly, waiting.

"I guess . . . I guess the bird goes to be with God. The bird goes to heaven," she said. If Mary hadn't wanted Josie to make decisions about her son's shoes, she sure wouldn't want Josie making decisions about his faith. She had no idea what Mary believed other than that she had been raised some mild version of Episcopal. She had never heard her talk about God or religion, and they never went to church, but Tyler was attending a Christian day school, and Josie was sure they had at least mentioned heaven.

"How do you know?" he asked.

Josie pressed her fingers to her temples. Who knew what happened after death? It was a futile question, and all anyone could really do was concentrate on who and what was left. "I *don't* know, Tyler. But we can bury the bird. We can give it a funeral."

"What's a funeral?"

"It's when you put the bird . . . the body of the bird . . . in the ground, and you say some things about the bird, and you say some prayers."

"Why?"

"Because . . . because . . ." Because it helps the living deal with death, she wanted to say. Instead, she took a deep breath. "It helps the bird get to heaven," she said.

He was silent, still staring intently at the bird. The black circles of ants had grown.

"Come on. You can measure the box and the hole, and make sure everything is straight and equal." She put her hand on his shoulder, and he shrugged it off and dropped the stick.

"It's too sunny out here. It hurts my eyes," he said.

"We'll get your sunglasses," she said. "And we can use that new shoebox for the bird."

He stood for a minute, nudged the stick with his foot, and then sighed. "Okay," he said. "But you have to dig the hole."

They found the shoebox, lined it with balled-up toilet paper and some grass Tyler insisted she pull from the lawn, and took the box, a measuring tape, and a spade back outside. Tyler watched as Josie gingerly scooped the bird into the box and closed the lid. Digging the hole was more difficult, and Josie struggled with it until Tyler was sure it measured a perfect eighteen inches.

"Do you want to put the box in the ground?" Josie asked.

He said nothing and turned the tape measure over and over in his hands.

"All right, well . . . I guess I'll do it." She placed the box carefully in the hole and stood. "Now we have to cover it up with dirt."

Tyler stared at the tape measure, and Josie wondered if he was counting the rotations.

"I'm assuming you don't want to do that either," she said.

He was silent, and she knelt and filled the hole and then patted the dirt with the back of the spade. "Well," she said, and stood, "that's it. It's done. We can go inside."

"You said you have to say some things about the bird, you said you have to say prayers." He didn't look up, and Josie stared at the silver measuring tape in his hands, watched the sun glint off the corners.

"Right. Okay." She dusted the dirt from her knees and took a deep breath. "He was a good bird," she started. She was sure she had watched this scene on some bad sitcom. If she had thought to put a piece of bread or seeds in the box, she could have spoken about the bird's journey, how he would eat the food on his long trip to the afterlife. She could have given a Ghanaian funeral, made the bird an Akan cardinal. "But now he's someplace better," she continued. She glanced at Tyler. He had stopped playing with the measuring tape and was now staring solemnly at the patted earth.

"Is he in heaven now?" He looked up at her, and she felt a spasm of guilt. He looked so small, so young, and she wondered if she had been that believing when she was four, and her brother Matthew died. She imagined she had. She had been sent to Sunday School a handful of times, and the family had gone to church on a few Easters, but that was before Matthew's death. After, no one seemed to care about Jesus or redemption, and Josie thought Matthew had probably gone to heaven not because her parents told her so, but because she remembered how, at Sunday School, she had colored a picture of heaven with smiling winged babies floating on clouds. But she had learned soon after that souls didn't float around in some cosmic or heavenly sphere. When she was eight, she had watched an after-school television special where a teenage girl had told her mother she hated her before she left for school one morning. That afternoon, the girl came home to find her house surrounded by police cars and ambulances, and her mother dead. Josie couldn't remember what happened in the middle of the program, but at the end, the mother mystically appeared at the foot of the girl's bed one night to forgive her daughter. Josie had no idea that someone who was dead could appear again. She had been told that Matthew was never coming back, but here was this woman returning to grant forgiveness. The idea was astounding, and for weeks she whispered "Matthew, I hate you" out her bedroom window at night. But of course, Matthew hadn't appeared, and one morning, when she once again woke up with no visit from her brother, she went downstairs and hurled every throwable object she could find at the television. After that, Josie knew that dead meant dead, and it was the people who were left that you had to deal with. That's who funerals were for—the people left. It didn't matter to the dead what food or clothing or adornments they were buried with, whether the day and time of the service were auspicious, what each family member shaved or painted or tore.

But to Tyler it mattered, and the existence of someplace better suddenly seemed quite possible. The thought pricked her roughly, and she shook her head.

"Almost done," she said. She didn't know what to say next, but the idea of telling him that yes, the bird was in heaven with God watching from above made her palms damp and her heart quicken. "Do you want to say a prayer?" she asked.

"I don't know any prayers," he said.

"Don't you say prayers at school?"

"Only before we eat."

"Well . . . do you want to say that one?"

"It's only before we eat," he said, and pushed the hair out of his eyes.

"Come on, Tyler," she said. "You want the bird to get to heaven, don't you?" She couldn't believe she was coaxing him like this, but the thought of saying a prayer herself, putting the words 'please' and 'God' together made the blood rush to her head, and she wished Devesh was here, his hands firmly on her waist, keeping her steady and in place.

"Yes," he said, and began turning the measuring tape.

She watched him turn it, watched it glint in his hands. He turned it once, twice, three times. He was making her nervous.

All of this was making her nervous, and she had a sudden desire either to shake Tyler or be shaken herself.

"Come on, Tyler. Say it."

He turned the tape measure. Eight, nine, ten times, and with each turn Josie felt the blood pulse in her head. Finally on the twelfth turn, he started. "God is great," he said. "God is good." He turned the tape rhythmically with the words. "Let us thank him for this food."

"That's it," she said quickly. "We're done. Let's go inside." Her heart was still beating rapidly, and she couldn't understand how something as innocuous as a bird funeral could make her feel so . . . so . . . provoked. She cringed at what she had instinctively felt—the desire to shake him, to rid herself of the thought that something, someone, was looking down on them.

"Go inside, Tyler," she said. "I'll be there in a minute."

He walked across the grass, onto the patio, and then stopped.

"What?" she said.

"Now," he said. He looked up and past her, and she knew she should remind him to look at her. People know you're talking to them when you look at them, she should say, but she didn't want him looking at her. He stared past the tree, over the fence, and far, far away.

"Now the bird is in heaven," he said. He nodded his head, and Josie felt the motion in the pit of her stomach. No, she wanted to say. He's not. It's just for us. The funeral is just for us. But the trickle of uncertainty had begun to bleed into her, and instead she focused on the fence and began to count the posts.

*   *   *

That evening, when Josie arrived at Devesh's house, he was waiting on the porch.

"Turn around," he said. "Get in the car."

"Where are we going?"

He smiled mischievously. "It's a surprise."

She raised her eyebrows.

"Come on. We're going to be late." He got into the car, and she slid into the passenger's seat.

"Tell me," she pleaded.

"Nope," he said and switched on the radio. It was a country music station, and she groaned.

"Not this again," she said. The first time he tuned the radio to the country station, she thought he was joking. Instead, he gave her a lecture on the virtues of country music. "Each song is a narrative," he explained. "Conflict, crisis, and resolution all in three minutes. Where else can you get that?"

Now, she rolled her eyes and rested her head against the window.

"Next time I'll do it better," he sang. "Next time I'll do it right."

She shook her head. "If you're taking me to a country music concert, I'm going to kill you."

"You're going to love it," he said.

She sat up straight in her seat. "No, absolutely not. I refuse."

"Oh, you do, do you?" He raised his eyebrows, and she shrank back into her seat. "We're not going to a country music concert," he said. "Don't worry."

"Then where are we going?"

"Patience, patience."

She sighed and looked out the window. The trees were thick with kudzu, the vines spiraling up tree trunks, covering enormous birches and maples, making them look like giant topiaries. She watched the scenery whir by and felt the intensity of the day begin to lessen. He placed his hand on her knee, and she closed her eyes and smiled.

"I'm going to fall asleep," she said. "I always do. In cars."

"It's okay," he said, and stroked her knee.

The car rolled rhythmically beneath her, and she listened to the light twang of the guitars, felt the setting sun fall along her cheek, and drifted into a soft sleep.

When they arrived, the sun had set. Streetlights illuminated the sidewalk, but it looked like any other suburb—strip malls with dry cleaners, car dealerships, drugstores, and fast food restaurants.

"Where are we?"

"Amory," he said, and pulled into a parking lot.

She rubbed her eyes and sat up straight. "Why?"

"Look," he said, and pointed to her right.

It was a normal suburban movie theater, but the marquee read *Ek Pyaar*. She turned back to him.

"This is how a Bollywood movie *should* be seen," he said, and stepped out of the car. He was smiling brightly, and when he grabbed her hand, he squeezed it repeatedly.

At the box office, there was a line of Indians—grandmothers in saris chastising rambunctious little boys, teenage girls with bright lipstick and tight jeans, women speaking animatedly and shaking their gold-bangled wrists, young men, old men, toddlers, and babies. Josie felt suddenly shy, and she leaned into Devesh's side.

"Will it have subtitles?" she whispered.

"No, but this one has a good amount of English. You'll get it."

In front of them, a woman stood with her hands on a little girl's shoulders. "Give Auntie a kiss," she said, pushing the girl toward a woman in a bright yellow top, but the girl turned her face into her mother's legs. "*Arre*," the woman said; "suddenly she's shy. Come." The line moved forward, and Josie held tightly to Devesh. He paid for the tickets, and they followed the line into the packed theater.

"There are so many people," she said.

"They only play Hindi movies twice a month. Some enterprising family probably rents the theater. See that man selling Samosas?" he asked, pointing at an old man walking the aisles. "He's probably the grandfather. Do you want one?"

She shrugged, but he had already waved the man over. "Two," he said, and the man handed him two fried pastries. "How much?" Devesh asked and handed Josie the Samosas.

"Two dollars," the old man said.

Devesh paid, and they found seats near the back.

"Eat," Devesh said.

It was hot and spicy and greasy, and Josie ate it quickly.

"Good?" Devesh asked.

Josie nodded and wiped her fingers on her jeans. He smiled and put his arm around her shoulders.

"I'm the only white girl here," she whispered.

"The box office girl was white," he said, and kissed her cheek. "You could pass for a Parsi girl. Maybe." He looked at her and laughed. "Maybe not."

He smiled and squeezed her to him, and Josie realized she had never seen him so boyish. She could imagine him young, kicking his heels against the back of the seat, throwing greasy Samosa wrappers at his buddies.

The lights dimmed, and the theater was filled with heavy drums and the tinny sound of a sitar. The camera panned over a large city, spiraling closer and closer until the title appeared.

"Aren't there any previews?" she asked.

"The movie's already over three hours, *baba*."

"Three hours?"

"There's an intermission."

She sat and watched the city appear: huge apartment buildings, windows lined with laundry; shops with names like Shiva Electronics and Sri Ganesh Cycles; streets crammed with black and yellow cabs, buses, and motorcycles; tea vendors; men on street corners; packs of uniformed schoolchildren.

"This is Bombay," Devesh whispered.

The camera wound through the busy streets until it stopped at a tiny house. A young man stood in the doorway. "Rajeev," he yelled.

"Who's that?" Josie asked.

"The hero," Devesh said. "He lives with his widowed mother and his younger brothers and sister. But you have to watch."

"You've seen it?"

"Yes, yes, but sh. Watch."

It was an easy plot to follow: the poor boy falls in love with the rich girl whose father won't let them marry. There were lots of songs and people dancing on hilltops and in front of waterfalls despite the fact that it took place in the city, and Josie alternately watched the screen and Devesh. He would lean forward in his seat during the happy songs, and back and down during the sad. It made her smile, and despite the fact that she couldn't understand half of the dialogue, she didn't want it to end. She liked that the audience talked to the screen, that the babies cried, that the teenage girls giggled behind her. The theater seemed to swell with life. She felt it in herself, felt her heart grow bigger, and she wanted to lean over and whisper in Devesh's ear: This is what I feel for you. Instead, she held his hand closely and watched the girl on the screen cry into the boy's arms. The boy hugged her to him, and when the music swelled and he held her at arm's length and spoke, she knew it was important.

"What did he say?' she whispered.

"*Hamara saat janmon ka saath hai,*" Devesh said. "It means 'our togetherness will be for seven lives.' It means their karma is linked, even when they die." He squeezed her hand, and she stiffened. She knew about Hinduism, how one life affected the next, but with the textbook gone and the concept played out in fifteen-foot form above her, the idea of life after death suddenly seemed as possible as the pressure of his hand and the flutter in her chest. She closed her eyes, but her heart seemed to beat it. There's more, it beat, there's more, there's more, there's more.

She could hear the boy begin to sing, his voice strong and bright throughout the theater. Devesh leaned over and pressed his lips against her head.

"Do you like it?" he asked.

She nodded, eyes closed.

He kissed her again and pulled her close. "I'm glad," he said.

She could feel his arms around her, strong and solid, and she focused on his hold and tried to stay perfectly, painfully still.

CHAPTER SEVEN

THE NEXT DAY, JOSIE SAT ROCKING MADDY INTO HER DAILY NAP. It was gray and drizzly outside, and Tyler was sick with a cold. She had wrapped him in blankets and set him in front of the television, and now she listened to the drops of rain hit the roof and thought about the night before. Back at the house, Devesh had taken her over his knee and spanked her like a little kid. This was not something new, but it was what came before the spanking that was different. She had lain over his lap and listened to him lecture her for what seemed hours. Did she feel she needed to be disciplined, had she been good all day, had she made herself come without telling him.

She had gone hazy before he even touched her. It was the anticipation, the long relentless minutes when she knew what' was coming and couldn't stop it. Usually it took much more to get her to the place where she felt as if she were swimming in spiderwebs, her mind far gone from her body, but last night it had happened almost instantly. And then he began, slow, even smacks, and she counted them as if they were Christmas gifts. She felt her blood speeding through her veins, felt her body start to pulse, and then it began to rain. She could hear the drops slapping out of cadence with his hand, and abruptly her mind was driven forcefully back into her body. It was the rain. It made her think of Matthew, one quick thought, but enough to propel her back to herself, enough to have to work to not ask him to stop.

At Matthew's funeral, it had rained—a storm that came from nowhere in the middle of the summer. At the reception afterward, she wandered the house, staring at people's darkly clothed knees and listening to adult after adult say something about the peculiarity of the rain, but to her it had seemed completely appropriate. Her brother was dead. God was crying. Her nanny Alba had told her this, and although her mother had scoffed when she repeated it, Josie knew it was true. She had seen her mother cry, her father cry, but there had been no tears with the force of the ones outside. She figured God must be even sadder than her parents, sad enough to create enough tears to drown in. If God cried into a bathtub, she thought, it would fill up and she could cover herself in all that sadness.

Somehow, she managed to sneak outside. It was warm, and even in her sleeveless dress she wasn't cold. She unbuckled her sandals, tiptoed to the middle of the lawn, and lay down on her back. It was hard to keep her eyes open with the drops coming so quickly, but she could open her mouth. If the drops came fast and hard enough, they would trickle down her throat, no room for air, no room for breath. This was how her brother had died. Accidental aspiration. She said the words like a jump rope rhyme. Ac-ci-den-tal as-pir-a-tion. Their mother had given him a bottle and put him down for a nap, but when she came to wake him, she found him lifeless. He had thrown up and it had gone the wrong way—down his throat and into his airway—no room for air, no room for breath. Ac-ci-den-tal as-pir-a-tion. Josie had heard mumbled voices tell her mother that there was nothing she could have done, that hundreds of babies every year died this way, that they weren't strong enough to cough their throats clear, and Josie figured that at least some of their little baby airways had been filled with rain. She lay there for a long time, long enough so that when Alba finally found her, almost everyone had gone home.

Last night the memory had flashed before her. It was quick, nothing more than one burst of remembered water in her open mouth, but it had so immediately forced her back to her body that Devesh's hand against her skin was intensely painful, and she was grateful when he pulled her up abruptly and put her on her back.

Now, Maddy was almost asleep, and Josie realized that Matthew was eleven months—only three months younger than Madeline—when he died. He hadn't looked so little then, his body laid out in a sailor suit, but with the baby across Josie's lap, she imagined how small he must have been. She had kissed his forehead at the funeral. She remembered the way her father had lifted her and she had placed her lips on Matthew's skin. It felt exactly the same as it always had, but she understood that he was dead, that there was no more Matthew. And then there had been the service. She hadn't been interested in the funeral then. She had played with the paper program, twisting it into a bow tie, wondering when she could look at the picture book of horses someone had brought her; and then back at the house, the rain. After, when Alba found her outside, she bundled Josie in flannel pajamas and an assortment of quilts and left her in front of the television. It was an adult show, a soap opera, and she lay on the couch and for a short time

watched the people talk animatedly about something, but she
was hot under all those layers, and she remembered that she
peeled off her pajamas and cocooned herself in the quilts. It
was warm, and the quilts made the fading light muted and hazy,
and she felt alone, but safe.

Madeline was asleep now, but Josie continued to rock
her. She looked at her own hand under Maddy's tiny head
and thought of Devesh's hands. They were large and full of
ropy veins, fingers that tapered at the tips, and a ring on his
left pointer finger. She closed her eyes and saw his hands run
down her belly, the silver of the ring glinting like a tiny explosion. Then her eyes opened. The ring. It was hers, tiny and
silver, something she had picked up one day in town, but she
had imagined it on his finger. Her heart quickened. She
wanted to put Maddy in her crib, but she felt stuck to the
chair. Her ring on his finger; so what? But it made her anxious, the idea of her hands that huge. She swallowed hard and
looked at her hands. Tiny. Her hands had always been this
small; that day under the quilts, with the hazy light streaming through, she had looked at her hands and thought them
small. No. She had thought them huge and wished them
small, and when they stayed exactly as they were, still pruned
from the rainwater, she let them fall beside her thighs and
was not angry but frustrated, and sad and something else,
something that enabled her to go outside her quilt-bundled
self, tiptoe around her body until the fuzzy images that were
lurking in the background became clear—someone huge,
someone enormous, was lifting her gently onto his lap, over
his knee, and then he was spanking her, hard and long and
mercilessly.

Now, Josie gasped. That had been the first time she thought those things, the first imagined punishment. From far away, Josie heard Tyler call her name, a hard jarring sound, and she jumped. Madeline awoke and whimpered, and Josie's breath shortened. Now, she felt the marble in her heart throb. The fantasies had begun then. And after that, they became routine, daydreams in class and hazy nighttime images.

She stood and made her way down the stairs, and the baby began to cry. Tyler called again, and then quickly began to whine.

"Make her stop crying!" he yelled.

"You stop," she said.

"Stop, stop, stop!" he cried, and banged his fists against his knees.

"Be quiet."

"Stooooop!"

"Quiet!" she yelled. She held tightly onto Madeline's torso, and the baby cried louder. Josie could feel her palms begin to sweat, could feel her body expand.

"Stoooop!"

The noise was overpowering. It grew rapidly and tornadoed around her until she felt picked up and shoved forward.

"Stop, stop, stop!" he yelled.

She took a step, and another, and then she was grabbing Tyler, yanking him up by the arm until he was stumbling before her. He cried, she held tightly, and it wasn't until her other arm, still wrapped around the baby, crackled with the desire to slap him, that she realized what she was doing.

And then she was motionless, and their cries seemed far away, and Josie put the baby down on the floor, walked out of

the room, slid herself into the corner of the hall, and felt the
world slip from its axis.

For a few days after, Tyler refused to talk to Josie, and she was
glad that Mary was gone nearly twelve hours a day, attending
this month at the hospital. Josie tried to apologize to Tyler, to
woo him with a book on animals of the rainforest, but he ignored her until one morning he woke up and seemed to simply forget. She was grateful and tried to convince herself that
she hadn't gotten enough sleep, that she was coming down with
Tyler's cold, that she'd drunk too much coffee, but she remembered that same vicious feeling from when they had been burying the bird, and a few days after the second incident, it washed
over her again.

It was Sunday, and Josie had been at Devesh's since Saturday morning. She thought the kids were at the neighbor's
and Mary gone to work in the lab, so when she came home to
pick up a change of clothes and found the three of them in the
living room, she was surprised

"You're home," Josie said.

"For a bit," Mary said.

Mary had bought Halloween pumpkins, and although it
was only September, they had carved them into lopsided jack-
o'-lanterns and were now taking pictures in front of the fireplace. Mary had dressed Tyler in overalls and Madeline in a
red dress and sat them in front of the pumpkins, but Maddy
wouldn't hold still and Tyler was intent on counting the number of lines on the pumpkin shell.

"There's guts inside the pumpkin," Tyler said.

"Yes, yes, I know," Mary said. "But Tyler, please; just hold her on your lap for one picture."

Tyler sighed. "All right, but no guts, no glory," he said, and it was so funny that both Mary and Josie couldn't stop laughing.

"Where did you learn that?" Mary asked.

"TV."

"Who's letting you watch that on TV?" she asked Josie, but Mary was smiling, and Josie shrugged. "Someone *else* needs a break from T-Y-L-E-R every now and then, I see," Mary said.

"Hey, that's my name!" Tyler shouted.

"One picture," Mary said. "Sit up straight and hold the baby properly." But Tyler wiggled around and held Maddy with one arm.

"Here," Josie said and walked over to them.

"No, no, I'll do it." Mary rushed over and set the baby straight.

Josie brushed Tyler's hair out of his eyes.

"I said, I'll do it," Mary said sharply, and Josie felt it like a punch in the gut. She took a step back and tried to will herself to let it go and casually walk to her room.

"There," Mary said and snapped a picture. "One more."

"No, Mommy," Tyler said.

Maddy struggled, and Tyler tried to keep hold of her.

"She's hurting me," he said.

"Damn it. The batteries died."

Tyler whined.

"Sit still and stop being such a baby!" Mary yelled. Josie winced, and Mary ran up the stairs. "Just watch them while I get more batteries," she said.

Maddy squirmed, Tyler held her tighter, and Josie felt their struggle hit her hard in the chest. She told herself she should take the baby from him or just walk away—out of the house and away from all three of them—but she stayed, her feet cemented to the floor. She watched Tyler's face contort, watched Maddy squirm desperately in his arms, watched the red of her dress and the blue of his overalls twist together; Maddy's fist, small and soft, on his chin; Tyler's palms, flat and determined, against her back; and then the baby was tumbling, landing bottom down on the floor, and Josie's vision tunneled. She saw only Tyler's shoulder, one overall strap fastened securely on his chest, and in one swift movement, she grabbed it, swung him close to her, and with her other hand tilted his chin up to her. "You," she said. She dug her fingertips into his soft skin, and he began to cry. "You!" She could do it, slap him squarely across the face. But instantly, Mary was in front of Josie, the empty battery package still in her hand, asking Tyler what in the world he was crying about, and Josie felt thrown back into herself, her hand still entangled in Tyler's overall strap, her nails dug into her palm.

"All right; fine. I guess that's the end of the pictures," Mary said and picked up Madeline. "Jesus, Tyler, what are you crying about now?"

Tyler covered his face with his hands, and Josie had to restrain herself from crying out and pulling him tightly into her arms.

"Well?" Mary asked.

Josie could feel the shame seep in, and yet along with that was something else—gratitude. Maybe it would be over now. The confrontation the entire household had been recently inching toward could lie just ahead. Tyler could tell Mary, and in a few minutes Josie could be packing her bags. Instead, he lied, mumbled into his palms, and said, "Maddy hit me."

"Hit you? She has no muscle in her arms; that's what you're crying about? Ridiculous. Go wash your face."

And he did. And Mary set the pumpkin that had been knocked over straight. And Maddy giggled as her mother bent over. And Josie slipped out the front door and slid onto her bike and rode. She rode past the park, past Devesh's house, past the university, and out of town and onto the roads with few houses and large pieces of land. She would ride until her legs gave out and she had reached someplace entirely unfamiliar, and then she would lie down in a ditch and hope the ground would swallow her.

She had nearly done it, knew her intention, felt the impulse and the charge, the instinct to hurt him. Just like when she was young and her temper flared. Once when her mother refused to let her have chocolate milk for breakfast, she had clawed four bright pink lines down her mother's forearm. "You're an *animal*," her mother said, and the way she spit the word, and the pinpricks of blood on her mother's golden skin, made Josie know her mother was right—the wrong child *had* died. Josie was wild, and unpredictable, and bad. And now she could see that she hadn't outgrown any of that, or perhaps it had just grown back.

It was starting to get cold, but there was no rain, and she rode until she reached a small tobacco farm. An old drying shed sat in the corner of the field, grayed wood barely held together by rusty nails. She stopped. Her legs cramped violently, and she realized she must have been riding for a very long time. She laid her bike down on the ground and made her way to the shed. The door was gone, and she stepped inside. Moss had grown on the floor and worked its way up the baseboards, and the smell of wet wood permeated the air. The roof was still there, but planks were missing, and the gray sky made the ceiling look like a gloomy patchwork quilt. It was surprisingly warm inside, and Josie took off her sweatshirt and sat in the center of the room. The shed was no more than twelve feet across, and with the soft moss underneath and the quilt of a ceiling above, Josie felt she was in the middle of a gigantic bed. She bundled her sweatshirt under her head and lay on the ground.

Phillip once told her that, during harvest, farm workers often came down with green tobacco sickness. After a full day of handling the plants, they would pass out in the fields. Now, Josie wished she could simply slip into unconsciousness. She turned on her side and pushed her forehead into the hard ground. It felt comfortably solid underneath her, and it reminded her of when she was twelve and slept on the floor of a cabin for almost an entire summer. Josie and her cousin Natalie had convinced their parents to send them to sleepaway camp. Natalie had only gone for two weeks, but at Josie's insistence, her mother had signed her up for six straight weeks. It was only an hour up the coast, but even then Josie thought that if she just removed herself from Santa Barbara, she would be happier, and she had been, sort of. No one put bleach in her shampoo bottle or told the other girls she wet her bed. She made friends. She learned to ride a horse. But it was also the summer she first dreamt the dream. In it, she was falling, arms and legs spread, the wind rushing down rather than up. And as she rushed toward the ground, her body seemed to split into two bodies, one that fell and one that lay on the bed waiting to be crushed. Her mind would zoom into the Josie on the bed, and she would feel the suffocating weight of her body, her limbs filled with iron. She would stare helplessly up at her rushing other half until the split second before the two collided. Then whatever had held her loosened, and she threw herself out of the way and onto the cabin floor. After a week of bruises the size of plums and bunk mates complaining that she was making too much noise, she had started sleeping on a blanket on the concrete floor, sneaking off her bed after everyone went to sleep, and back again near morning after she rolled away from her plummeting self.

Now she wondered what it would feel like to crash into yourself, one self converging with the other. She closed her eyes, and when she opened them again, the sky was dark.

It seemed like minutes, but Josie knew she must have been asleep for hours. She was cold and stiff and her legs ached so much that when she stood up she thought they might give out under her. Riding her bike was impossible, and she walked it down the long road to an old gas station on the corner and called Devesh from the pay phone.

When he drove up, she could tell he was angry. "It's not safe going so far out."

"I have to tell you something," she said.

He hoisted her bike into the car. "You didn't even bring your cell phone."

"Sometimes . . . lately," she stumbled, "I've been wanting to do bad stuff." She knew that if she didn't say it now, her courage would evaporate on the ride home. "To Tyler. I mean, sometimes I want to hit him."

He looked at her over the roof of the car. "Get in."

She slid into the front seat and looked at her hands, and the same enormous feeling washed over her. "I want to hurt him. I want to . . . I don't know . . . but it's bad. It's very bad."

He looked at her. "Have you?"

"No."

"When he misbehaves, you mean."

She nodded.

He put his hand on her knee. "I think that's normal. I mean, I don't know, but it seems like a normal impulse."

"No," she said. "It's not normal."

"But you haven't."

She shook her head.

"Children can drive you crazy," he said. "As long as you didn't do it, and you didn't—"

"I want to hurt him," she interrupted.

"But you didn't."

"I want to slap him . . . I . . . I want to spank him." She looked at Devesh and held his gaze. There was a long silence, and she knew she had admitted something she could not take back.

"You think it's because of the games we play."

She could hear the defensiveness in his voice. She shrugged.

"Fine; then we won't play them anymore." He started the car.

"No."

"Then what, Josie?"

"I don't know."

"If you can't leave it in the bedroom, we'll stop. We'll just stop."

She was afraid he would take it away from her, that he would see what was growing inside her and think he could stunt it.

"No," she said. "No. I can. I can. Maybe you're right. Maybe it's just the stress—Mary and the kids. And I didn't do it, you're right, I didn't actually do it." She didn't believe what she was saying, but she didn't care. The thought of him taking away what she had thought she could never have was enough to pull the lie from her chest. And maybe it wasn't a lie after all. Tyler had blamed his tears on Maddy. Maybe he knew for sure what Josie didn't, that she would never really do it.

Devesh looked at her for a long time and then pulled her close. "What happens between us, that's just . . ."

"I know." She didn't want to hear anymore, just wanted to believe that Tyler knew more than she did, that at least for Devesh this dark thing wasn't always there like an inner stain, that the games they created were just games, made up out of nothing, just to play with.

CHAPTER EIGHT

AFTER MATTHEW DIED, JOSIE'S PARENTS TRIED TO ADOPT A BABY. Josie found out even before her parents announced it, when Alba informed her that she was going to be a big sister. Looking back now, Josie wondered how anyone could tell a child the things Alba had. Everything she gleaned from Josie's parents, she relayed, as if the two of them were siblings or Josie another employee. Her father liked to tell the story of how one Friday when he was writing a check for Alba, Josie stood expectantly waiting for hers, and when he explained that Alba was paid to take care of her, Josie simply asked why she wasn't paid to be the daughter. Her father would tell the story and people would laugh, and Josie would smile and make a crack about how she was only perfecting her business skills, but that wasn't it at all. She *had* felt she was doing a job, pretending to be her parents' daughter, holding Matthew's place until he one day returned. So when she was told the news that her parents were going to adopt a baby, she wasn't surprised.

Nevertheless, the baby never arrived. The adoption fell through, and Alba told Josie that it was a good thing because to have trouble come into your house was one thing, but to ask it in was something entirely different. The baby clothes were put away and the crib given to charity. No one ever spoke of a baby again, and it was almost as if Matthew had never been born. But Josie could feel the way he held tight to her mother's hand. It was most noticeable when Josie's temper flared. Her mother would turn unbearably calm, and then Josie would feel Matthew there in the room, the child who should have lived staring into the eyes of the one that had.

It was when she exploded like this that her fantasies were most violent. Her mother would send her to her room, and Josie would crawl under the blankets to the bottom of her bed, wedge herself tightly between the sheets, and imagine violent, terrifying things. The fantasies started small, just an image of being spanked, nothing but a hand, but they had grown, and Josie soon imagined paddles and belts, and then she was tied and sometimes gagged.

At first she used the thoughts only to soothe herself. She would twirl them in her head and feel her body hum, her mind anesthetized, but by the time she was fourteen, she found herself slipping her hands shyly down her belly, and then, one night, between her legs. She had gone next door to babysit and arrived to household chaos. The little boy she took care of refused to eat his peas. He banged his fists on the table and kicked the chair, and his father, calm at first, finally picked the kid up by the scruff of the neck, marched him to his room, and told him to stay until he could behave. The boy eventually settled down, came back and ate his dinner, and his parents kissed him goodbye and left for the evening. It had resolved peacefully enough, but the scene rooted in Josie's brain, and that night, after the boy went to bed, she found herself imagining the boy's father, his hand on her own neck. She could see him marching her down the hall, his grip firm and determined, but instead of telling her to stay until she could behave, he followed her inside and told her to strip.

She had sat on the couch in their living room and felt the need between her legs. It scared her, and she gripped a cushion, afraid of where her hands would go, but the image was insistent. It urged her shorts to her knees, her hands under her panties. She saw the father removing his belt, saw him order her over his lap, and then the strokes, hard and unrelenting. He was punishing her for having dirty thoughts, he was punishing her for wanting a spanking, he was punishing her just to punish her. Her hands moved easily, faster and faster, until she knew exactly why those girls moaned so loudly in the movies.

That was the first time the thoughts had turned sexual, and from then on, she played these scenes in her head whether she was alone or with someone else. She never told her boyfriends. Instead, she pretended to be present until the moment when she could feel herself building to orgasm. Then, if she was in the right position, she could push her face into a pillow, go limp, then far away in her head.

This was what was so intoxicating about sex with Devesh. It was *real*, at least for Josie it was. But she worried it was this realness that was making her feel so violent. It had definitely brought on the uneasy thoughts of Matthew. Once, Devesh and she had been sitting on the couch watching TV. They were only kissing, but when she leaned her head back and Devesh softly bit her neck, she gasped, felt the air fill her lungs, and then she was her four-year-old self swinging Matthew around by the arms. She remembered that it was something she was forbidden to do, and that was part of the joy, but so was the way it made him giggle—hysterical fits of laughter. Josie saw the image like a strip of super-eight in her head, flickering slowly but insistently. She did not like Matthew in her head at all, but in these circumstances it was unbearable, and it made her push Devesh away, something she never did. He had sat up and looked at her with such indignant surprise that she melted under him and pretended she was just trying to initiate a game. It worked, and immediately all images of Matthew faded from her head. Still, it unnerved her, and she found herself worrying that Matthew would slip into the bedroom and hover above the bed, ruining Devesh for her just as he had ruined her mother.

But one night as she was falling asleep, her head on Devesh's warm chest, he grazed his lips against her ear and whispered that he loved her, and in that moment, something changed. He loved her. A dark, passionate man who could crawl inside her head and revel in all the dirty thoughts that had been piling up for ages loved her. She was dizzy with surprise and sheer gratitude. Around Devesh, she felt a new gravity that spun Matthew out of her head and kept the fantasies in the bedroom, just as Devesh instructed. And he instructed so well. He was wickedly creative in his discipline, and it *was* discipline. Good girls were disciplined. Bad girls were punished, and punishments were not something to be desired. She had learned this quickly.

One evening, Devesh told her he needed to work on a grant proposal. He would love for her to stay, he said, but she needed to let him work. She had agreed, but she was bored with her reading and annoyed with the stupid sitcoms on television, so she draped herself over his lap and nuzzled his neck.

"Josie," he said. "You need to let me work."

"Play with me," she murmured.

"Not now," he said, and pushed her to standing. He went back to his papers, and she stood there, staring. She willed him to look at her, to pull her close to him, to at least let her wrap herself around his feet, but when he didn't look up, she finally sighed and left the room. It wasn't fair, and there was nothing to do. She sat in the dark living room and watched the clock. Five minutes went by, then ten, and after twelve minutes, she couldn't take it anymore. She slipped down the hallway and hung on the study door frame.

"Out," he said.

"I just wanted to ask you if you wanted some *chai*." She knew he would say no, that the caffeine would keep him up all night. He didn't look up, didn't answer, just pointed his finger toward the door.

She sighed heavily, stomped her way back to the living room, raised the volume on the television, banged pots around the kitchen, sent a shelf full of books accidentally to the ground, and then he called her.

"What?" she yelled.

"Come here."

She knew she was in trouble, could hear the calm irritation in his voice, and she felt the sudden rush. Now it would be real. She walked into the room and crossed her arms over her chest. "What?"

"That's enough," he said, and looked at her sternly.

She stood defiantly in front of him. Now he would punish her, now he would beat her for disobedience.

"I'm not doing anything," she said.

"You're not, huh?"

"No." She could feel the charge between them, and she set her jaw determinedly and crossed her arms more tightly.

"If you're looking to be punished, you're on the right track."

She felt her breath quicken, felt her body hum. "Punish me then. I don't care."

He sat for a moment, stared at her, and then slowly and methodically placed his pen on the desk. He stood, put his hand on the back of her neck, and walked her out of the study and into the hall. She felt her heart beat, her breath quicken, and she wondered if he would leave her untied, demand she stay still and take her medicine, but instead of making her bring him a paddle, he walked her to the front hall.

"Put on your shoes," he said.

She was confused, and when she hesitated, he picked them up and pushed the shoes and her bag into her arms.

"Bad girls are not beaten," he said, and walked her outside. "They're sent home." He kissed the top of her head and shut the door behind him.

She stood there, stunned. This was not what she expected. He was supposed to spank her and make her stand in the corner, but here she was outside and barefoot.

The new moon hung like a too-bright smile, and she felt mocked. She stared at her feet on the pavement, and understood that any punishment he dished out would be truly painful. Still, she had spent her life desperate for punishment. But why? Strong, intelligent, independent women did not want to be spanked as if they were little girls. But they did. She did. And here he was telling her that it was all right, it was normal, it was natural, and here she was starting to believe it. But this was discipline, not punishment and even now when she knew he would never strike her in anger, she could not let go of that need.

She walked home, but the thought of entering the Griffins' house made her body hurt. To go from that warm, safe world to what was slowly becoming a cold, lonely place—this was, very definitely, a punishment. She felt a lump rise in her throat and then the deep pain of being alone. It was the same feeling as when she was eleven and angry at her father for not allowing her to see some R-rated movie. They had fought on the drive to school, and when they arrived, she slammed the car door and stomped away. But after three steps, the lump in her throat and sudden pain in her chest made her turn and run after the car until she was breathless and all she could see was the glint of the bumper shining brightly in the sunlight.

Now she wanted to run back to Devesh and beg him to let her come in, but behind this desire was a stronger feeling, an understanding of the rightness of what he had done. This was what she wanted—to be taught and cared for and handled appropriately. The thought made her slightly uneasy and yet unmistakably secure. Things were falling steadily into place. The world that had only a few weeks ago seemed precarious, and barely under her control, now seemed solid, steady, and hers.

And the rest of her world seemed on track as well. Maddy was doing baby things; she could drink from a cup and stand on her own. Tyler had started second grade and could already add three-digit columns by the end of the first week, but he had also become clingy, asking Josie to do things for him he normally insisted on himself, staying close by her side, crying when she dropped him off at school. She tried to hide these from Mary, but Tyler made it impossible—insisting Mary call Josie at Devesh's so he could say good night, claiming only Josie prepared cereal correctly—little quirks that Mary had once thought sweet. But now they meant that Josie was overindulging him. "No more cartoons," Mary said. "They're making him violent." And no more ice cream in the afternoons, no more conceding to his demands of only wearing sweatpants, no more measuring tape at school. It was after this last demand that Josie waited for Mary to walk out the door and then threw Tyler's dirty orange juice glass against the wall. Tyler watched her and cautiously asked why she had done it. When she told him his mother made her crazy, he asked if he could throw a glass too. She let him, and after, he turned to her and said, "Maddy makes me crazy, too." She handed him another glass, which he threw and then said, "And school." They went on like this until all the orange juice glasses were smashed, and then sat on the floor and looked at what they had done. They were quiet a long while when he finally sighed. "The whole world makes me crazy," he said, and Josie looked at the little boy beside her and wished she could relieve him of that permanent ache.

But Josie had to admit, she was grateful for Tyler's new desperate attachment. If he was behaving, she would have no provocation, and if she wasn't provoked, she would neither think nor do the things she was afraid she was capable of doing. But the underlying knowledge that she could have—would have—often unexpectedly pricked her. One day she picked him up from school, and he told her a story about a little girl who had been hung by her panties from a flagpole because she had bitten another child. It was a strange, made-up story, and when she told him that he was lying, he said, "No I'm not, and she deserved it." It suddenly felt a hundred degrees in the car, and she wanted to convince him that, even if it was true, no one deserved that. "Tyler, lying is bad," she said, but then thought about how he had lied to protect her, how he had lied to his mother to keep her safe. "Tyler, I'm sorry," she said, "I'm sorry." He rolled and unrolled the window and didn't say anything, and the thought that perhaps he hadn't lied to save her at all crept into her head. Perhaps, like the little girl he had fabricated, he thought he deserved whatever it was she had been planning to dish out. But he didn't deserve it, and she wouldn't do it. "Let's get you some ice cream, Ty," she said. "We'll get some chocolate mint." "Okay," he said. "O-O-O, K-K-K."

Her studies were going well. She had long since given up the plan of a book a day, but at least she was reading, which was more than she had been doing the first month after she met Devesh. And real progress was made when Devesh introduced her to two Ghanaian doctors who were visiting for the semester. She still needed to narrow down what community she wanted to study, so she set up interviews with each of them at the hospital.

Devesh was back attending at the hospital the day of her interviews, and she planned to meet him in the Intensive Care Unit and then go to lunch. She waited at the nurse's station, feeling self-conscious in her civilian clothes, and tried to peer into the open rooms. She knew there was a burn patient he was caring for, a man who tried to save a baby in a neighboring apartment and was burned over 80 percent of his body. There were articles in the paper the month before, and she had been saddened by the story and confused by Devesh's lack of interest in the articles. "Aren't you curious?" she had asked him. "I can't be," he said.

Now, Devesh rounded the corner, and she smiled. He looked boyish in his green scrubs, a kid clad in his pajamas and father's dress shoes. He hugged her to him and introduced her to the nurses.

"Is that man here?" she whispered to him. "The burn patient?"

"Yes, do you want to see him?"

"I don't know."

"Let's not then."

The stories in the paper had talked about the man's heroism, how he had emigrated from Cuba to make a better life for his children, how he had been assisting immigrants for the last thirty years. Now there was a fund to help him get back to the devoted family man and citizen he was.

"No," she said. "I want to."

"Morbid curiosity?" he asked.

Josie shrugged. But it was more than that. Here was a man who was willing to sacrifice himself for someone else's baby, a child he didn't even know.

"All right; we'll have to get you some scrubs," Devesh said.

He took her to a closet-sized room behind the nurse's station where she draped herself in a large blue gown and hairnet. She felt like she was playing dress up and she giggled and turned to him for inspection.

He laughed softly. "Charming."

Through this room was a bigger room, and she followed him closely. Large machines on wheels cluttered the space, and she had to push one to the side to stick near to him. On the walls were hundreds of pictures of family and friends collaged around homemade cards and a deflated Mylar balloon. Along the wide window hung a computer-printed banner that read "Te Amamos." A crayoned parrot on a square of pink construction paper squawked "Abuelo! Abuelo!"

And then there was the bed, the body tucked neatly in up to the chin. The only thing visible was the face and head, a stretched mass of polished red—the skin wet and furrowed and angry. The eyes were large and glassy, forced open like a doll's; and from beneath the covers, one hand peeked out, bandaged in a large gauzy mitt.

Josie stared. She felt the room slowly roll and she grabbed a chair beside her and shook her head violently. It was horrible, the worst thing she'd ever seen.

"He's sedated so he doesn't feel the pain," Devesh said. "And a ventilator is breathing for him."

"I can't touch him," she said.

It was a statement but Devesh answered. "No."

There was a long pause, and then Devesh spoke. "They brought his grandson in this morning," he said. "His eighty-year-old mother comes every day. And there's a blind cousin that comes with his wife," he continued. "The cousin doesn't speak any English, but he had someone write a thank-you letter to all the doctors."

"Okay," she said.

Devesh nodded and started for the door, but he had misunderstood. She had only wanted him to stop talking. She

didn't want to know anything more, and she understood why
he had been so uninterested in the news articles. How could
you reconcile the act—this man's heroic deed—with this mass
of burnt flesh. It was too awful, too much.

"What happened to the baby?" she asked.

"She died."

She stepped to the side of the bed and grazed a single finger lightly against the top sheet. She wanted to whisper something numbing and comforting, but instead she ran her finger
back and forth, back and forth.

CHAPTER NINE

SHE HAD THOUGHT HERSELF IN LOVE BEFORE. TWICE. THE FIRST time with her college boyfriend, J. D. Henry, a Midwestern boy who thought in scientific equations. He was the first boy she ever brought home, and when they drove up the long, winding driveway to her childhood house, he quietly surveyed the huge property and then said, "What kind of watering system have your parents installed?" She loved him for this and thought that no matter what happened that weekend, she would be okay if she thought about watering systems. But to her surprise, the visit went reasonably well. Her father tried too hard to impress him with his collection of antique maps, and her mother was relentless in her questioning of what J.D. intended to do when he graduated, but there were no major eruptions until Sunday night.

Her parents had gone to a dinner party, left fifty dollars on the kitchen table, and told them to go out to dinner, but Josie pocketed the money, and they raided the refrigerator and wine cellar. After drinking two bottles of expensive cabernet, they were drunk. They tried to open a third bottle, broke it, and then mangled the cork of a fourth. Josie wanted to ditch that bottle too, but J.D. thought it silly to let it go to waste, so he broke the bottle neck and poured the wine through a strainer and into a crystal pitcher. They sipped from the pitcher and stumbled from room to room, looking for the cigarettes Josie knew her mother hid. When they got to the library, J.D. surveyed the long shelves of books, laden alternately with expensive antiques and extravagant art from her parents' many trips, and said, "You're rich." She giggled and agreed. "And you're hot," she said, and pulled him onto the fainting couch that her mother had upholstered with imported French brocade. He sloppily licked her neck and pulled off her shirt and his pants, and they were rolling around on the expensive Persian rug that was not to be walked on with shoes when she saw her mother's thin heels on the hardwood floor in the doorway. It took Josie a few moments to realize first that her mother was watching her and second that she was half naked, but when she did, she froze. J.D. must have felt the immediate change in her body because he looked behind him, said "Oh, shit," and grabbed for his pants, but Josie dug her nails into his back to keep him close, and tried to think about watering systems. She clawed at him and prayed her mother would go away, but she stood there long enough that Josie could chant "watering systems" twenty-five times. It wasn't until J.D. said, "Sorry, ma'am," that her mother finally did anything, and what she did was step farther into the room. Josie could hear her mother's shoes clip slowly across the floor, and she closed her eyes and prayed her mother would stop. Instead, her mother picked up Josie's shirt from the rug and stood beside them. No one moved, and Josie thought they would have stayed like that perpetually, her mother looming over them, but her father came in and after an initial "Jesus Christ" told her mother to let them be. "She's *your* daughter," her mother said and walked, with

Josie's shirt, out of the room. Her father closed the door, and J.D. gave Josie his shirt to put on. They left the next day, and that night, when they were back at school, Josie knocked on his door and, without even coming into his dorm room, broke up with him. Then she went back to her room, called her mother, and said simply, "I wish you were dead."

The second time she had thought herself in love was with the owner of one of the hotel jobs she had breezed through before graduate school. Charlie was older, and she teased him about being a cradle robber. The day he had her fired, he also asked her to dinner. She went and, for a brief period of time, found herself enjoying the glitz of dating someone with both power and money. There were one-hundred-dollar dinners almost every night, and weekend trips to spas in Ojai and Carmel. She had been raised with these things and learned to detest their opulence, but somehow with him it seemed all right. Charlie had grown up poor in Alabama, hitchhiked to Santa Barbara to surf after college, and ended up a personal assistant to a hotel financier who helped him invest in his first property. Charlie was sweet, and he overtipped and intentionally made faux pas that Josie loved. He would pick his teeth during meetings, and ask if the waiter could replace his salad with a side of fried apples at business dinners. She loved his accent, his freckles, his scarred hands from working his way through college as a cook. But he was also a drunk, or in his words a good ole boy who liked his whiskey, and when he was drunk, he did not have Josie on his mind. The first time she caught him with another woman, he cried and begged and swore fidelity, and she took him back, but a few months later at his birthday party, she went to use the bathroom and found him kissing a leggy blonde while getting a blow job from what could have been the leggy blonde's twin sister. He looked at her and simply said, "It's my birthday, baby." Josie's knees felt locked solid, and she stood there watching until he pulled up his pants and the girls giggled their way out. She managed a brief rant, but the truth of the matter was that she felt calm and astonishingly unaffected.

But with Devesh it was different. With Devesh, she felt simultaneously idolized and truly seen. It was as if he could look inside her and see the mess she had made of herself and love her more dearly for it. He told her to crawl to the bedroom, and she knew he understood how much she needed to feel both deeply wanted and nearly insignificant. Every day she felt like getting down on her knees and thanking him, but the most she could manage was to entangle her fingers in his dark hair and cling to him. She wanted to tell him she loved him, to grab him by the shoulders and insist on it, but the hugeness of the feeling was suffocating. And behind it was something else— the shame of deception, as if she was hiding something more than her money and background, as if her tightly wound past could unfurl like a roll of butcher paper to reveal something darker than what he already saw.

One night, grocery shopping, they walked around the store going over Hindi words: banana: *kela*; apple: *sev*; milk: *doodh*. She pointed to things and then repeated the word, and he laughed.

"Your pronunciation is horrible," he said. "Maybe you'll do better with Tamil. You can practice on the kind South Indians if you come with me to Chennai in November."

She was surprised. He hadn't mentioned this before, and the thought of him sweeping her off to a world she knew only through him both scared and excited her.

"You're going?" she asked.

"Yes; for a month, for my cousin's wedding."

"Oh." She looked at the boxes of cereal lining the shelves.

"I'm not going to leave you," he said, and pulled her to him. "We can go to Delhi for the wedding, and then they've asked me to help with an emergency medical center at a hospital in Tamil Nadu. We can stay a whole month."

He bent down and kissed her forehead.

"Oh." She wasn't sure what to say or even what she felt. "But what about work?"

"You haven't had a holiday in a year now."

She looked at the bunch of bananas in the cart, the bag of deep red apples. *Kela*, she said to herself. *Sev*.

"My brother has a huge house overlooking the water in Chennai—we'll stay there."

"That's an awful long time to stay with someone."

He laughed. "You obviously don't know the ways and workings of Indian families."

She nodded, but what she had meant was that a month was a long time for them to be gone, to be away from this cocoon they had somehow managed to spin into being.

"Maybe we'll go to Goa for the weekend," he said. "Or would you rather see the Taj Mahal?" He smiled, and her heart stumbled. If she went, she would be surrendering herself to his care completely.

"I can't," she said.

"Why?"

"I can't leave the kids," she said.

"They have a mother, you know."

"Lately, not a very good one." She looked down at the thin yellow wedges of dried paint under her nails. Yesterday, they had painted Tyler's toy chest, then decorated it with Maddy's blue handprints. The baby had laughed and banged her little palms into the tray of blue paint, and Tyler hadn't even cared about the paint that flew onto his clothes and arms. But when Mary came home, tired and grumpy, she only noticed that Tyler had stained his new sneakers and that Josie had left them unwashed. "She's gone all the time now," Josie said. "She's attending, and on call twice a week."

"Well, she's their mother. She'll have to find a way to deal with it." He took a container of yogurt from the shelf. "*Dahi*," he said, and handed it to her.

She looked down at the container in her hands, tried to focus on the red cartoon cow on the lid.

He took it from her, put it in the cart, and held her hands. "I can help you with the tickets."

She shook her head and slid her hands from his. "No . . . I mean, thank you . . . I know you would, but I can't."

There was a long awkward silence, and she wished there were no India, that everything he needed was contained in the sixty-five inch space of her body. She put her arms around him and squeezed tightly. "The next time," she said. "I'll go with you then."

Still, that night, she waited for him to fall asleep and then sat in front of the computer for an hour, searching airline sites and nearly buying her own ticket. A few thousand dollars would barely put a dent in her father's account, and perhaps if she bought her own ticket, she could keep hold of herself. She could go for two weeks and come back virtually unchanged.

But it was more than that. It was also something else. Something she had felt sitting in the movie theater with him, surrounded by people who believed that what she had done in this life would be played out for eternity.

So, instead, she listened to Devesh detail what the wedding would look like—the flowered *mandap* under which the ceremony would take place, the bride's arms draped in thin gold bangles, the trays of *samagri*—fruits and grains and sweets—the world an explosion of color.

She imagined it all and said that she wished she could go.

"Then come," he said.

They were sitting on the couch eating ice cream and watching *Company*, a Hindi gangster movie.

"Why do the gangsters sing songs?" she asked.

"Everyone sings songs," he said quickly. "Why won't you come?"

"And *everyone* dances?"

"Yes; now, why?"

She put her ice cream bowl down on the table. "The kids need me."

"Not this again."

"I need the money."

"We've gone over this. I told you I'd pay for everything." He held her hands, and she looked at him. "Please," he said.

His face was round and soft, and she wished she could crawl onto his lap and rest her cheek on his, but instead she looked at her hands. "I can't."

"Fine," he said, and switched off the TV. "I'm going to bed."

"Devesh," she called after him, but he ignored her, and she sank down into the couch and sighed. She knew he saw beneath the excuses, that he could feel her pushing away with every rationalization, but she would go the next time, would meet his family and see the house he had grown up in. He had a small album of black-and-white pictures she had looked through again and again. It sat on the coffee table, and she picked it up now and opened it. The album was full of formal pictures of serious-looking people—Devesh and his family posed under large leafed trees, Devesh in his cricket uniform amid a group of gangly looking boys—but her favorite pictures were a series of Devesh as a chubby three-year-old. In one, he was posed with his brother and sister. An older girl held a baby brother on her lap, and Devesh stood beside them, his eyes round and huge, staring straight at the camera. The little boy's gaze was so clearly Devesh's, penetrating and powerful. It unnerved her, and she found herself covering his eyes with her finger, trying to make him look more childish. She closed the album and laid her head back on the couch. Next time she would go with him; next time she wouldn't be so afraid.

Two days later, she was sitting on Devesh's bed, looking at the photo album, wondering what kind of elaborate sexual fantasies he had constructed in his head as a child. She was staring at Devesh's little-boy face and trying to get inside his little-boy head when he ran his hand down her back, and she shivered.

"Cold?" he asked.

"No."

His fingers grazed her thighs, and she let out a breathy sigh.

"Sexy girl," he said, and lay down facing her.

She smiled and nosed her face into his neck. He pushed his other hand through her hair, turned her head to him, and kissed her softly. Lately, their lovemaking had been softer, sweeter. To anyone else, the change would have been unnoticeable, but Josie could sense the shift, and although she liked it, liked his strength coupled with the new tenderness, at times she missed feeling as completely at his mercy as she did that first night they had played.

"Have you been a good girl?" he asked.

She shook her head, and he wove his hand more deeply into her hair and then made a fist. "Get up." He pulled her to her feet. "Into the kitchen." He led her down the hallway, and she felt her skin prickle.

"I think some discipline is in order." He guided her into the kitchen and stood her in front of the sink. It was dark, and he switched on the light. In the sink, were a stack of dirty dishes.

"I want you to wash these," he said.

She looked at the handful of silverware, the mug she drank from this morning, and suddenly felt deeply embarrassed. She had felt this before. Once, he had made her look at herself in a mirror, tied over a stool, wrists and ankles bound, legs spread. She had blushed terribly, but he had smiled and looked so intensely pleased by her humiliation that she almost cried. But soon there was the familiar haziness, and she focused on his hand firm on her back and quickly was lost in the play.

Now she was glad he was behind her.

"Turn on the water," he said, and slipped his thumbs into the band of her panties. She tensed. He was going to beat her here, in the kitchen.

"I'm waiting."

She didn't move.

"All right then." He pulled her underwear quickly down her thighs, pushed his knee between her legs. "We can do this the hard way, if you wish." He grabbed her wrists, stuck the sponge in one of her hands, and turned on the water.

She rarely washed the dishes in his house. She would cook and he would clean up. Still, she would do it. She would, she wanted to say, but then, could they please go back to the bedroom where he could do anything he wanted to her? She was afraid, and yet she could feel her body heating, her insides beginning to blister.

"Now," he said, and took the dishwashing liquid and squeezed some over the sponge, "you're going to wash these dishes."

"No," she whimpered.

He took his wet hand and brought it down on her thigh. "Do as you're told," he said. "And you're going to be very quiet and very good, do you understand?"

She could feel the tears beginning to gather, the lump rising at the back of her throat, and she was afraid to open her mouth.

He pushed his knee roughly between her legs. "Do you understand?"

"Yes," she managed.

"Yes what?"

"Yes, Sir."

She could feel her muscles contract, could feel her knees get weak, but when he reached toward the dish-drying rack and grabbed a wooden spoon, her vision went cloudy, and when he brought the spoon firmly down on her skin, her brain was vacuumed from her skull. She could feel the biting cold water and the slick soapy glass and the rough tongue of the spoon hitting her over and over and over, and then his hands were on her body, his fingers exploring everywhere. She whimpered, and he slipped his hand over her mouth. He had caught her with no air in her chest, and she could feel the dull pain of her empty lungs get larger and larger, and when she thought she would either have to fight him or pass out, she realized first that she could sip air easily in through her nose, and second that she had never felt such overwhelming pleasure. She closed her eyes, held her breath, and slipped easily into the sensation. It was terrifying, and yet with each new wave of panic came a blast of rapture, and suddenly, she was back in her canopy bed, made to lie still. She was little and the spankings were harder and the punishment worse because it was fantasy and not Devesh being careful. She was small and deserved it, but no, it wasn't her, it was some other child being beaten—a boy or a girl, she wasn't sure—and it was she who was bringing the spoon down, listening to the whistle of the wood, feeling the power of her swing, swinging it hard, harder, harder until she came more violently than she ever had before.

Even when her body stopped shaking, she felt herself going round and round on a pinwheel, stuck like a butterfly, and it was only when Devesh took her chin in his hand and kissed her on the forehead that she realized she was a grownup and that the man she loved was doing these things to her. Her head was still spinning, and she was somewhere between there and here, still trying to catch her breath, and this had never happened before. She had never gone so far away that she was startled to be brought back, but the worst part, the part that made her want to tear her fingernails down her forearms, was that she had orgasmed from thinking that thought, seeing that vibrant image of herself and some child play itself on the screen of her skull. She had to close her eyes and clench her jaw to keep from throwing up.

"That was lovely," he said, and held her.

Her skin puckered under him. "Let go," she said.

"No." He kissed her head, and it felt like knives across her scalp.

"Let go," she said, and knocked a clean glass into the sink. It shattered, and she pulled away from him.

"Josie," he said.

"What?" She reached for her panties and pulled down her tank top.

"What's wrong?"

"Nothing."

"Nothing?"

She swept her hair back into a ponytail and stretched the rubber band from her wrist around it. "No, nothing." She took a step out of the kitchen, and he grabbed her by the arm.

"Tell me what's wrong."

She looked at him and wanted to slap his beautiful face. "You tried to suffocate me." She knew it wasn't true, but she wanted to be mean, to spite him.

"What?"

"You put your hand over my mouth. You made it so I couldn't breathe." She hated him for doing this, making her body react the way it had, but she hated herself more.

"What?" He was confused, and she could feel his grip slacken.

She jerked her arm from his hand. "Maybe one time you can make me come without beating the shit out of me."

He looked at her, shocked, and she wanted to hurt him even more, to make him feel dirty and humiliated, but she didn't know how, didn't know how to push into him the shame that was expanding inside her like a thick fog.

"Nothing, forget it," she said, and started for the bedroom.

"Don't walk away from me," he said, and grabbed her wrist.

"Let go." She squirmed, but he held tight.

"What is going on?"

"Nothing; just let go."

"Absolutely not," he said, and held her.

She looked at him, felt her wrist pinched tight in his big fist, and suddenly she felt unbearably tired. She didn't care if he held onto her, she just wanted to sit down. She slid to the floor, and he crouched beside her. She had been afraid he would take it all away from her, and now she was afraid he wouldn't.

"This needs to stop," she said.

"What needs to stop?"

"Everything," she said, and tucked her knees into her chest.

"Everything? Everything what?"

"The playing . . ." She paused. "I can't . . . I can't do it any-more." She rested her forehead on her knees. "It's bad, Devesh. It's just bad."

"What's bad?"

"The things we do. They're bad."

"Oh, sweetie," he said, and took her hands in his. "They're not bad. They're just games."

She looked up at him. "Do you think that? Do you really think that?"

He looked at her and then looked at her hands in his.

"They're not just games; they're not," she said. She shook her head and pulled her hands away. She felt like she was unplugging a plug from its socket, so immediately changed was the space between them, and he must have felt it too because he grabbed for her.

"Then we won't play them anymore."

"You couldn't do that," she said, but she wasn't sure. There had been a handful of times where she was pretty certain he had wanted to make love to her the way millions of people in millions of bedroom around the world made love, or at least he wanted to try, but she had turned it dark. Once, he had placed his hand on her chest and then raised it, a quarter inch away, and traced her body. She had closed her eyes and felt the heat of that concentrated love, but within moments she grew too hot, too close to him. She could feel him begin to slip under her skin, begin to root around her insides, and she kept her eyes closed and said, "You don't beat me hard enough." There was a moment of complete stillness, and she hoped and waited for him to bring his hand down hard on her thigh. Instead, he pressed his lips to her forehead for a long, long time.

Now the memory breathed bitterly into her lungs. "You need it," she said.

"No, I don't," he said.

She could hear the same desperation in his voice that she had heard in her own the day he threatened to take it all away. It made her feel enormous and powerful, and she hated him for this.

"You're lying," she said.

"I'm not."

"Yes, you are. All those toys. You think you could give this up like it was cigarettes? Go fuck someone else," she said, and got up.

He grabbed her strongly by the wrist, and for a moment she could feel that familiar pull in her belly.

"That's enough," he said, and stood.

"It's true."

"What's true? That I have those toys? That I like using them on you? Yes, Josie, it's true, but what do you think is happening between us? Do you think this is just lust? Is that what you think?"

She didn't know what to think.

He tightened his grip, and as much as it ached, she couldn't pull away. She could feel her bones disintegrating, her body somehow held up by just his hand on her. "Why?" she asked.

"Why what?"

"Why do you want to beat me?"

Immediately he loosened his grip. He looked at her, and for a fragment of time, she thought she saw what she had only felt in herself, that tidal wave of shame that clogged her head and made her chest dense and heavy, but then it was gone.

"We've discussed this before."

But she had seen it in him, knew it was there, an ache beneath the surface. Even if it was only the disgrace of what his old-fashioned Indian parents would think, at least it was something. She felt each of her tendons and muscles untwist. It was within him too—the same shame that her mother could make her feel, the same shame that she wore like a black birthmark. She felt magnetic, her negative to his positive, and she fell into him.

He hugged her to him. "We'll never do any of it again if you don't want to."

She loved him for saying this, but she doubted she could do it. Once she felt the pull in her belly and that syrupy intensity began to drip like an IV, her body controlled her head, and her body needed to feel her wrists in cuffs, the whip on her skin. But why? The question pitched inside her like a rocking horse, aching back and forth, back and forth. She steeled herself and shook her head. Maybe if they stopped for a while, maybe she could somehow steer herself back, and it wouldn't matter why. He was leaving for India in two days. She would have a month to push all that darkness—the uninvited images and thoughts and actions—into oblivion.

She laid her head heavily on his shoulder. "I need a break," she said. "Just for a little bit."

CHAPTER TEN

THE NEXT DAY, JOSIE PICKED TYLER UP FROM SCHOOL AND TOOK him to the grocery store to buy supplies for his Halloween costume. He wanted to be an astronaut, and they had designed a costume that required tinfoil, spray paint, and a football helmet.

They walked through an aisle stocked with candy, the bags brightly colored and piled high above his head.

"It looks like a candy house," Tyler said. "A candy spaceship."

Last night, she had dreamt that she was chasing Tyler, a game of some sort, and when she caught him, instead of him pulling away, they went tumbling to the ground in a heap of giggles. She felt no dread at touching him, no fear that she would want to hurt him, but when he rolled on top of her, he had smacked her across the face with the same wooden spoon Devesh had used on her.

Tyler pulled a bag of Pixie Stix off the shelf. "What are these?"

She smiled. "They're gross. They're just flavored sugar you pour into your mouth. We can get them."

He put the bag onto Maddy's lap.

"Oh, Ty, she'll want to eat the bag." She put the bag in the cart and handed the baby a pretzel.

"Okay, let's see what we need," she said.

"I know!" he said, and then he did something strange. He walked over to her, kissed his palm, and then pressed his hand to hers. "One," he said.

Josie felt an unexpected surge of love and need, and she had to put her hand over her heart to still the swell. Tyler hated kisses, and yet he had figured out a way around the sloppy mouths and close proximity, figured out a way to make them soothingly numerical.

"Tyler," she said.

He had turned back to the shelves, and although she wanted to grab him, to gather him up into her arms, she stayed where she was.

"Tyler," she said again. "It's okay to count, and to measure." She needed him to know this, needed him to feel her kiss him back. "Don't let anyone ever tell you it's not."

He stood where he was, staring at the giant boxes of cereals, when a woman pushing a shopping cart stopped to baby-talk to Maddy . She was about Josie's age, and a baby, a boy, was sitting in her cart, gurgling to himself and waving a set of plastic keys.

The woman smiled. "How old is your baby?" she asked.

"Fifteen months."

"She's so cute," she said. "Daniel is sixteen months."

Josie smiled at the boy and tried to get Maddy to wave.

"And your son?"

"He's seven."

"You're lucky to have a boy and a girl."

Usually Josie was quick to say that the kids weren't hers, but this time she realized she felt a deep longing for this.

"I have another boy; he's five," the woman said.

Josie smiled and encircled Maddy's ankles with her thumb and forefinger.

"Is your son in first grade?"

"Second."

"Tinfoil," Tyler said, and put the box in the cart.

"Your mommy says you're in second grade," the woman said. "Do you like it?"

Josie's heart quickened, and Tyler looked at his feet.

"Do you have a favorite subject?"

"The moon is two hundred and thirty-nine thousand miles from Earth," he said.

"Well," the woman said. "You're a smart little boy."

Tyler shifted his weight from foot to foot. "We need paint," he said.

"Yes; okay," Josie said. She smiled at the woman and wheeled the cart down the aisle. They found the silver spray paint, duct tape, a few more bags of candy, and a pack of metallic markers, and Josie unloaded the cart and paid the checker. On the way out, Tyler stopped in the parking lot.

"She thought you were my mommy," he said.

"Yes; she did."

He nodded. "It's okay," he said. "I think it's okay."

She didn't say anything, but she felt her heart expand in her chest, aching to hold tight to his.

* * *

When they got home, Josie helped Tyler get into his space suit. It was really just a gray sweat suit, but it didn't scratch at him, and it was the right color. She figured she could write NASA on the front with a black marker, duct-tape some metallic stripes, and no one would question him.

"Last year I was a dinosaur, and this year I'm an astronaut," he said.

"You need your helmet," Josie said, and placed it on his head.

"It's hot."

"You can just hold it then," she said, and took it from his head. "Put your candy in it."

He held it in both hands and stared down at the empty insides.

"Say trick or treat."

"Trick or treat," he said, and she emptied a handful of Pixie Stix into the helmet.

"Candy," he said.

"Yes, and when someone gives you candy, you have to say thank you. Let's practice. You go first."

"Trick or treat."

Josie took two Pixie Stix from the bag and dropped them in his helmet. "Happy Halloween," she said.

"Are you going to come trick-or-treating with us?" he asked.

"You forgot to say thank you."

"Are you going to come trick-or-treating with us?" he repeated.

"No."

"Why?"

"Because." Josie opened a Pixie Stix and poured the green dust into her hand.

"Because why?"

"Just because." She licked the dust from her palm.

"But you came last year."

"Yes." But last year everything had been different. Last year they had gone first to the mall with Phillip and Katie, and later that night out with Mary. The night had been warm and windy, and Tyler dragged his dinosaur tail from house to house collecting candy while Mary pushed the sleeping baby in the stroller.

The streets were dotted with ballerinas and cowboys and skeletons, and the buzz of the night had made Josie brave. She rested her hand atop Mary's, and Mary leaned her head on Josie's shoulder, and Josie wondered if there was ever a more perfect night.

"When I was little," Mary had said, "my mom would cover the trees with masses of spiderwebs. I wouldn't walk under them without someone holding my hand."

Josie smiled. "What else?"

"We would have a pre-trick-or-treating party every year, and my mom made this punch she called Witches Brew that I'm convinced had brandy in it."

"What else?"

"Ummm . . . I was a cat for four years straight, and then a gypsy, and then a cheerleader."

Josie tickled her cheek with Mary's hair.

"What about you?" Mary asked.

"My dad had a haunted house built on our property each year."

"A real house?"

"All these workmen would show up in the morning with a giant tent, and by the time I came home from school it had turned into a real house—with turrets and everything," Josie said.

"Wow."

"Every year there was some different theme. Once he had two dozen animated zombies programmed to raise their arms and howl when he flipped a switch. It was his own personal *Dawn of the Dead.*"

"Where did he get all that stuff?" Mary asked.

"Some prop shop in Hollywood."

Mary looked at her. "That must have cost a fortune."

Josie was silent. She had told Mary that her father was an accountant, that she grew up on the outskirts of Santa Barbara in a town full of strip malls and fast food joints.

"He was really into Halloween," Josie said.

"That's some serious dough," Mary continued.

"Yeah . . . I don't know. . . ." She fiddled with the zipper on her sweatshirt.

Mary knew Josie was being evasive. Josie once told her she could only lie with her back to someone. Otherwise her palms sweated, she swallowed hard, and couldn't stay focused.

"I don't know," Josie said, and bent down to tie her shoe. She could sense Mary's hurt. "My dad owned some property," Josie said. "We sometimes had a little extra money from that."

"Oh," Mary said, and paused. "What did your mom do?"

"She was a housewife." Josie wondered how she had managed to avoid this conversation for over three months.

"And what does she do now?"

"Same," she said.

They had walked along in silence, feeling the wind whip their hair against their shoulders until Tyler was ready to go home. Then they put the kids to bed, and Mary lit a fire and snuggled up with Josie. Josie thought she would like to be suspended in the moment forever, but it had, of course, been too tender to last.

A year later, whatever was pure and sweet between them was slowly being coated with a thin film of muck. Mary could ask Josie to address her as Dr. Griffin in public, tell her not to sign Tyler's permission slips anymore, insist on taking Maddy to her doctor's appointments, and Josie would still feel an invisible thread tied tightly around her heart and planted firmly in Mary's hand. Mary could tug ever so slightly, and instantly Josie was five again, unable to escape her mother's gripping hold.

Now Tyler put the helmet on the bed. "I want you to come trick-or-treating," he said.

"I know you do," she said, "but I can't."

"Why?"

"I have a lot of stuff to do."

He looked up at her and then rolled his eyes. She had never seen him do this before, and she tried not to smile.

"Where did you get that?"

"What?"

She did it back to him, and he giggled. She did it again, and he laughed harder.

"You're an eye roller," she said.

"*You* are," he said, laughing.

"No, you."

"No, you." He was giggling wildly, and Josie was rolling her whole head along with her eyes when Mary opened the front door.

Mary wasn't supposed to be home until the evening, and Josie scrambled to sit up straight. Tyler bounded to the door and stopped in front of Mary.

"Make Josie come trick-or-treating with us," he said.

Mary ignored him and set the mail down on the hallway table.

"Mommy, please." Tyler tugged on her sleeve. "Pleeeease."

"Stop it, Tyler." Mary flipped through the mail and pulled out a letter.

"I want Josie to come."

"*I'm* going with you," Mary said. "Now stop it."

"I want Josie!"

"Another time, Tyler," Josie said.

"Josie," he yelled. "Josie, Josie, Josie!"

Mary walked toward the closet, but Tyler had tangled himself in her legs, and Mary had to catch herself on the wall to keep from falling. "Fine!" she yelled. "Let Josie take you!"

"Yay!" Tyler squealed.

"Ty . . ." Josie started.

"No," Mary said. She paused for only a second, but Josie could see what was coming, could see Mary's eyes light up. "Why don't you go? He obviously doesn't love me anymore." She was still standing in the hallway, her briefcase in one hand, her coat in the other. "Isn't that true, Tyler?" Mary asked. "You don't love me anymore?"

Josie wanted to pull Tyler to her and cover his ears, and yet directly behind came an even worse feeling. The air became denser, and Josie was abruptly outside herself, looking down on the room—Mary and her face-to-face, Tyler between. They were dolls being put roughly in place. Mary was being positioned, being made to take Tyler's chin in her hand. "You think Josie's your mommy?" she asked. "I'll show you who your mommy is." Mary's doll arms were grabbing Tyler's shoulders, turning him toward Josie. Then Mary dropped her briefcase, and Josie came tumbling back.

"I asked you a question, Tyler," Mary continued.

Josie steadied herself against the wall and managed a "Don't."

"Don't what? Don't make him tell the truth?"

Tyler cowered between them.

"Should I hand over custody now?" Mary said. "You want to steal my children too?"

Josie felt the heat building in her hands, felt it seep through her body.

From the other room, Madeline began to cry. Josie had laid her down for a nap in the playpen only fifteen minutes before. Her cries built until Josie instinctively went into the family room and lifted her out. Maddy immediately quieted, but Josie felt the heat pour through her body. She had Mary's baby in her arms, and even if Tyler ran to his mother, Josie had the baby, the child Mary loved most. Mary had started it, and now she would get what she had asked for. Now Josie would wound Mary so deeply, she would carry it in her heart forever.

She walked back to the hallway. Tyler had pressed himself against the wall, and Mary had done nothing more than drop her coat beside her briefcase.

"Give her to me," Mary said.

"Why, so you can ignore her?" Josie turned abruptly toward the stairs. "Come on, Ty." She took each stair forcefully, and Madeline started to whimper.

"Josie!" Mary yelled.

"She doesn't even know you're her mother anymore," Josie said, and walked into Madeline's room. Mary followed, and Tyler stood in the doorway, alternately calling for Josie and his mother. "She thinks you're just some woman who comes in to kiss her good night." Josie turned to set Maddy down on the changing table, but before she could, Mary snatched for the baby, clumsily grabbed a handful of pink jumper, and pulled. Maddy's head snapped back against Josie's shoulder and then forward onto Mary's chest, and Josie heard the baby's head thump heavily against Mary's breastbone. It was a dense, terrible sound. Mary gasped, and for a fraction of a moment Josie thought that Mary had snapped the baby's neck, but then Maddy shrieked. Josie took a step back, and it took Mary only a second to put the baby over her other shoulder and regain her composure. "You think you're some beacon of goodness?" Mary said. "You're not fooling anyone."

"I didn't steal your boyfriend, Mary."

Mary laughed. "Oh, you can have him. I don't need to be beaten by the men in my life."

Josie froze.

"You don't know what you're talking about," Josie said.

"Oh, please," Mary said. "I've seen what he does to you. I've seen your bruises. You've had them all down your thighs. What does he do?" She laughed. "Find a hairbrush and take you over his knee?"

Josie was stunned, and all she could do was shake her head.

"You might think about not wearing a skirt when you've been a bad girl."

"No," Josie said.

Mary set the baby down to be changed and pulled out a clean diaper. "It's sick, you know that? It's sick what you do."

Madeline's toys looked too big, the colors too bright, and Mary's words mixed with Madeline's cries until the noise sounded like needles in her ears.

"Did your parents spank you when you were little? Is that what happened? I bet they did. I bet they spanked you, and you liked it."

The world shrunk. Mary's words circled the room, growing bigger and bigger until they were colossal, sucking air and space. They were swallowing the room, and Josie felt unstable on her feet. She steadied herself against the crib and tried to breathe, but it was as if Devesh's hand were once again tightly over her mouth.

Mary's pager beeped. "Shit. I don't have time for this now." She fastened Maddy's jumper. "I just came home to pick up a file, but I think it's time we discuss our current situation." Madeline had quieted down, and Mary grabbed a pacifier from her crib and stuck it in the baby's mouth. "Take her." Mary pressed the baby into Josie's arms, and when she did, Josie felt the air forcibly thrust into her lungs.

She heard Mary take each stair quickly, heard her drop her keys, bang her briefcase, shut the door. And then nothing. Tyler stopped crying. Maddy held the pacifier still in her mouth.

Josie felt dizzy and was suddenly afraid she would drop the baby, but the idea of moving even an inch of her body seemed worse. To take a step from this moment would set the world in action again, and she suddenly wished she could be put to sleep—her finger pricked, the world frozen for a hundred years. She could almost feel the sweet languor, feel her body funneled with sand, but then Tyler called her name, and she looked up. He had stopped crying, but when she stared at him, he began to sob again, and she sank to the ground, put her head on her knees and let the baby crawl from her arms.

Tyler cried long, whimpery cries, and with each wail, Josie grew more and more exhausted. If Devesh were here, he would carry her home, wrap her in blankets, and call her his baby. And then he would beat her. She would beg him to do it, and he would. He would beat her marvelously, and with every strike she would thank him. Gratitude would pour from her body like tears, buckets and buckets of tears, all for him. It was her gift. Why did it matter how she offered it? It was her body to do with as she pleased, and if Mary were here now she would tell her this. She would tell her this, and she would tell her that she wasn't sick, and that her parents didn't spank her, and that in fact it was a very natural urge to want to be beaten, an evolutionary adaptation that came down through the apes, who built societies on very explicit negotiations of dominance and submission designed to maximize genetic reproduction. But these were Devesh's words, and the truth was, Mary didn't even need to peer into Josie's heart to see that what Josie was trying to call a gift was really no gift at all. It was a sickness, and Mary had seen it and wanted her gone.

Tyler stood in the doorway, whimpering repetitively.

"What?" she said.

His hands were tight little balls, and she could see he only wanted to be quieted. All she would have to do was sit him down on the floor with his plastic animals and measuring tape, and he would be fine. If she could manage it, he would occupy himself aligning and measuring, but the thought of his voice—high and tinny—repeating animal after animal, statistic after statistic, made her clench her teeth to keep from screaming.

"What?" she said.

He didn't say anything, just stood there crying half sobs.

"You can speak, can't you?" The minute she said it, she felt her stomach lurch. She tried to think of her wrists in Devesh's fist, but Tyler continued to cry. "Go to your room," she said.

He didn't move, and she felt the familiar simmer in her chest. It bubbled, and she breathed deeply, trying to push it down with each inhalation. "Go to your room!" she yelled.

He stood there for a moment, just enough time for Josie to push herself to stand, and then he ran to his room. Josie felt her head cloud, and she had to grip the crib again to keep upright. She tried to focus on her breath, tried to count each inhalation and exhalation, but she could feel the heat building. If she was so sick, why had Mary left her children alone with her? Obviously Mary was the sick one. Obviously Mary was the one in need of punishment. She would like to see Devesh beat Mary until she was covered in red palm prints, and if Josie couldn't have that, well, then she would have to dole out her own punishment. She thought of rulers and wooden spoons and belts. She thought there was a flat palm-sized hairbrush in Mary's bathroom. But, oh, God, she couldn't think these things. She would count. She would count the strands of carpet, the toys on the shelves, the flowers on Madeline's jumper. She pushed herself against the wall and tried to imagine her ankles and wrists cuffed in place. Madeline had crawled to the other side of the room and was playing with a set of plastic blocks. There were two blue blocks, four red, two yellow, three green. The rest, she knew, were in Tyler's room. He had arranged them on the bed so that they formed a kind of cage, and inside sat a bunch of his animals. She had owned a set like this when she was little. She remembered because she had chewed the tails off all the animals and then collected them in a jar she hid beneath her mattress and shook like a snow globe before she went to bed. One night her mother saw her pushing it back into its hiding place. When asked for an explanation, Josie had been dumbfounded. It just seemed like something she needed to do. Her mother chastised her and called her father in to see what his daughter did with her toys, but her father laughed it off, complimented Josie on her ingenuity, and asked if she wanted to apply for a patent. Josie had loved him for this, but it also brought about the same feeling she had felt that day at the beach when her father had buried her in the sand, the feeling that she had done something very wrong. It was recurring, something she felt whenever her father sided with her, and inevitably that sensation of total weakness would come over her and she would feel helpless—wedged between her parents like a doorstop—and then unbearably angry.

It was the anger that was hardest to control. It expanded in-side her like a balloon, growing bigger and bigger until it popped, making her throw dolls and smash crayons and tear pages from books.

Earlier in the day, Josie had sat on Tyler's bed and exam-ined each animal; the elephant with the missing eye, the tiger that Tyler placed at the front of the pack. She was holding the giraffe when Madeline cried out, and Josie had slipped it into her pocket and went to get the baby. Now she put her hand inside her pocket and felt the giraffe. She fingered its slender neck, the ridge of plastic along its back that remained from the mold. It felt tiny against her fingertips and she had a sudden urge to put it in her mouth—to feel it solid against her tongue, to hold it tightly between her teeth.

She was pulling it from her pocket when Tyler came back into the room, and she shoved the giraffe guiltily back into her pocket. His face was still puffy from crying, but all his need had evaporated. He stormed in holding a large plastic truck.

"I told you to go to your room," she said.

"Where's my giraffe?" he demanded.

She was taken aback, and for a moment she was terrified that he could read her thoughts.

"Go to your room," she said.

"I want my giraffe." He stood defiantly in the doorway, banging the truck softly against his knees, staring intensely at her hands.

The thought of the giraffe firmly in her mouth had calmed her, but now she felt the simmer again, her bones swelling be-neath her skin. He had been so good lately, obedient and almost sweet, and she thought that somehow the two of them had agreed

to an unspoken pact—they would be sweet and obedient together. But then again, she had not lived up to her side of the
bargain. She had dreamt things and thought things, and she
wondered if he had somehow plugged into her so that now here
they were, connected by some kind of internal current.

"Tyler," she said. "Go to your room." She had wanted to
sound forceful and commanding, but it came out as a plea, and
he stood his ground.

He stared through her pocket to the giraffe cradled in her
hand. "I want my giraffe, I want my giraffe, I want my giraffe!"
he yelled, and in one swift move, he slammed the truck to the
ground. It skipped across the floor—cab, then wheels, then
trunk—and then it was striking her bare foot, banging along
her toes and across her shin. The pain was sharp, a current
which singed first her foot and then traveled fiercely along her
leg until it reached her heart, where it splintered, sending elec-
tricity through her veins.

And then time seemed to stop. It waited for her to do
something, and this time she did. The door in her head opened,
and she took a decisive step inside.

"Fine," she said. She swept past him—down the hall, into
Mary's bedroom, and into the bathroom. She was no longer
near explosion. Her breathing wasn't labored. To her surprise,
she felt a tremendous amount of relief, and she settled into the
easiness of it all. She opened each drawer and finally, under
the sink, she found the hairbrush she was looking for. It was
dark wood, palm-sized with a short thick handle, and it was so
old that Josie thought Mary must have had it since she was a
little girl. She held it tightly in her hand and walked back down
the hall to Tyler.

"Do you know what this is?" she asked.

He had his back against the door jamb now, and he stared annoyingly past the brush in her hand.

"A brush," he said.

"And do you know what it's used for?"

He had not expected this, and she could see his puzzlement.

"It's used for spanking naughty little children."

His eyes widened, and he crumpled.

"Have you been naughty?"

She thought he might run away, and she was prepared to chase him, but instead, he just leaned more tightly against the doorjamb.

"Look at me," she said. She wanted his eyes fixed on hers, and she walked to him, took his chin in her hand, and turned his face up to look at her. "Look at me," she repeated. She could hear Devesh's tone in her voice, the flat force behind the command, and she wasn't surprised when he did.

"I asked you a question," she said.

He was silent.

"I asked if you've been naughty," she said, and held his chin firmly. This time he whimpered and looked past her, and she tightened her grip. Her hands itched, and she wanted to pull her palm back and slap him, but she gripped the hairbrush tightly. "Answer me," she said.

"I don't know." She could hear the fear in his voice, but he didn't cry.

"You don't know?"

This time he answered quickly. "No."

"Yes, you do, and now you're lying to me." She let go of his chin, put her hand on the back of his neck, and guided him down the hall. She could walk around the whole house with him this way, tell him she was going to teach him a lesson. She could put him in the corner, she could make him bend over the couch. The images flickered in her head, and the IV began to drip, drip, drip into her veins. She felt enchanted, as if she had been stroked with a magic wand.

"I'll show you what happens to naughty children." She led him past Maddy's room, closed the baby's door, and then directed him into his room. She sat on the bed, and the plastic blocks and animals tumbled to the floor. "I'll show you what they get." She pulled him swiftly across her lap and laid the brush beside her. "Little boys who don't behave get spanked." She tugged his pants down and then his underwear. "They need to be punished for being bad."

She picked up the brush. It was a conductor, and she would plug the two of them to it, feel the current travel from his backside to her insides. She knew to let the brush linger in the air, to heighten the anticipation, and she knew to bring it down first across one cheek, then the other, and then lower at what Devesh called the sweet spot. She centered it on his back-side, and when she did, he flinched.

It was only one tiny movement, a small contraction of his shoulder blades, but it sliced her fingertips and knocked her back to the brush in her hand, his little body across her lap, the rapturous and dizzying ache of what she was about to do.

She dropped the brush to the floor, stood up, and he tumbled to the ground. The blocks had toppled around him, and now he kicked at one and struggled with his underwear and pants.

She gasped and brought her hand to her mouth. She had nearly done it. Not in her head. And now he sat with his knees drawn to his chest, crying real tears into his very real knees. This was *not* what happened in her head. This was *not* what happened with Devesh.

She stepped back toward the door and out into the hallway. She was shaky, and she put her hands to her face and tried to think clearly. She had left the brush in the room. She should go back and get it. She could hide it in her underwear drawer. She could throw it in the neighbor's trash. Maybe if she took Tyler in her arms and cried her apologies, it would be all right. Or maybe there was no need to apologize, maybe he wanted it. Oh, God, that was sick. Little boys did not want to be spanked. Their heads did not cloud and their bodies melt at the idea of a beating.

She looked at Tyler, framed by the door. He was curled against the bed, the plastic animals spread around him. Her hands burned so violently it felt as if the skin had been grated off, and she knew that if she had to look at him, she would tear herself to bits.

She closed his door slowly, stood there, and wished she could go back in time. If she could go back in time, she would do it right. Just ten minutes would allow her to shut him in his room, thirty and she could storm out on Mary, a whole six hours and she could have quit and left the damn giraffe alone. If she hadn't pocketed it, he wouldn't have come storming into Maddy's room, and if he hadn't come storming into Maddy's room, she wouldn't have erupted, and if she hadn't erupted, she wouldn't be standing here now, the world irreparably changed. But this was ridiculous thinking. The giraffe had not created this in her. That darkness had burrowed its way into her belly long ago. She felt her heart throb and her stomach seize. She was going to be sick. She could feel it, could feel that her insides would push their way out at any moment, but she made herself walk to the bathroom, made herself lift the lid slowly and kneel carefully. And then she vomited, and when she did, it came out forcefully, one spasm after the other until she was sweaty and drained, and she couldn't drive anything else out, and she leaned against the cool tile of the bathtub and shut her eyes.

When she heard the front door open, she jolted. She was still in the bathroom and had no idea how much time had gone by. She knew she had fallen into a hazy half sleep, but whether it was fifteen minutes or two hours, she couldn't have guessed. She stood and the blood rushed quickly to her feet. From the bathroom window, she could see that it was dark, and she wondered if both Tyler and Maddy had fallen asleep.

Her head was pounding, and she walked tentatively into the hallway. Tyler's door was still closed, but even the sight of it—his name plate with the trains, the watercolor pictures he had painted and she had tacked up—made her shaky. She heard Mary walk into the kitchen, and Josie wondered if it would be possible to sneak down the stairs and out the front door without Mary seeing her. She heard the refrigerator open, close, a glass clink. She took a few steps, but then Mary's feet were on the stairs, and Josie could do nothing but stand there and wait, and it seemed like every step Mary took was slow and intentional, trudging closer and closer, until finally Mary appeared, and Josie readied herself to be broken, but instead, Mary breezed past her. "I'm too tired to deal with you tonight," she said.

Josie didn't move. She didn't place one foot in front of the other and run. She didn't turn around and shoot her confession into Mary's chest. She just stood in the hallway, outside the room of a boy she had nearly beaten, and the injustice of what she had almost done overcame her like a sudden fever. She forced herself to imagine the stairs, and her feet on them, and then she made herself take one step, then two, and then she was walking—hall, stairs, hall—and then outside on her bike, and finally at Devesh's door, knocking—scraping her knuckles raw against the door because she had forgotten her key—and when he answered, she must have looked changed because he grimaced, ever so slightly, and she knew she was once again transparent.

"I want you to beat me," she said quickly and walked directly into the bedroom. His two large suitcases were laid on the floor, open and half packed for India, and she stepped around them and opened the chest where he kept his toys. He didn't say anything, but she could feel his unease. She took everything out—the paddles and whips and ropes—and arranged them all neatly on the bed.

She pulled her shirt, bra, and jeans off and turned toward him. "Panties on or off?"

"I thought we had decided not to do this right now."

She pushed her thumbs between the elastic of the waistband and her skin. "On or off?"

He didn't say anything.

"Off then," she said, and slid them down her legs. She picked up a coil of rope and two wrist cuffs and held them out for him.

"What exactly is going on?" he asked.

"I changed my mind. You can decide the implement."

He was cautious with her. "This seems sort of a radical change from last night."

"Are you going to do this or not?"

He looked at her, and it seemed an interminable amount of time before he spoke. "No," he said.

She felt shaky. If she couldn't get him to take the rope, to bind her and beat her ruthlessly, she might explode. She took a deep breath and tried to focus on the goal. "Please," she said. "I need you to do this."

"Why?"

She wouldn't tell him, couldn't tell him. "I just need it . . . tonight. Please."

He stared at her, and she knew whatever came out of his mouth next would be a definitive decision.

"Give me the cuffs," he said.

She exhaled softly and handed them to him.

"Will you tie me?" she asked. "Tightly?" She thought she could control her mouth, but she was unsure of her body, and she wanted no way for her to stop him.

He didn't speak, just took her wrists in his hand and slowly fastened the buckles and threaded the rope. She could feel her impatience building, and she clenched her teeth and closed her eyes. He pulled her slowly to the bed and bound her wrists to one of the tall bedposts. It seemed to take forever—each knot meticulous—and finally she couldn't stand it any longer.

"Hurry," she said.

He looked up at her slowly.

"I said hurry."

His eyes blazed, and he slapped her across the face. Her hands went instinctively for her cheek, but the rope held her tightly. She looked down. The carpet rolled beneath her feet and then seemed completely gone. She was suspended in the thick murky air. She shook her head. She was not ready to go so far away so quickly. She wanted to be present in the moment, body and mind beaten together.

"You want to beaten, huh?" He stepped back.

"Yes," she said, and instantly he snatched a light cat-o'-nine tails and brought it down firmly across the middle of her backside.

"You're sure?" he asked.

"Yes."

"I'm not sure you'll be saying that shortly. I think you'll be begging me to stop."

"No, I won't." But she knew if he did it as hard and as long as she wanted him to, it would eventually push whimpers, cries, and then words up from her belly. She would have to bite something to keep quiet, and now she wanted him to gag her.

"Gag me," she said. She didn't think he would. He would tie her or gag her, but doing both left her no way to signal him to stop.

He didn't say anything, just walked behind her.

"Gag me."

"I suggest you watch what you say."

"Gag me!" she said.

He brought the cat-o'-nine tails down quickly on her thigh. She jumped, but she knew that light whip would do little more than stripe her back.

"I said, 'I suggest you watch what you say.'"

She stamped her foot. She needed to make him angry—really angry—to make this beating come from someplace violent and unfamiliar, to enrage him so much that he would finally punish her.

"I don't want you to use that," she said.

"I don't care what you want," he said, and brought it down again.

She caught her breath but held firm. "That's a baby whip," she said.

"Then it's perfect for using on babies."

"Use something harder," she said.

"No." He brought it down again, and she gritted her teeth.

"I'm not asking, I'm telling."

"Stop it," he warned.

"Coward!"

And then she heard the whip drop to the floor with a thud, the whistle of his belt through his belt loops, the swish of the leather through air, and then the searing pain on her right thigh.

"Is that hard enough for you?" The next blow cut her other thigh. It was equal in intensity, and she had to work not to cry.

"No," she said.

This time it caught her squarely across her backside, and she thought she had been cut to the bone. This is a punishment, she told herself, but she could feel the heat between her legs. "Not hard enough," she said. She heard him bring the belt swiftly back, and she wrapped herself around that sound because she knew, to tolerate the next, she would have to cling to something, and then she felt the air rush around her shoulders and the wind knocked out of her body. She sucked for breath and instinctively tried to pull out of the ropes, but he had tied her tightly, and she could do nothing but let the blows fall swiftly on her body. She could hear each cut through the air, again and again, but worse were his soft grunts, how hard he was working to beat her. The pain was intense, and she tried to focus. This is what you almost did to Tyler, she told herself, but soon it was just pure pain and with each blow she cried out until she was crying, real tears, her body being thrashed, his body thrashing hers, harder and harder and harder.

Then, as quickly as it had begun, it stopped. He dropped the belt and walked out of the room.

She stood there and suddenly felt more alone than she had ever been. She slid to the ground, her wrists still tied tightly to the bedpost and cried. Her nose was running and the tears mixed with her snot and saliva, and she couldn't wipe her face. She sobbed and pushed her forehead into the hard wood.

It was a long time before he came back, and when he did, he bent tentatively beside her and rested his head heavily on her shoulder. They stayed like that for what seemed hours. There was nothing to say or do except breathe, and when he finally spoke, his voice seemed far away and unfamiliar.

"I'm sorry," he said.

"Don't . . . please."

"I . . ."

"Please, Devesh, please."

He nodded and untied her wrists, and she realized she must have been pulling hard on the ropes because her skin was red and rubbed raw along the circles of bone. He pulled a blanket off the bed, wrapped it around her, and pulled her close to him. He reached from behind her and intertwined his hands in hers. His arms were the same dark brown, his fingernails the same milky white. Nothing had changed, and she realized that the world which she had hoped to tip had barely quivered.

In the morning, she woke up feeling ill. Her head hurt and her body felt as if it had been filled with lead. He was already out of bed, and she could hear him in the kitchen. She made her way to the bathroom, turned on the shower, and stood under the stream of hot water until it began to turn cold. He was leaving for a month, and she wasn't sure if she was glad or terrified.

They had fallen asleep on the floor together, and she had only woken up when she rolled on her back and felt the throb of her upper buttock. She went to the bathroom and looked at the damage. From her lower back to above her knees, she was bruised and swollen—welts the size of thick fingers peppered her skin and when she ran her hand across her backside, she could feel the swell of purpled tissue like Braille across her fingertips.

She turned off the water, got out of the shower, and he was standing in the bathroom.

"I made you some *chai*," he said.

He hadn't made her tea since the day she had appeared on his doorstep, wet and unexpected.

"Thank you." She took the cup and sipped. "Not enough cardamom," she said.

He smiled.

She put the cup on the counter. The towel dropped from one hand, and he looked at her thigh and grimaced.

"Oh, God, Josie." He reached and turned her around. "Does it hurt?"

"A little," she said.

"Oh, bunny," he said and pulled her into him.

"I know, Devesh, I know. Please. Please, let's not talk about this. You're leaving in a few hours."

He closed his eyes and rested his head on hers. "I want you to come with me," he said.

She stiffened and pulled slightly. "No," she said. The thought of going to a country of penetrating stares, and knowing gurus, and gods with hands and eyes enough to see into every crevice of her heart was enough to make her turn physically away from him. "You should finish packing," she said. She wrapped the towel tightly around herself and walked into the bedroom.

When the cab picked him up at the house, he hugged her close, kissed her forehead and told her to be good, and for a moment it felt as if last night had never happened, but when he slammed the car door and left her standing there all alone, the reality of yesterday returned, and she wanted to run after the cab and breathlessly beg him to get her as far from here as possible. He could wrap her in saffron and dip her in the Ganges, and she would be forgiven—all karmic sins washed clean—but that was silly, another ridiculous ritual. Redemption did not come from a river and it did not come from a belt.

She locked the front door and got on her bike. She wondered if Tyler had told Mary what had happened. She thought he must have, yet she wasn't afraid to go back to the Griffins'.

Rather, she wished she were already there, enmeshed in what she justly deserved.

When she arrived at the house, she propped her bike against the garage and felt stuck, her hands glued to the handlebars. She simply had to put one foot in front of the other, she told herself. She would knock on the door instead of using her key. Mary would answer, and then it would begin. Maybe Mary would send Tyler to his room. Maybe she would hold him by the shoulders and use him as a prop. Josie could feel her heart accelerate, her breath grow shallow. She pushed her back against the garage, dug her hands into her pockets, and tried to steady her breathing.

She looked at the trees. They were enormous, and she realized that somehow without her knowing they had lost all their leaves. It was unnerving to think that hundreds of hours of time had simply slid by. She tried to calculate how many. She could remember helping Tyler make a collage with brightly colored fall leaves. That must have been in September—forty days ago? Fifty? And there were twenty-four hours in a day. Twenty-four multiplied by fifty equaled one thousand? She wasn't sure. If she added up the hours one by one, it would be easier to calculate. She could start with the first of September.

She had started to count when she heard the front door open. She froze, and then Mary turned the corner carrying a garbage bag.

"Jesus, you scared me," Mary said.

Josie was silent. Mary's hair was pulled back in a ponytail, and Josie could see the strawberry birthmark on her neck. She concentrated on it and waited.

"Listen," Mary said. "Your father called."

"What?" Josie asked.

"You need to call him." She paused. "Now."

Her father only called on the Griffins' home phone when she didn't return the messages he left on her cell phone.

"Oh," Josie said. She was confused and taken off guard. "All right."

"You need to call him now," Mary said, and threw the garbage bag in the trash can.

"Fine." She stood still for a moment, waiting for Mary to add something, but she didn't. Josie walked tentatively into the house. Mary followed and went immediately upstairs.

Josie felt she was in some kind of light dream, aware that she could wake up at any moment. She walked into the kitchen and picked up her cell phone from the counter. Upstairs Madeline shrieked, and Josie listened to her giggle. She dialed the number, and it rang, six, seven, eight times. Finally a woman answered.

"Who's this?" Josie asked.

"Josie? Oh, God, honey, we've been waiting for you to call since last night." It was her Aunt Steffi. "Hold on. Let me get your dad."

Josie stared at the sink. Tyler's crusted cereal bowl sat among two sippy cups, an assortment of silverware, three plates, and a coffee mug. She hadn't done the dishes yesterday morning because Tyler was running late. He had lost a sneaker, and they had searched but not found it, and he eventually went to school in socks and sandals.

She was wondering if she would see Tyler, if he would even stay in the same room with her, when her father got on the line.

"Sweetie," he said. She hadn't heard his voice in a long time, and she had a quick jab of homesickness. "Sweetie, your mother . . . I have to tell you something," and then the rest seemed to pour like honey from a tiny spout, slow and continuous.

Josie listened. "Uh-huh," she said. "Yes, okay," she said. "Okay, yes, tomorrow." And then she placed the receiver gently back on the cradle.

CHAPTER ELEVEN

ON THE PLANE THE NEXT MORNING, JOSIE WATCHED THE LITTLE girl next to her play with her dolls. She was six or seven, and her hair went so far down her back that she had to drape her braids over her shoulders to avoid sitting on them. She changed the dolls' outfits, brushed their hair, and talked to them about the ocean in California and how to avoid sharks. They had been flying for over an hour and a half and so far the little girl had only stopped chattering to her dolls to drink a can of ginger ale.

Eventually the girl's mother leaned over to Josie and said, "She can play by herself forever."

Josie smiled.

"Are you vacationing in California?" the mother asked. The woman looked like she was from Southern California—blonde hair, brown skin, and designer clothes. Josie realized that she hadn't seen a designer bag or a hundred-dollar T-shirt since she left Santa Barbara.

"No," Josie said.

"Business?"

"A funeral." Talking to this woman was not what she wanted to do at this moment, but she felt a sense of obligation for ogling her daughter.

"Oh, I'm sorry. Not someone close, I hope."

"My mother."

The woman gasped, and Josie warmed with the charge of shocking her.

"I'm so sorry."

Josie didn't say anything.

"You must still be in shock."

Josie knew she was not in shock. Rather, she felt disembodied. It was the same feeling she'd had during that last fight with Mary, the same feeling her childhood dream drew on. She was outside herself, but this time she was watching an aquarium of her insides, different feelings swimming by, one after another. It was hard to dwell on one for any period of time; each was more curious than the next, and yet it was all dully familiar.

"And your dad? Were they still married?"

Josie nodded.

"It's good your father has you," the woman continued.

Josie tried a smile, and the woman reached over and squeezed her hand.

"Are you staying long?"

The woman's daughter had begun to sing, and Josie looked at her watch. "Just for the funeral."

She was dreading the funeral. Not so much the service itself—the loving eulogy and endless hugs from her mother's wide circle of friends—but the physical viewing of her mother. She knew she would break at the sight, snap wide open, both sides of her body pulled apart. No matter how many strained memories of their relationship she held in her head, seeing her mother's body was sure to make her crack. It had happened even when her mother was alive. Whatever icy exterior Josie managed to fabricate, the fact was that her insides clawed and scrabbled and begged for any piece of her mother. And now that her mother was dead, now that there was no chance of ever climbing into her mother's heart, Josie was afraid of what would expose itself if she split in two.

The irony of the last few days did not escape her either. Although her father hadn't told her exactly what time her mother had died, Josie knew it had happened the day before Halloween in the early evening, and Josie knew what she had been doing in the early evening—nearly beating Tyler. Karma, she told herself. The more she thought about it, the more her guilt piled up like a towering stack of baby blocks.

According to Josie's father, her mother had gone to the doctor for a checkup—for the preceding two weeks she had been sluggish and her arms had been tingly. The doctor did a series of tests and told her she had heart disease, told her to quit smoking, and gave her a prescription. After the appointment, she had filled the prescription, and as she was pulling out of the pharmacy parking lot, the pain struck. She managed to pull the car to the side of the road, but soon after, the attack gripped her. She had even tried to get to the pills, managed to get the safety top off, but her heart had given out just outside the pharmacy, the bright yellow pills dotting her thighs like happy suns. And the worst part, her father told her, was there were no cigarettes in her purse. "No cigarettes, Jojo."

"You'll get through it," the woman said.

Josie wished the woman would leave her alone now, and she was thankful when the little girl across the aisle tugged on her mother's blouse. The woman gave the little girl a cookie, and Josie watched her eat it, watched her nibble around the exterior in a circle just as Tyler did. She thought about changing seats. The more Josie watched her, the more she felt crushed by the leaded weight of what she had almost done. She could feel it coat the inside of her body like an internal shell, heavy and oppressive. She wondered if Tyler thought she was going to give him what he deserved. Once he had asked her if his daddy would come back if he stopped measuring everything. She had looked at him and sadly shaken her head, and he had nodded and gone back to playing with his measuring tape. "Ty," she said, "it's not your fault." He kept his eyes on the tape in his hand and told her he knew that, but she had already sensed his guilt, knew he was carrying it like a lump of coal jammed tightly in his throat.

Now she wondered if he had linked the two together—his crime with her punishment. The thought made her nauseated, and she was glad of her body's reaction. You're the kind of person who would beat a child, she told herself, and yet she couldn't help thinking that Devesh should also be held responsible. He had promised her that what they did was just play, but these were not games they were playing at.

When the flight attendant came around with the drink cart, Josie ordered a vodka tonic. She drank it, then ordered and downed a second, and finally felt the sharp edges of the world filed away.

They landed at 10 P.M., and Josie waved goodbye to the little girl and let the girl's mother give her a hug. Her father was meeting her outside the baggage carousel, and she walked as slowly as possible. He had sounded bad on the phone, skipping from one thought to the next, crying, hiccuping. She had seen him like this only once before, when Matthew died.

Now, Josie came down the terminal escalator and saw him immediately. He pulled her to him and buried his face in her hair. She had not been this close to him in over a year, but his shape and smell were so familiar and the alcohol made her so fuzzy that she had to shake her head to remember she was a grown-up.

"Jojo," he said. When he hugged her, he had knocked his baseball cap to the floor, and she bent to pick it up. Without it, she could see where his hair had become thinner, and she forced herself to look down at the cap. He was old. It had been hard to see before, but now she could see the age spots on his forehead, his already thin hair now brittle and gray. He held her by the arms and looked at her. "I'm so glad you're here," he said. "You have no idea how much I missed you." Unlike her mother, he had held tightly to her when Matthew died, and for a long, long time she had tried to cling to that.

She knew her father loved her. When he returned from his business trips he would bring her back gifts—a piece of fossilized wood, a battery-operated cable car, a blue casino chip—and take her to a movie or the beach, but this affection always seemed to dissipate, and within a few days he was back in his office, answering two phones at the same time and gently shooing her over to the main house. She would refuse, sprawl face down across his desk, until he laughed and agreed to a quick game of hangman. Still, it had always been a desperate kind of love, too precarious. For years, she felt as if she were carefully binding the two of them together with fragile netting, and some morning she might wake up and find it snipped through.

"I missed you too," she said.

"The house is a mess. I'm a mess. Everyone's a mess." He took a handkerchief out of his pocket and blew his nose loudly. "I'm just glad you're home."

The word sounded strange. She hadn't thought of their house as home for a very long time, but she nodded, took a deep breath, and followed her father into the parking lot.

On the way to the house, the palm trees whizzed by, and the lights twinkled in a mass of cityscape. She felt bulleted along the freeway, the film sped up to make the audience aware of itself, and she was very aware of herself. Every inch of her body felt in the wrong place, and it made her twitch and jolt and feel like she had the weekend she was sixteen and had decided to see what it would be like to be a coke addict. Then too, she'd felt tumbled onto a movie set. She had given a boy in her class a fifty-dollar bill, and he presented her with the goods. She didn't know whether she was being ripped off or how to go about getting the stuff up her nose or what to do once she did, and she kept the Baggie in her pocket until Sunday morning when she spied the gardener's son. She was lying by the pool on a chaise longue, bundled in a too-warm coat, fingering the Baggie and trying to work up the courage to do something with it, when he appeared with a trash bag full of grass cuttings. "Do you do this?" she had said, and pulled the Baggie from her pocket. He smiled. His front tooth was chipped, and when she wondered what it would be like to run her tongue along it, she tumbled into someone else's film. She was directed to the guesthouse and instructed to sit on the kitchen floor, and she was glad it was a silent movie because it was easier to watch yourself without the distraction of spoken lines. They cut and snorted, cut and snorted until she felt shot through with candied energy and zoomed her way first to his mouth and then down his chest. It was a montage of body parts, and she watched and thought that perhaps the film would stay focused on the two of them rolling around on the brown linoleum, a teen love flick, but it hadn't, and instead the old standby had flickered on, and she watched herself beaten with the always reliable belt.

Now, the Porsche slid into the driveway, and Josie gritted her teeth. She was drifting through a series of movies, each more stylized than the next. She had tumbled from the weepy family drama of the airport to the Gothic styling of Montecito. Her father keyed in the security code, and the gate lurched open. They drove slowly up the driveway until the house appeared, huge and ominous. Illuminated by the security lights, it looked like some filmmaker's version of a Victorian mental ward. Standing beneath it, all twenty-one rooms and two staircases towering above her, she felt that if she walked through the door there was a very good chance she might never walk out again.

"Your Aunt Steffi's been staying with me," her father said. "I think she set you up in the blue room."

Both her aunt and her mother had moved from Ohio to Los Angeles for college, roomed together, and then married within a year of each other. When Josie's father had quadrupled his income in under a year, he had tried to get Aunt Steffi's husband interested in investing, but he was overly cautious, and then resentful when the windfall came. Aunt Steffi insisted it wasn't the money, but the disintegration of the marriage seemed to coincide, and soon Josie's father had found Aunt

Steffi a three-bedroom bungalow in Summerland, close enough for the cousins to bike back and forth.

Josie's father carried her suitcase to the room and hugged her good night.

"I'm glad you're here, baby," he said.

She nodded. She knew he was longing for something from her, any bit of emotion that he could snatch up and cling to as proof that her mother's death affected her, proof that the family he intermittently tried to squeeze together had really existed, but she only felt drained.

"I'm exhausted," she said.

He nodded and kissed her forehead. She waited until she couldn't hear his footsteps anymore and then closed the door. It was late, and although she was tired, her mind was spinning thoughts, and she felt banged around in her own head.

She was glad not to be in her childhood room and wondered if her aunt had purposely done this. It would be just like Aunt Steffi to read her with such pinpoint accuracy, and Josie felt suddenly grateful, and pained that she had not returned any of her aunt's recent e-mails. When she was young, she had loved her aunt with such intensity that once she had punched her cousin Natalie in the mouth when Natalie simply asserted that Josie had her own mother. Her mother and her aunt were markedly similar, and yet the quality she loved so deeply in her aunt, the ability to anticipate what Josie would do and think, was exactly what made Josie crack plates against dinner tables and kick holes in doors when it came to her mother.

Josie changed out of her clothes. It was almost 1 A.M. In India it would already be afternoon. Devesh had promised to call when he arrived, and she assumed he had tried, but her cell phone had died. She had his parents' number, but the idea of picking up the phone, let alone actually talking to him, seemed unmanageable. In the forty-five hours they had been apart, Josie felt as if the space between them had grown far greater than eight thousand miles. She imagined he was in Delhi by now, fawned over and catered to by his mother and sisters. She had snuck his photo album into her suitcase, and now she pulled it out and crawled into bed. She flipped the pages and looked at the women. His mother had been beautiful. She had Devesh's wide eyes and intense stare, and in each photograph she was draped with ornate saris and elaborate jewelry, regal and formal. Josie imagined her a goddess, attendants massaging her feet with oils. On the wall of Devesh's study was a painting of the four-armed Kali, a sword in one hand, the head of a demon in another, the other two arms encouraging her worshippers. The painting always scared her—all that control and destruction. Now Josie imagined his mother this way, a necklace of skulls around her neck, her foot on Devesh's neck, but she knew this was pure imagination. Devesh told her that his mother pampered and gushed over him, would fill his plate before he was done and make his bed the moment he stepped out of it. Still, Josie preferred to think of her as she looked in the photograph, distant and aloof, and with everything that had gone on in the last two days, the image of Devesh's neck resting firmly under his mother's foot was strangely comforting.

She turned the pages of the photo album and stopped on the photograph of Devesh and his sister. She looked at the little boy. When she was that age, Matthew had still been alive, and there was no violence and no horrible thoughts. She looked at

Devesh's baby face and wondered if his baby head had gotten its way around such violence yet. She had once asked him how old he had been when his fantasies had begun. She asked tentatively, but he answered as if she asked him the time. "Four, five, seven?" he said. "Sadomasochists usually report having had these fantasies for as long as they can remember." She had cringed at the clinical terminology and the ease with which he used it.

She placed her finger on the photograph, dug her nail into his dimpled chin, and marked him with a crescent moon. Then she closed the album and shoved it deep within her suitcase.

CHAPTER TWELVE

THE FUNERAL HOME WAS A LONG STONE BUILDING WITH SOMBER-looking columns and marble stairs. Josie could remember playing on these steps, her and her cousins trying to out-jump each other until some grown-up told them to stand quietly.

"The funeral director's name is Steve Steller," her aunt said. Steffi had woken Josie early and persuaded her to come help make the funeral arrangements. Josie had tried to get out of it, but her aunt had insisted. "Your father's been a mess," she said, "sitting in your mother's closet, not washing the dishes because she might have eaten off one. Do this one thing for him," and Josie had caved.

"Steve Steller. Sounds like a car salesman," Josie said.

Her aunt sighed. "Think about what color the flowers should be."

"Black."

Her aunt gave her a sharp look. "Be good."

They walked up the stairs and opened the tinted glass doors. Inside, the anteroom was dark, and because Josie had not taken off her sunglasses, the funeral director seemed to materialize out of thin air. He grabbed her hand, and Josie jumped.

"I'm so sorry for your loss," he said and pressed first her and then her aunt's hand firmly in both of his.

He was a skinny, balding man who had obviously been meticulously taught what to say and how to say it. He led them to his office, and Josie sat in the overstuffed chair and thought how carefully someone had planned this room. The chairs were a warm shade of rose, and the arms seemed to enfold her. There was no desk; instead, they sat around a low coffee table that held a variety of glossy brochures and a vase of cheerful-looking pink lilies. The flowers matched the chairs that matched the trim of the wallpaper; even the funeral director's tie was a gooey pink.

"As you know," he said, "we have a variety of packages to help make this difficult time easier."

Josie bit the inside of her cheek but took the brochure he handed her. On the cover was a collage of photographs, mostly of grandparents and children and flowers and ducks. There were no coffins or black-clad guests dabbing their eyes with handkerchiefs, and Josie had a strong urge to ask Steve Steller what package the ducks and children came with, but she was attempting to behave, so she skimmed the brochure trying to discern the differences between the Serenity, Devotional, and Harmony packages.

"There will be quite a few people," her aunt said. "How many does your chapel seat?"

"One hundred and fifty."

Her aunt nodded and flipped the pages of her brochure.

Josie listened to him talk about organists and limousine services and bronze memorial tablets, but when he pulled out

the catalog of caskets and suggested either the Aurora or the
Majestic, Josie's palms began to sweat, and when he asked
whether it would be an open or closed casket, the room seemed
to grow fifty degrees hotter.

"Excuse me," she said, and walked outside.

The night before, she had found an old pack of cigarettes
in the kitchen and slipped it into her bag, thinking that, if nothing else, at least she would have something to do with her
hands. Now she lit one and inhaled deeply. It burned, but she
held the smoke in her lungs for as long as she could. Her
mother's dead body was already in that building, being em-
balmed, or having its lips painted, or its hair curled and styled.
She wasn't quite sure why the sight of the body was so terrifying to her. Her mother was, after all, dead. Dead, dead, dead.

Josie dropped the cigarette and ground it into the marble
with the toe of her boot. It was cold out, and she hadn't brought
a jacket. She put her hands in her pockets and felt the scrap of
paper with Devesh's phone number. She wondered how long
it would take for him to become worried, and if he would call
Mary to see where she was. If he had been here, he would have
told her that her mother wasn't really dead at all, that her soul
was strapped to the revolving machine of the material universe,
going around and around like a Ferris wheel, each life a new
rotation. They had discussed this on the way home from seeing the Hindi movie. He told her about Krishna's explanation
of life and death, and although in the theater, she had felt the
possibility as keenly as his hand in hers, with the car carrying
her solidly home and the world speeding by her window, it
now seemed foolish, and she laughed at him and questioned
how a doctor, someone of scientific mind, could believe that

nonsense. He grew quiet and said it was a metaphor, but for the first time she knew she had wounded him.

She did not like to think about the possibility of a spinning Ferris wheel of life, nor did she like to think about karmic retribution.

The door swung open and her aunt walked out.

"You okay?" she asked.

Josie nodded and lit another cigarette.

"Do you have to smoke those?"

"Yes."

Her aunt sighed. "Great; we can have a double funeral." She put the brochures in her purse and took out a map. "I want to look at the gravesite. I think it's just up this hill. We can walk."

Josie followed her aunt and watched her thin black heels clip the asphalt. From the back, she looked so much like her mother—the same over-processed blonde hair, the same broad, strong back that tapered to a tiny waist, firmly cinched by a belt.

Her mother and her aunt had owned what, when she was young, seemed a million belts. And the belts had been perfect playthings. Josie would grab an armful from her mother's closet, fasten each, and lay them on the floor. They were hopscotch squares. They were rings for seals to swim through. Josie would play in the dressing room as her mother dressed to go out, not wanting her mother to leave but not knowing how to say it. Josie could remember the sharp, biting smell of her mother's perfume, how sometimes her mother would let her put a little on each wrist, and later, when Alba put her to bed, Josie would press her nose to her arms and fall asleep with her mother still on her. That smell. Even today when she caught a whiff of it, she could feel the familiar pull in her belly, and for the first time, Josie was overcome by a deep and heavy sadness. Her mother was dead. There would be no night visits, no forgiveness granted. What Josie wanted more than anything in the world would never, ever happen. The realization overwhelmed her, and she crumbled to the curb.

Her aunt turned around. "Honey, what's the matter?"

All air seemed to have left her body and, along with it, her blood, bones, kidneys. Never had she felt so empty, a dry calyx.

"Josie?" Her aunt bent beside her. "Talk to me."

She wanted to squeeze her fist around herself, crush her thin, papery casing and dust the ground with it, and then, as if on cue, her aunt took her chin in her hand.

"Listen to me. I know . . . I know you two had your issues, but you have to know your mother loved you."

"I don't care."

"Well, *she* did," her aunt snapped.

Josie wanted to shake her aunt, wanted to ask if she was blind, wanted to shout that her mother had seen her, seen her violence, her cruelty. She *knew* me, she wanted to scream.

"It was just hard for her to show it," her aunt continued.

"Not always."

"No; of course not, sweetie." But that was not what Josie had meant. What she had meant was that before—before Matthew died—it had been different. She could remember how her mother had washed her hair with strawberry shampoo, wrapped her in her pink silk robe, and let her fall asleep right next to her—right *next* to her. *Before,* her mother had been different. And *before,* Josie had been different too.

"Before Matthew died," Josie interrupted. She hadn't heard his name spoken aloud in years, and she felt like she had forced open a rusted lock. The entire cemetery grew brighter. The world was too green. There were too many trees. Too much grass. "Before Matthew died it was different," Josie said.

There was a long silence, and then her aunt spoke. "Yes."

"Before he died it was different," she said again. She needed her aunt to say it aloud. "Right? Before, it was different."

"Yes." She paused. "Before, it was different."

Josie could feel each second tick by like the clicking of a metronome in her skull, each tick an insistent question.

"Losing a child," her aunt said, "I imagine it changes you. After the baby died, when you were living with us, she fell apart for a while."

Josie looked at her. "What are you talking about? When did I live with you?"

"You were very young."

Josie was silent.

"Just for a month," her aunt said. "After the death."

Josie could remember so much of her childhood, and the memories after the death, as her aunt called it, were *too* bright, *too* in focus. It was inconceivable that this memory had somehow slipped away. "I don't remember," she said.

"Well, you were only four."

Josie's stomach clenched, and she had to put her chin to her chest to stop the dizziness. Her aunt put her hand on Josie's lower back. "It was only for a month," her aunt said. "Your mother just didn't know what to do. She was in so much pain, and you—I don't know, I suppose it was hard to be around any child." She paused for a moment, and Josie could hear her aunt's heels grating against the asphalt, the birds chirping at a thousand decibels. "She bought you this stupid stuffed dog and told you to hug it when you needed her."

Then Josie remembered. She remembered the dog. It had been white with long ears and a red ribbon around its neck. The dog's nose had somehow come loose, and she had lain in bed one night twisting it around and around and around. She was cold and for some reason afraid to ask for another blanket, and she shivered under the sheet and twisted the dog's nose until it suddenly came off. It surprised her, and she almost cried, but she knew crying would bring someone to the room, so she pressed her lips tightly together and stuffed the nose under the mattress, hoping no one would find it. But the dog looked at her with his big sad eyes, and this made her angry, made her pull the stuffing from its nose, and then maneuver her finger into the hole, widening it until she could rip his snout in two. Then she ripped down his back, along his legs, under his belly, ripped until the entire contents of the dog lay on the bed.

"I ripped it up," Josie said.

"Yes."

"The dog had sad eyes."

"You had a temper." There was a long silence. "But, your mom got through it, I guess. You, on the other hand, still have a temper."

Josie tried to smile.

"Your mom was good with you though, you know. She could get you under control in a snap."

Josie swallowed hard.

"I don't know how she did it; your father couldn't, I couldn't, but she knew what you needed."

Josie stood up. "Let's go. I want to get out of here." She didn't want to talk about this anymore—not stuffed dogs, not Matthew, not *before* or *after*, and certainly not her temper.

"All right," her aunt said, "all right."

They walked silently to the parking lot. Josie lit a cigarette and imagined inhaling mustard gas.

That night she dreamt the dream. Her body fell in halves like a splitting nucleus, each Josie becoming its own fully formed entity, and then one Josie was falling, careening toward the other, who seemed to be pinioned to the bed by a hundred thousand tiny nails. The dream went on and on, and finally when the two bodies were within a millimeter of crashing violently into each other, she jarred awake. Her eyes shot open, and she saw a rocking chair silhouetted against a milky blue wall next to a sheer curtain, translucent in the moonlight. She sat up. She hated that dream. It made her feverish and disoriented, and she wished that just once she would smack into herself and be done with it.

The moon was almost full, and from where she sat she could see the outline of the monstrous sycamore trees. When she was little, she had tried to build a tree house in one and got as far as nailing the first board to the trunk when her father hired two workmen to build it for her. At first she sat, pouting, and watched the workmen pull two-by-fours and sheets of plywood up into the bowels of the tree. She had wanted it to be a secret, a hideout of sorts, but a week later, when the workmen finally emerged, and she first climbed the sturdy steps with the rope banister and set foot in what no one would ever describe as *just* a tree house, she was delighted. It had a high domed roof with a skylight, and a ladder that led to a loft with a secret panel which you could open to lower and raise a basket attached to a pulley system, and it had real floor-to-ceiling windows on each wall so that if you sat in the center of the room, it was possible to think yourself afloat in a forest.

Now, she stood up and went to the window. She couldn't make out the tree house, but it was easy to see the grounds laid out before her—the meticulously groomed gardens full of still-blooming flowers, a blanket of purple and pink. Her first winter away from Santa Barbara she had been stunned by the complete lack of greenery. She would walk outside and feel as if the world had been stained brown. She understood that most of the country had seasons, but she had not expected the complete lack of life. Now she thought it odd that anyplace could be so perpetually alive. It seemed wrong, and yet appropriate that the world would be vibrant for her mother's funeral. The flowers would bloom. The birds would sing. And Josie would feel the strength sucked out of her, her mother controlling her even from the grave.

Her aunt had wondered how her mother had done it, how she could so easily get Josie under control. It was a simple thing, really. You just saw things and understood things and never spoke them, but you knew. And like a bullet, her mother's knowing went straight to the tight bundle of shame in Josie's heart. But what was hard to admit was that along with the pain came a speck of pleasure, a pinch of blissful intoxication at being controlled, and the two sensations, swirling around in her body, more often than not made her crawl to the bottom of her bed and imagine far more horrific punishments. In college, she had taken a physiology class where the professor lectured on the amygdala. It sat nestled in the middle of the brain, and its job was to prompt good feelings in response to behaviors like eating or having sex. Josie was taken by the concept. To survive you needed to have sustenance, you needed to reproduce, and the brain knew to encourage these behaviors. How logical. How clever. But why had her brain paired punishment with pleasure? Why was this need in her so essential? It wasn't for Devesh. His need for domination was not an addiction. Sure it was a natural urge, but ultimately he could choose not to give in. He had made that clear. If some kind of Darwinian theory *was* correct, this giving and receiving of pain was merely an evolutionary adaptation. But more than likely, Devesh said, there *was* no explanation, and her job was not to try and fasten one, but rather just to accept what was. She wished it were that easy, but her needs insisted on forcing themselves outside herself. She thought briefly of Tyler. Her mother wouldn't have even been surprised. "Yes," she would have said, "that *is* something you would do."

She looked at the clock. It was 2 P.M. in Delhi. She would have to do it eventually, and so she dug the number out from her discarded jeans' pocket. There was no phone in this bedroom, so she crept down to the kitchen and sat at the table with the slip of paper in front of her. She looked at the number—his handwritten twos and nines so distinctly non-American, and above the number, an uppercase "D." To anyone else that "D" was just an initial, and the number just digits

dialed to contact the owner of that initial, but Josie saw the
capitalized "D" and knew that if he had written her name
besides his, it would have begun with a lower-case "j," a little
"j," a submissive "j." But Devesh's "D" was enormous. "D" for
Devesh. "D" for Dominance. And the number—it belonged
to him. It made her stomach pitch.

She picked up the phone and dialed. She wondered if
there was a way not to tell him about her mother. She did not
want him to feel sorry and offer condolences. She knew he
would be sincere, that he would be genuinely sad, and at this
moment, she wanted no tenderness from him. The phone rang
many times and eventually a woman answered.

"Hello," she said.

Although she had heard Devesh speak English to his parents, she was taken aback, and she stumbled. "Umm, yes, is
Devesh there?"

"One moment please." The woman used Devesh's same
precise phrasing, the same semi-British accent. She had to be
his sister. The woman called his name. There were bits of loud
conversation in the background, lots of voices, and she wondered if she was interrupting a party.

When he answered the phone, his voice sounded very
deep and very far away.

"Hi," she said.

"Josie?"

"Yeah."

"Finally. I called my house and your cell; I even tried
Mary's, but no one answered. Where are you?"

She paused. She looked at the kitchen. She looked at the
black marble countertops and the Sub-Zero freezer. She looked

at the pizza oven her father had installed and the shiny copper pots that hung from the ceiling.

"In the kitchen," she said.

"In what kitchen?"

She paused. "A big kitchen?"

"Josie, *where*?"

"My parents'."

"In California? Why?"

"Um," she said. She would say it and the words would zoom through thousands of miles of optic cables, and she would not be able to get them back. "My mother died." She had not said it aloud, and she swallowed the m's and dropped the last d.

"What?"

"My mother. . . ." She had spoken little of her mother, and then only to tell him they weren't close. "She died." The static on the line seemed to jump onto her tongue.

"Oh my God. Oh, Josie. When? Are you all right?"

"Yes; I'm fine."

"Josie. Oh, God . . . I'm sorry." He was saying all the things she knew he would, and she wished this were a cordless phone so she could go outside and smoke a cigarette. "I'll fly out there tomorrow. I'll try and get a flight."

"No." She knew she had answered too quickly and too resoundingly.

"Why not?"

"Just because."

There was a long agonizing pause, and Josie could feel his restraint through the phone line.

"How did it happen?" he finally asked.

"Heart attack."

"Oh," he said. There was another pause and then, "I'm sorry. I'm just . . . I'm so, so sorry." His concern was making all the muscles in her neck contract.

"I should go," she said.

"No."

"It's two-thirty in the morning here."

"Are you sure you're okay? You sound . . . I don't know . . . unwell."

"My mother died, Devesh."

He was silent. She knew that at any other time he would have told her that was enough, that she was being rude, but instead he said, "I'm flying out there."

"No." Even as she said it, she knew she was insincere. She wanted him to make her say yes, to force her into acquiescence, and yet the thought made her heart contract, made her next "no" even more determined.

"All right," he said. "All right, but will you call me tomorrow?"

"I have a lot of stuff to do tomorrow."

"Then the next day."

"The next day is the funeral."

"Josie . . ."

She said nothing.

"Okay," he said. "Well . . . call as soon as you can."

"All right." She hung up the phone before he could say anything else, and as soon as she did, she wished she could get him back. She picked up the phone, then set it down again. She felt as if her heart were being pulled apart by two work-horses. She wanted him here so badly, and yet she was glad she had been cruel. But it was hard, and she put her head down on her forearms and was counting the number of hours she would have to be here, when her father walked in. He switched on the light, and she jumped.

"Josie! Good God, you scared me," he said.

She quickly got to her feet. "I was just getting something to drink."

"Don't go."

She sat awkwardly and then snatched Devesh's number off the table.

"What's that?" he asked.

"Nothing; it's nothing."

"Were you calling someone?"

"No." She knew it was obvious she was lying. "Yeah. Just a friend."

"A boy?"

Josie smiled. The idea of Devesh as a boy was ridiculous, but her father had always called her boyfriends boys; even Charlie with the graying temples had been a boy. "Um, yeah."

"Is it serious?"

"Um, maybe. I don't know," and it was true. Right now she wondered who she would be if it were possible to erase the previous six months. She wished she could just fall into a deep sleep. She took a deep breath. "I'm exhausted. I'm gonna try and go back to bed."

He nodded. She could see the need in his face, but doing this father-daughter thing was too much right now. It was easier to add his disappointment to the giant mass already in her stomach.

"I'll see you in the morning," she said, and left the room.

CHAPTER THIRTEEN

EVERY MINUTE JOSIE SPENT IN THE HOUSE, SHE FELT MORE AND more smothered. Her father so badly wanted her close to him, and the air in the house seemed to deplete every time he mentioned how much Josie's mother had loved her. This morning he had tried to get her to look through the many photo albums her mother kept in the upstairs sitting room, but she had refused. It wasn't so much the pictures as the room itself. It was bright and small, and she was sure it would still smell of her mother's lavender hand lotion. Her mother would often sit there and knit, the one remnant of her Midwestern upbringing. Josie had liked to lie at her feet and unwind the yarn from its skein as her mother needed it. Sometimes her mother would tell her stories about when she was young, about the flounced dresses and stiff hats she wore to church, the award-winning rabbit she raised for 4H, the basement that her parents had turned into a ballet studio for her and her sister. Josie would wind the yarn around her fingers and try and imagine her mother small. She loved that room when her mother was in it, the way it hugged the two of them close, but without her, it made Josie uneasy precisely because of its size—one wall was two body lengths, another four, and if she stood on a chair she could graze the slant of the ceiling with her fingertips. It made her feel giant, capable of smashing entire towns with her big toe.

She discovered this by accident during a game of hide-and-seek. She had hidden in the sitting room many times before—behind the dark wood chest, the yellow gauzy curtains—but this particular time, she realized she was tiny enough to wedge herself beneath the large white armchair and be unseen. Once there, protected by the skirt of the chair, she was a squirrel in its den. She went a whole half hour before she was found, and only then because Natalie recruited Alba to help. But one summer afternoon when Natalie and her brother were playing, everything changed. Josie ran immediately to the room, but when she tried to push herself under the seat of the chair, she found her chest too big, her shoulders too broad. She tried again, this time feet first, but with the same results, and eventually she lay flat on her back, her legs squeezed, her hips scrunched to one side, and cried, not because she had lost her favorite hiding spot, but because she had grown too big, swelled like a twisted ankle. The pencil markings her father drew on her doorframe may have measured how tall she was, but the kind of growing that made her too big to fit under the chair was the inside-out kind. She was huge and this was bad.

So instead of looking at family photos, Josie placated her father by running as many errands as possible: she dropped a check off at the caterer, picked up black stockings for her aunt, took the funeral program to be copied, bought the liquor for the reception, and finally, when there was no other reason for her to stay away, turned off her cell phone and drove to the beach.

It was chilly, and she huddled beneath an abandoned life guard station to shield herself from the wind. She realized that she had, without thinking, driven to Butterfly Beach and then down to the beach below the Biltmore, the hotel where her parents brunched every Sunday. When she was little, she had loved going. She would eat chocolate chip pancakes shaped like animals while her parents sipped Bloody Marys, read the *New York Times*, and chatted with the other high-society regulars. When she was done eating, she was allowed to play on the sand below, and as long as she stayed where her parents could see her from their booth at the window, she could do as she pleased. She was used to playing alone, and usually she didn't mind, but one morning she had wanted her father to come with her. He had been away on business for the last few weeks but, the Sunday before he had left, he taught her how to skip rocks across the calm ocean.

"Please," she said, and tugged on his shirt. "I want to show you how good I am."

At first he smiled and agreed, but then Josie's mother interrupted.

"I haven't seen you in weeks," she said.

"Neither has Josie."

Her mother looked at her father, and Josie knew that there was something more at stake than who her father chose to spend the next twenty minutes with.

"You can spend time with her when I go to play tennis; she can play by herself now."

"Carol . . ." he said.

"Fine, do what you want," her mother said, and raised the Arts section of the *Times* to cover her face.

Her father sighed and started to get up.

"I don't want you to come," Josie said.

"Jojo . . .," he said, and stood.

She hated her mother in that moment, but she hated her father even more. He had chosen her, and it made her feel dirty and shameful. She knocked a water glass to the floor and ran out and down to the beach. They didn't follow her, which she expected. She knew they thought she behaved badly for the attention, but this wasn't it at all. What she wanted was no attention, to be invisible, and yet at the same time, she wanted her mother to take her by the scruff of her neck and scold her fiercely. She wanted to feel her shame magnified, blown up so big that all there was room for was a ribbon of pleasure. Her mother could then dismiss her, go back and snuggle her father, and Josie could lace this ribbon through her head, think of being spanked, and the ribbon would lengthen until it filled first her brain and then her body. But instead they sent her mousy friend Rachel down to play with her. She had never liked Rachel—she refused to take her shoes off because she was afraid of jellyfish, and she had once tattled on Josie for throwing rocks at the empty lifeguard station. Rachel was pale with thin blonde hair, and she was clingy and wouldn't play any of the games Josie wanted to play.

"Go away," Josie said.

"No," Rachel said.

"I don't want to play with you."

"Why?" Rachel whined.

"Because you don't know how to play."

"I do too."

"Fine," Josie said, "then you have to play what I want, and do what I say."

Rachel agreed, and Josie spent the next half hour ordering her around. She made her move rocks and then move them back; she made her stand on her head and, when she fell, do it again, and Rachel whined, but obeyed. Josie didn't know why she did it, and when her parents called the two of them back, Josie felt sick and, on the way home, threw up in the car. It was the bossing around, all that power and aggression with no space for imaginary punishments.

Punishment. That was all it was then, something to counter the dark dirty bruise inside her. The thought made her wince, and she pushed her thumbs deep into her temples.

CHAPTER FOURTEEN

THE NEXT MORNING, JOSIE WOKE UP TO THE PERSISTENT RING OF her cell phone. She had set it on the nightstand, and now she picked it up.

"Bunny," Devesh said.

She was shaken and didn't answer.

"You there?" he said.

"Yes," Josie said and sat up in bed.

"How are you?"

"What time is it?"

"It's eight your time."

"A.M. or P.M.?"

"A.M."

She closed her eyes and wondered what would happen if she just flipped the phone shut. "I was sleeping."

"Oh."

She knew he wanted to be reassured that everything was okay between them, and it was a struggle not to succumb. "Did you need something?" she asked.

There was a pause.

"I wanted to check on you," he said.

"I'm fine," she said. It was painful, and she gritted her teeth. "Look, I just . . . I can't talk to you right now," she said.

"Why?"

She wondered if he thought she didn't love him anymore or perhaps he thought she was just overwhelmed by grief, and she wanted to tell him that neither was true. "I have to go," she said.

"Let me fly you to India after the funeral."

Her chest ached, and it was as if he had reached through the phone and worked his fingers insistently between her ribs.

"No." It was enormous work to say the word, and she rested her head on the headboard. If he had just insisted she go with him from the start, stolen her away even a week earlier, perhaps the whole thing with Tyler could have been avoided. Everything could go back to the way Devesh insisted: thoughts would just be thoughts, no reasons, no repercussions. But this was not how things had happened, and trying to convince herself that a week's absence would have prevented the whole business, was as ridiculous as believing that he had implanted the marble of shame she carried inside her. He hadn't. It had been there long before him. Her mother had known it was there, had known who Josie was and what she was capable of from the time she was a very little girl. And now her mother was dead and no one was there to know who Josie was but Josie herself.

"I can't do this right now," she said. "I . . . I'm going."

"Josie, no," he said. "I need to tell you something. Just listen for a minute. The other night . . . what happened between us . . . I never wanted to do that. Do you understand?"

She could hear his need, and she gripped the phone.

"What we do," he said. "It's *leela*."

"What are you talking about?"

"It's *leela*," he said. "It's divine play. It's up and down, yin and yang, both sides playing with each other. It's what Shiva and Shakti did . . . it's . . ."

She laughed, and she felt herself grow stronger. "Jesus Christ, Devesh. You think you're some Indian love god, and what *you* do . . . is somehow holy? You beat women and you're a mystic? You beat women and it's divine? No Devesh, it's not divine. It's not *leela*."

"Yes; yes it is."

"No it's not, and I don't think even *you* believe this. I think at least part of you thinks that it's wrong, that it's bad."

"No," he said.

"Admit it. You've thought about it. You've thought that maybe you shouldn't be doing these things. I know you have. I've seen it in you." She wanted to hurt him, to tell him he disgusted her, but she clenched her teeth and waited. There was a long silence, and she could hear someone laughing in the background.

"Yes," he said. "I've thought that. But it's just one of many, many thoughts. It doesn't take precedence simply because it occurred to me. This is who I am, Josie. It's not bad, or good. It just is."

She laughed. "Yes, *guruji*."

"Don't say that."

"Whatever you say, Devesh, *I* know. *I* know it's violence and anger and punishment."

"No," he said. "It's not. That's not what it is. That's not what I want."

"It's what *I* want."

He was silent, and she knew she needed to hang up before he said another word. "I'm going now," she said. "I'm going." She closed the phone and threw it hard across the room.

She would not have it. She would not listen to rational-
izations and excuses for her behavior. She knew who she was.

There was a knock on the door and, when she didn't answer, her aunt peeked in.

"We need to leave in about an hour."

She put her head down on the bed. "What if I don't go,"
she said.

"Josie, don't do this now."

"I don't—"

"Just get up, get dressed," her aunt interrupted and tossed
her mother's diamond tennis bracelet on the bed.

 They arrived late. Josie's father insisted he drive, and it took
them forty minutes to make a trip that normally took twenty.
The lot was already half full of cars, and Josie knew there was
no slinking off into a corner before anyone came. It made her
nervous, and her heart felt like a mechanical hammer—beating her from the inside.

The funeral director greeted them at the door and led them
into the chapel. There were already around seventy-five people
there, and although she recognized faces, Josie couldn't remember how her mother had known most of these people. A woman
who she thought might be her mother's tennis partner hugged
her, and then it seemed like an endless series of hugs and shoulder squeezes and back rubs: a distant cousin, a next-door neighbor, a woman Josie was sure she had never met but who knew

her name and where she was living; and Josie thought that if one more person touched her, she would scream. She looked for her father. He was sitting with her aunt in the front pew, surrounded by well-wishers. In front of him was the casket. It was a dark mahogany with brass handles, and on top rested a bouquet of white roses. There were other bouquets including one of those giant wreaths with legs and a banner that read ETERNAL REMEMBRANCE that Josie knew her mother would have thought tacky. She wondered if it had a card, and she thought that if she read all the cards on all the bouquets very slowly, she might be able to avoid being touched by anyone else, but next to the bouquets was also the casket, and from where Josie stood, she could see it was open, could see a slice of white satin interior, a puff of her mother's blonde hair. If they expected her to walk by the casket, they were mistaken, and if they insisted, she would simply refuse. They couldn't make her. She wasn't a child, and she wouldn't be forced to offer goodbye kisses. She felt her head grow light and her stomach lurch, and then her cousin's hand on her shoulder, and she jumped.

"Steady there, soldier."

She hadn't seen Natalie in over a year, and she looked rounder and happier than when Josie had left. "Nat," she said.

"Come with me," Natalie said, and pulled Josie out of the chapel and into the funeral director's office. Natalie closed the door and gave her a hug. "You okay?" she asked.

Josie nodded.

"Yeah, well, we all know how well you and your mom got along. Guess this whole dying thing will make it a little easier?"

Josie giggled, and was glad that someone was able to state the obvious without also trying to convince her that underneath the friction there had been some stalwart devotion. She took a deep breath and sat in one of the overstuffed pink chairs.

"Your mom made me come with her to make the arrangements," Josie said. "I felt like I was picking out wallpaper."

Natalie sank into the other chair and put her feet up on the low table. "Are you going to speak at the service?"

"You must be kidding."

"Didn't think so," Natalie said.

There was a long pause and Josie scratched at the fraying threads on the armchair.

"I haven't seen you in a long time," Natalie said

"I know."

"I missed you."

Josie nodded. When they were very little they had fought constantly, but at thirteen when Josie discovered boys, Natalie discovered her brother's porn collection and the two would hover by the television with their fingers on the stop button, ready if a parent came home. Natalie was the one who gave Josie a congratulations card after she lost her virginity, the one who helped her plan imaginary ways to torture her mother, the one who held her hand under the Christmas dinner tablecloth when Josie wanted to pound her plate against the table. "Is it not way too pink in here?" Josie said.

"Yep."

"I feel like I'm inside a bunch of cotton candy."

"Or a wad of bubble gum."

There was another long pause, and Josie looked at her hands. "Thanks for dragging me in here."

"It looked like you needed it." She reached into her purse. "And I have a surprise for you." She pulled out two miniature bottles of vodka.

Josie smiled. For a long time they had competed for how many miniatures they could swipe from the liquor store on San Ysidro. "Did you steal those?"

"Yep."

"From San Ysidro?"

"You're two behind me, baby."

"Oh my God. Natalie, you are so bad."

Natalie smiled, and opened one. "Here."

"Now?"

"Do you know a better way to get through the next four hours?"

Josie took the bottle and downed it. "Yuck," she said, and wiped her mouth.

"What? You don't drink anymore?"

"Not straight vodka, you lush!"

"Remember when my mom caught us drinking?" Natalie asked.

"Which time?"

Natalie laughed. "At that pool party at your house. When my brother taught us to empty the bottles into Coke cans."

"Yeah."

"And remember how our senior year, your mom got us out of calculus and took us to the Four Seasons? Remember? She insisted we were twenty-one and made the waiter bring us Navy Grogs," Natalie said.

"On the way home, we stopped at the park on Olive Mill, and my mom picked those roses," Josie said.

"And put them all in your room."

"I forgot that."

There was a long pause, and Josie could feel the alcohol start to soften her brain. "Sometimes my mom wasn't so bad," she said. She had stuck the tennis bracelet in her pocket, and she realized she had been fingering it for the last ten minutes. "Look," she said, and pulled it out.

"I remember that bracelet."

The diamonds looked luminous in her palm, but Josie knew they were only chips; her father had bought her mother the bracelet long before he made his first million.

"Here," Natalie said, and took the bracelet. "You should wear it." Natalie encircled Josie's wrist and fastened the clasp.

It fit more snugly than it had on her mother's tiny wrist, but Josie was surprised by how similar her hands were to her mother's, the pale skin and brush of freckles. "I don't like it," she said, and held out her hand.

"It looks nice."

"No."

"Put that hand back in your pocket and take this." She held out the other opened bottle of vodka.

"I'm not drinking that."

"Yes, you are."

"No way; you drink it."

"It's for you," Natalie said, and pushed it on her.

"I'm already buzzed. I'm not drinking it."

"Oh, yes, you are." Natalie tried to force it into her hand, but Josie held her hands away from her body and behind her back.

"I'll pour it into your mouth," Natalie said, and tried to grab Josie's chin. They were laughing and wrestling and trying to keep the bottle from spilling when the bells chimed. Josie pulled away and gripped the chair. She was sure they would make her sit in the front row, and if she sat in the front row, she would glimpse her mother's closed eyes and red fingernails and freckled arms that looked very much like her own. "I don't want to go."

"I know," Natalie said, and stood up. She recapped the vodka, put it back in her purse, and took Josie's hand.

"No."

Natalie held Josie's hand and looked at her. They said nothing until the bells chimed again, and the funeral director entered.

"Oh," he said. He wore the same gooey pink tie, and Josie had an overwhelming desire to pull it tighter on his pale little neck. She wondered if he had ever kicked anyone out of the funeral home and what it would take to make him do so.

"The service is beginning," he said.

"Yeah," Natalie said. "We were just going." She pulled Josie to stand. "Just walk," she whispered.

The air was heavy, and Josie felt like she was wading through the shallow end of a swimming pool, but she focused on Natalie's hand on her lower back and allowed herself to be led to the chapel. She had to will her feet over the threshold, but when they hit the green carpet, she stopped. "I'm not going any farther."

"Josie."

"No." She spoke too loud, and a couple in the last pew turned around.

"All right, all right. Let me just tell my mom."

Josie watched Natalie walk to the front pew, watched her aunt and then her father turn around. Even from the back of the room, Josie could see her father's hurt, and she wished she could send a twin to sit and hold his hand. He whispered something to Natalie, and she nodded and walked back.

"Your dad says he'd like you to stand at the casket with him after the service."

"No fucking way," Josie said, and turned around.

Natalie grabbed her arm. "All right, all right, all right. Just stay here."

If Devesh were here, Josie would have had him stand behind her and wrap his palms and fingers tightly around both her fists.

"I'm not staying." Josie said it without conviction, and when she pulled gently away, Natalie tightened her grip, and Josie softened. If Natalie kept her hand firmly on her arm, she might make it through. And she could count things. The number of blonde heads, the white checks on Natalie's dress, the hairs on her arms.

A gray-haired man stood next to the casket and rested a notebook on the lectern.

"Who is that?" Josie whispered.

"The reverend. Sh."

"We don't know any reverends." She listened to the man talk about life and death and God, but when he started to speak about heaven, the marble in her chest began to throb and a small tornado began to circle in her belly. She felt it sweep its way around her insides, and she began to count. Seven windows in the room. Eighteen bouquets of flowers. Twenty-nine men with bald spots. And there were thirty-seven pews. She, in fact, had counted them when she was four, walked up and down the aisles tapping each one until the service had started and her aunt set her in the front pew and gave her a pen and a program to draw on. She tried to draw a baby on a cloud, but the letters on the program got in the way and instead she worked at covering the whole page in blue ink.

"Are you sure you don't want to sit down?" Natalie asked.

Natalie's mother stepped to the front, and Natalie let go of Josie's arm.

"No," Josie said. And she wanted Natalie's hands back on her. She shifted from foot to foot and imagined she could count the thin blue lines on her aunt's note card. At Matthew's funeral, no one spoke, and the casket was white and decorated with stuffed teddy bears, and the carpet had been brown then. Yes; she remembered because her shoes had also been brown and when she pointed this out to her aunt, her aunt said nothing, and Josie realized that this was how it was going to be for a very long time. It made her sad and she began to cry softly into her aunt's sleeve, and this seemed to make her aunt, who was sitting on one side of her, and her father, who was sitting on the other side almost happy, and she knew they thought she was crying because she missed her baby brother, but the truth was, she was crying because she knew no one would smile and say "That's right," when she pointed out that her shoes matched the carpet, or laugh and applaud when she sang the alphabet song, or tell her how adorable she was when she held her braids out and pretended to be an airplane, and she knew that they would be right in not doing so.

"When is this going to be over?" Josie asked.

"I don't know," Natalie whispered, "but you need to be quiet."

Her aunt dabbed her eyes and returned to her seat, and when she did, her father stood. He had told her he wasn't going to speak, but there he was putting one foot in front of the other, standing behind the podium, wiping his brow with his hand.

"I don't want to listen to this," Josie said.

"You have to."

"I can't."

"Just try."

Her father gripped the podium tightly. He was silent for a minute, his eyes closed, and when he opened them, he spoke. "I'm not really sure what to say, but I wanted to say something." He wiped his brow with his palm again and rested his elbows on the podium. "I wanted to talk about how wonderful Carol was. I wanted to talk about how much we'll miss her, and I think I speak for both Josie and myself."

The tornado in Josie's belly grew. A few people turned around and gave her consoling smiles.

"I want to leave," she said.

"No."

If Natalie wanted her to stay, she would have to do more than that. "Yes," Josie said. Her voice was getting louder, and the funeral director looked over at her. She looked down at her hands, and her mother's bracelet glinted in the harsh overhead lighting. The gold seemed too brilliant, the diamonds too luminous, and the bracelet hugged her wrist tightly.

"I guess . . . I guess maybe I'll tell a few stories," her father stuttered. "We all know about Carol's great sense of humor. I think she could make a stone laugh." There were some chuckles from the audience, and Josie felt the churning in her windpipe. If Natalie wasn't going to drag her out and give her a stern talking to, she would have to do it on her own. "I'm leaving," she said.

"No."

"Yes," Josie cried, and stomped her foot.

And then the room contracted. She felt her insides suctioned up, and she knew she was going to be sick.

She ran out of the chapel, out the front doors, and vomited on the steps. She gagged, but only bile and spit and vodka came up, and she clutched the handrail and wished she had eaten the toast her aunt offered her this morning. Someone was on the steps, and Josie retched again and then felt Natalie's hand on her back.

"Go away," Josie managed.

Natalie held Josie's long hair in one hand and rubbed her back with the other.

"Please. Please just go away," Josie said. She pushed on her stomach and spit on the steps. "If you don't go away, I'm going to scream."

"Scream if you want to," Natalie said, and held her hair tightly. "I'm not going anywhere."

"I don't need you to help me." Josie stood up and wiped her mouth with the back of her hand.

"Well, too fucking bad; sit down." Natalie pushed her to sit on the steps. "Your mother just died, Josie. You're storming out of her funeral, you're throwing up on the steps . . . and your shoes for that matter."

Josie looked at her feet; they were speckled with yellow spittle.

"You obviously need something," Natalie said.

"You don't understand," Josie said.

"Then explain."

Josie looked at Natalie. She wanted to, wanted to have Natalie see what her mother had seen, have her grab the long coarse rope that coiled at the base of her spine and pull it up through her mouth and out like a tapeworm, make it stop eating her insides.

"No," Josie said. She rested her head in her hands. Natalie sighed, but said nothing, and they sat there in silence. The tornado in Josie's stomach had made its way back down to the root of her abdomen, but it still rolled gently around her insides, and Josie pressed hard on her belly. There would be the interment service and then the reception at the house and then some forced goodbyes in the morning, and then she could vanish. But vanish into what? She seemed to have taken so many steps away from Africa that she thought she might not be able to find her way back. Devesh had eclipsed everything, made Ghana a distant smudge. Devesh—even his name in her head made her catch her breath. She pushed the heels of her hands into her closed eyes and felt book-ended into this one moment.

When the doors opened, the metal frame nearly hit Josie across the lower back, and she stood quickly, walked down the steps, and into the parking lot. Natalie followed.

"Did you drive?" Josie asked.

"We're not leaving," Natalie said.

"I just want to sit in the car."

Natalie gave Josie the keys and they made their way to the car. It was parked close to the funeral home, and Josie had to slide down in the passenger seat to keep from being seen. Still, from where she sat, she could see the steady stream of black-clad bodies make their way to their cars, and then she saw her father. He looked tiny even with her aunt's thin arm around his shoulder, and he looked tired and old. Josie forced herself to imagine him dead, laid out in a dark mahogany casket identical to her mother's. Besides his work, her mother had been his life, her mother and herself, and now her mother was dead, and Josie had excommunicated herself, and now he would have no one. She could easily imagine him as one of those perfectly healthy men who die shortly after their wives. He would die, and she would add another baby block to the already towering stack of guilt.

She watched her father and her aunt stand beside the hearse, its back doors wide open like a gaping mouth. Then four men emerged from the back door of the chapel with the casket. They transferred it easily, the front carriers using only one hand, and Josie wondered if her mother was still inside. When Matthew died, she had watched the casket lock shut, heard the clicks of the brass brackets, and then followed the men outside. Now, Josie watched the men slide the casket into the hearse, watched her father blow his nose in a handkerchief, watched her aunt looking very much like her mother with her puffs of blonde hair and red painted fingernails, and imagined this was what would have played out if she had managed to drown herself the night of Matthew's funeral. She would have joined Matthew in the soft ground, their skin drying up like old orange peels, their bones replicas of each other—brother and sister, sister and brother.

Natalie turned the ignition on.

"No," Josie said.

"We can drive behind the other cars."

"I don't want to go up there."

"You can stay in the car."

Josie put her feet on the dashboard and leaned the seat back. As they drove, she could see the too-green slopes of endless grass from the corners of her eyes, and when they stopped, two tall cypress trees jutted up beside her.

"I'm getting out; are you coming or staying?"

"Staying," Josie said. She felt the rush of cool air, heard the door slam shut, and immediately felt the complete stillness of the sealed car. She looked up. Natalie had parked far enough away that there were no cars behind, but close enough so that if Josie stretched out of her seat, she could just make out the crowd of dark bodies engulfing the gravesite. She watched Natalie walk quickly toward the crowd.

Natalie had asked Josie to explain herself, but to explain a piece would mean she would have to explain the whole. It was not enough to say she was probably the one who had stopped her mother's heart long before it had given out, not enough to swear that if she could, she would tear out her own and place it on her mother's coffin—an even exchange, a barter of body parts. If she told Natalie this, she would have to tell her what came before, and this was what she didn't know. What she did know was that her mother had hated her, and the reason was sure to make the sky fall in thick jagged pieces and the earth open up and swallow Josie whole. And now her mother was dead. And now there was no chance for either discovery or contrition.

She got out of the car, walked slowly to the outskirts of the gravesite, and leaned against one of the cypress trees. If the crowd parted down the middle, she would see her mother's grave and next to it the glint of Matthew's brass memorial tablet. She knew that the casket was placed on a sort of pulley system, and that a funeral-home worker would turn a crank that would lower the casket into the ground. And the funeral-home worker would have a thick black mustache, and he would give her a mild smile, and she would turn her face into her father's dark coat pocket not because she was shy but because he looked very much like one of the men who came to take Matthew's body away. Her father had tried to keep her in her bedroom while the men rushed into Matthew's room with a small gray box, but Josie sat in the hallway and listened to her mother cry, "My baby," over and over and over. The cries were horrible, small animal wails, and then there was no sound, the world frozen around her. Josie tried to convince herself that this was a good thing, but she had already seen Matthew's flaccid body, his arms and legs spread open like a limp teddy bear, and she had felt the heavy weight of something settle forever in her heart. Still, she concentrated on her father's tan shorts and pale legs, and counted. There were four pictures on the wall and six lamps on the ceiling and her father had two feet, but when she began to count the flowers on her dress, her mother's voice pierced the silence. This time she screamed. She screamed "No!" She screamed it over and over and over again. She screamed it even when Josie's father entered the room and one of the men left. Her mother screamed and screamed, and Josie counted nineteen flowers on her dress and when she

couldn't count any higher, had forgotten what came after nineteen and started back at one and again reached nineteen, her
mother's screams once again turned to cries, and then there
was only soft weeping. The man who left returned, and soon
both men came out of Matthew's room. The first man carried
the small gray box, and the man with the mustache carried a
soft white package. Josie knew what it was and looked at it hard
because she knew she would want to remember. She tried to
memorize the size and shape of the bag and how small it looked
in the man's huge hands. She memorized how the man held it
close to his chest, how it glowed next to his dark blue shirt,
and while she was memorizing the man's face, how a small
white scar ran the length of his chin, he looked straight at her,
smiled the same mild smile the funeral-home worker would
smile, and Josie thought—this man cannot see inside me.

That night, Josie had gone looking to kiss her mother good
night and found her in Matthew's bedroom folding his blankets and sheets. Josie had stood in the doorway and waited.
She watched her mother fold Matthew's soft blue blanket in
half, and then in half again. She watched her fold his sheets
with the trains, his tiny pillowcase, and when she finished, she
unfolded and folded again. Josie counted—one, two, three
repetitions—and finally, when she finished the fourth, her
mother stopped. And then, in a moment that Josie would play
over and over again, play it with such pinpoint accuracy that
she knew the angle of her mother's head, which shoulder her
mother's shirt had slid from, which fingernail's polish was
chipped, her mother turned and handed Josie her blanket, a
neat yellow square—six stars, two moons, four corners. "This,"
her mother said, "is yours." Josie felt her chest burn, and she

knew not only that she was transparent but that, in this one moment, her mother had branded her forever unlovable.

Now, Josie circled the crowd, carefully stepping over gravestones. There were easily one hundred people here, and they sat and stood facing the casket and looking solemn. At the edge of the white folding chairs, her two little cousins played. They were Natalie's brother's kids, and Josie had only seen the little one once, but the older one, Alex, she had babysat a handful of times. He sat at his father's feet and waved at her, and she lifted her hand and then shadowed herself behind a tree.

At Matthew's funeral, there had also been an interment ceremony, and Josie had sat on her aunt's lap and listened to the minister talk about Jesus taking the little children in his arms. She wondered if he was going to take Matthew, if at night he would come and scoop him out of the ground, and she cupped her aunt's ear in her hands and whispered the question. Her aunt closed her eyes for a long time and then slid Josie from her lap. "Go play by the trees," she said, and Josie walked slowly around the back of the chairs and then away from the service. She walked amid the graves, running her hand over the cold stone and stopping every now and then to trace her fingers atop the chiseled names and dates. Some had memorial tablets set into the earth. They had engravings of angels or crosses or flowers, and one even had a picture of a dog. She sat next to this one and put her finger on his brass coat. She wondered if Jesus only came for children, and why he didn't come get people before they were buried. Maybe there was a secret tunnel under the earth; maybe that was the only way Jesus could find them. That's why they were put in the ground. That's why you had to make sure they were buried. From where she sat, she could just make out her brother's funeral—the chairs looked like dollhouse chairs, the standing minister like a daddy doll—but she couldn't see the casket. She stood up and squinted her eyes, and when she saw something move, something small and white being lowered slowly into the ground, she ran. She ran hard—her patent leather shoes clicking rhythmically against the memorial tablets, her breath burning deep in her lungs—until she reached her father. He was standing now, and he caught her firmly against his side and held her close. She breathed ten deep breaths into the rough tweed of his coat pocket and then turned her head. The casket had been lowered, and the brilliant white contrasted sharply against the dark earth. Now they would fill the hole with dirt, and tonight Jesus would find his way, and Matthew would be fine. He had been put in the ground and tonight he would go to heaven.

Now Josie looked out across the wide expanse of headstones. They seemed to stretch on and on like whitecaps on a gentle ocean. All these people had died, and all these people had been given funerals. It helps the living deal with death, she had wanted to tell Tyler when they buried the bird; it helps them control the uncontrollable. But now she wasn't so sure. How had it helped her? She had seen Matthew covered in earth, had helped rain handfuls of rose petals down on his coffin, and what had it done for her? Nothing. She was still who she was, twisting out from that moment like a spiraling helix.

CHAPTER FIFTEEN

BY THE TIME THEY ARRIVED AT THE HOUSE, JOSIE HAD FINISHED the second miniature of vodka and made Natalie stop off at the liquor store for two more. There were a number of cars in the driveway, and a valet took Natalie's car and gave her a ticket.

"Only the best for my mom," Josie said.

Natalie put her hand on Josie's shoulder and steered her into the entryway. Josie's father was standing beneath the front stairs shaking hands and receiving hugs, but when he saw Josie come in, he called for her. "Honey," he said, and pulled her gently into a back hallway. He rested his cheek on her head and embraced her. She could feel his fingertips on her lower back. She flinched and tried to pull gently away, but he held her.

"I love you," he said, and clutched her tightly.

"I love you too," she said, and squirmed uncomfortably.

"And your mother loved you."

She jerked forcefully away and had to take a step back to keep her balance.

"Josie."

She had wounded him, and her stomach twitched.

"She did, Josie. She loved you very much."

She knew she should just nod and stay silent, but his inability to see made her angry. "Whatever you want to believe," she said.

"It's true," he said.

She could see the tears forming in his eyes, and for a moment, Josie wished he could see whatever her mother saw every time she looked at her. The thought scared her, and she closed her eyes and remembered something she had read a long, long time ago in an encyclopedia of African culture: If the correct funeral rites were observed, the deceased would not come back to trouble the living.

"I don't want to talk about this," she said. "I'm going to get us a drink."

"I don't want anything," her father said.

"I'm getting you some coffee then."

He sighed and nodded his head, and she walked to the dining room. There was a slew of people making drinks and picking through cheese and crackers and little sugared cookies. She made herself a vodka tonic and her father a coffee. She took it to him, kissed him on the cheek, and rounded the living room. She talked to Natalie's brother about his kids, chatted with one of her father's friends about North Carolina, and graciously received condolences. She was beginning to feel strong and capable. Yes, she could never crawl back into her mother's heart, but neither could her mother root around in hers. For the first time in a long while, she felt in control.

She pressed her palm into her left buttock and tested the bruises. They had calmed some, but the tenderness was still there, and she wasn't sure what to feel. When Devesh had first begun to beat her, she wore her bruises like a prize. Now, they seemed an unreturnable gift, something she was unsure would fit, something she was unsure she even wanted.

Her little cousin Alex came up to her and wrapped his arms around her waist.

"Hey, tiger," she said. He was Tyler's size, and she put her hand on his head and felt comforted.

"I want to play with the pinball machine," he said.

The last time he had been here, she had taken him upstairs and held him while he tried to hit the tiny metal ball with the paddles. His arms had been too small to reach both buttons, and she had played one side while trying to hold him, and he had giggled and squirmed and eventually been happy with lying on top of the machine and watching the lights.

"Let's go," she said, and led him to the stairs. The front stairway was long and sloping, with landings in between each flight, and she watched Alex lope up the stairs. She followed behind and sipped her drink. She was surprised by how much she had drunk, and yet she'd stopped feeling the buzz of the alcohol at least an hour ago. The only effect that lingered was a kind of soft bordered edge to the world. People slid out of sight, and everything looked spongy and supple.

They made their way to the game room where her father held his weekly pool games and her mother a monthly bridge tournament. At the end of the hall, the house divided—her parents' bedroom, study, and gym down the left hallway, more guest rooms, the game room, and her mother's sitting room down the right. Josie was glad she and Alex didn't have to pass the sitting room to get to the pinball machine. The thought of her mother knitting coupled with that feeling of childhood enormity made her uneasy. She took a deep breath and imag-

ined Devesh's hand interlaced with hers and then quickly saw
herself tied to the bed the night before he left—back arched,
buttocks out, the heavy black belt coming down fiercely on her
skin. She felt her body flush and prickle. She hadn't imagined
a single violent thing since she had entered her parents' house,
and the sudden rush made her pause.

"Josie," Alex called.

She had stopped just outside the game room. "Yeah; just
a second." It felt as if she had been shot up with some powerful serum. Her heart beat hard in her chest, and her body
flooded. She ran her fist along her backside again, this time
digging each knuckle into a different spot, making it throb, and
yet now she could imagine nothing more pleasurable than
having the belt bite her skin. He would take her wrists in his
hand and push her into a corner, tell her to stay there with her
palms on the wall while he found something to beat her with.
And maybe it wouldn't be his belt. He might leave her alone in
the room and come back with a switch cut from one of the
backyard cherry trees. He would stand behind her and slowly
strip the bark from the branch until it was only white tender
wood. And it would sting. Unlike the belt that gave more of a
deep thuddy throb, the switch would cut quickly, making it
harder to keep in position.

"Josie," Alex called again.

"Go on," she said. "There's a chair you can stand on."

Alex scraped the chair along the floor, and she stayed in
the doorway.

She wanted so badly to collapse to the floor, to place her
hands between her legs and feel the heat. She hadn't realized
how little she had felt inside her own body since she arrived,

and the want was almost painful. Before she'd met Devesh, she had needed to make do with the fantasy, but now she could have anything her perverse head imagined. She wished she had her cell phone in her pocket right now. She would pay the huge phone bill, wake his family up in the middle of the night. She didn't care. She needed to tell him she was sorry for being a brat, that he should be sure to take her over his knee when they both were back in the safety of his bedroom. She would be good, and repentant, and obedient, a tiny kitten, and she would take every punishment he gave her. "Punish me," she would say. But this was exactly what she couldn't say. Bad girls were punished; good girls were disciplined. Punishment was something unpleasant; discipline was pleasurable. He had drilled this into her head the night he had sent her home, and after her first actual punishment, she was sure there would be no others. On the plane, she had needed to sit balanced on one hip to avoid the pressure of the seat on her backside, and when she dressed this morning, she saw the ugly green mess her skin had become, but now none of that mattered, and she thought she would like him to beat her until she was close to passing out from pain. Her body warmed at the image, and she had the startling thought that she needed to immediately lock herself in the sitting room, drape herself over the chair, and imagine things Devesh would never do to her. The shame of it all seeped through her skin.

Her head was now pounding from the alcohol, and she needed to lie down.

"Alex, let's go," she said.

"I just started," he whined.

"You can play again later."

He ignored her and kept playing.

"Alex," she said.

He kept his eyes on the blinking lights and didn't acknowledge her.

"Alex. Now."

He did nothing, and Josie could see how easy it would be to make him Tyler. It was all punishment, whether she inflicted it directly on herself or not. If she thought she could separate the "good" punishment from the "bad," she was sorely mistaken. The need traveled the same well-worn track—from her head to her sex to her heart—and it sprang from the same place, the same wicked place. So what if her mother could no longer pry her open with a single look? This ugliness was always there, not because her mother knew it, not because Devesh beat it into her, but because it was hers.

"Alex, I'm leaving, I'm going," she said and turned right and walked down the hallway.

The hall dead-ended at the sitting room and then continued on to the left. Down that adjoining hallway was Matthew's bedroom and, at the end, Josie's room. She rarely took this path to her room when she was young. There was a back staircase that led directly from the kitchen to her bedroom, and she would rather go downstairs and up again than go past Matthew's room. Sometimes there was no way to avoid it, and when this happened, she would guide herself along the wall with her eyes closed, playing blind. She made it a game.

Now, she stopped at the sitting room. It was one of the rooms that had not been redone, and she planted her feet outside the doorway and looked. It was exactly the same as when she left—the pale blue carpet, the large white armchair, the dark wood chest—but now it seemed even smaller than she remembered. She stepped inside and felt draped in wet towels. She was silly to think her heart would be washed clean, the marble disintegrated simply because there was no one to see it. It was hers, attached like a tetherball firmly to her heart. It would belong to her forever, and ever, and ever. She sat down in the armchair and let her drink fall from her hand. It spilled onto her black skirt and thudded to the floor, and she curled up in the chair and closed her eyes tightly.

This time the dream is different. This time it is very clearly her four-year-old self. She is flying, her arms spread, her little flowered dress ballooning around her hips like a parachute, and she is holding something. It is small and cold and round. She grasps it tightly in her hand, and with the wind rushing down and her hair in her eyes, she can neither open her fist nor peek between her fingers. The thing is very cold, and it feels as if it is a little mole burrowing a hole through her hand, but it is also strangely comforting—a piercing tickle, an icy hug. She gives in to the falling. She smiles. She giggles. She is flying really. She is a baby bird whose mother has just pushed her out of the nest. She leans into the wind and lets the air rush into her mouth. There is no blue sky behind her, no black night either, it is simply space, and it seems gentle and endless. But soon, a dot appears below her, a single black speck, and as she falls closer, it grows until she can see it is a girl, a woman really. She squints to get a better look, and when she does, she is sucked into this woman's head. She is not scared despite the fact that she is tied tightly to a hard wooden plank. She is strapped down with leather restraints, and this time, something is very different. This time someone has painted a perfect circle on her bare belly. She would like to touch it, feel the dried paint rough against her fingertips, but the restraints are very tight. She cannot move, and it is oddly reassuring. She stares into the space above her and breathes—over and over—not caring how many inhalations, not counting the number of exhalations, until a dot appears above her, a single black speck, and as it falls closer, it grows until she can see it is a girl. And then something strange happens. She is split in half, but not really in half. She is dissected like a cell, each with its own membrane, each with its own nucleus. The woman and the girl are wiggling their collective fingers, and biting their collective lips, and most surprisingly of all, thinking in tandem—one's thoughts following the other's like a row of dominoes going down, down, down. The one on the ground pulls at her restraints, the one in the air claws at the empty space, but they are stuck, as if connected by a single kite string being rolled tighter and tighter in each direction. The woman's belly grows. It reaches upward as if magnetized, and as it grows, whatever is in the hand of the girl grows colder, freezing the hand shut, plunging determinedly down until there is a moment of pure terror, a kiss of excruciating pain.

Josie slammed into consciousness and instinctively braced herself against the chair. She could still feel the restraints pinching her wrists, the deep pain in her belly, and she shook her head to focus. She was in the sitting room, it was dark, and there was a blanket someone had covered her with tangled

between her feet. She sat up. Her back and neck were slick with
sweat. Her hands stung, and she looked at her palms. It was
dark, but she could make out eight crescent-shaped moons.
They bled, and she pressed her palms to her mouth and sucked.

She wrapped the blanket around her shoulders and left
the room. The house was dark, and she realized she must have
been asleep for a very long time. Her body felt heavy, each limb
stuffed full of pennies, and she walked down the hallway and
down the front stairs. The house was unnervingly quiet, and
she almost expected to find a household of frozen guests—a
man pouring a glass of solid red wine, a woman mid-sentence,
her hand on a coat lapel. She was incredibly thirsty, and she
made her way to the kitchen and poured herself a glass of water.
She drank it, filled another, and downed it quickly. Over the
sink was a window, and she sipped at a third glass and looked
at the back gardens. The moon was full now, and it illuminated
the yard like a spotlight.

The view was the same as from her guest room window,
but from here she could see the details. Someone had planted
a new fruit tree, anchored its skinny trunk straight with wire.
There was a flat of unplanted petunias, a bag of unopened
garden soil, and a pair of gardening gloves on one of the
Adirondack chairs. Everything seemed flooded by the moon,
and Josie looked at her hands coated with light and had a sudden need to feel flooded too. She put her glass in the sink and
walked outside.

The cold hit her, and she wrapped the blanket tightly
around her shoulders and wished she had something on her
feet. The moon was huge and luminous. She couldn't remember the last time she had seen it full, possibly that first night

with Devesh at the stone garden, or maybe the night he had left her in the corner—when he finally pulled her out, she had snapped her head to look at him and seen his hair gleam, his eyes illuminate. Then, she had wondered what she looked like, what they looked like together, awash in moonlight, and she had fallen to the floor and kissed his ankles.

But she hadn't looked at the moon then, or maybe just not seen it. Now, it was so, so bright. It made her squint. It reminded her of something—something far away—and it made her chest ache. She looked down and the ache seemed to subside. She should be in her bed, she thought, wedged tightly between the sheets, but when she took a step, the pain worsened, and she pressed her hand quickly to her heart and stood still. Why was she feeling this? Her mother was dead. Josie's heart should be aching for *her*, not for whatever ugliness existed inside her own chest. But whatever was in her heart seemed to be digging deeper, tunneling a tender hollow. She needed to go inside, to get out from under this flood of light, but when she took another step, the pain returned. She whimpered and sank to the ground. "Fine," she said and hugged her knees to her chest. "Fine." She would stay wrapped up, a little ball. She tried to ignore the pain, but it throbbed throughout her body until she lay down on the cold grass like a baby doll. Her arms fell limp by her sides, her eyelids clicked open, her eyes focused. It was too, too bright, but with each breath, the hurt seemed to gradually subside until it was only a dull ache. She breathed into the pain, and let the cool silver light penetrate her. It poured through her veins and made her aware of every inch of her body. And it made her remember.

*   *   *

It is a scorching hot summer, hot enough that the newspaper recommends keeping children inside. All day she has been very good, played nicely with her toys and shown her brother pictures in storybooks, and as a reward, her mother has taken the two of them outside for a nighttime picnic. The moon is full, and as a tribute, her mother packs a basket of only round items— cookies and oranges and small white bowls for lemonade.

She digs her hand into a bag of marshmallows and feeds them to her brother one by one. He eats each slowly, then opens his mouth for the next, and she laughs.

"He's a baby bird," she says.

Her mother smiles and stretches herself atop the blanket. Her mother is beautiful—her fine blonde hair pulled back in a loose ponytail, her tan arms perfectly freckled. She loves her mother so much that sometimes she imagines her gone just to feel the awful hurt and then the surge of happiness at realizing it's not true.

She holds a marshmallow in her palm and shows it to her mother. "Marshmallows aren't round," she says.

"Yes they are; you're just not looking at them correctly." Her mother pulls her close, has her pinch a marshmallow between her thumb and forefinger, holds her little hand next to the moon. The two look identical, and she is awestruck.

"Two moons," she says. She cuddles in close to her mother, breathes in the night, and thinks her mother can create worlds. She twists her moon in a circle, makes it orbit the real moon. "Moon," she says. She places her moon atop the other so that the two are swallowed into one. "Moon." She repeats the word, makes it long in her mouth, then short and clipped. It is a lovely word, and she could say it a billion times, but her mother puts a finger to her lips, and tells her to listen. She is quiet, but doesn't hear because the sound is muffled and seems far, far away. Then it becomes clear.

"Moon," her brother says, his mouth still full of marshmallow.

They look at him.

"Moon," he says again.

She is amazed. He has never said words, and now, here he is, saying a word, her word, and, like hers, it is soft and marshmallowy in his mouth. "Say it again," she says, but he doesn't, just cocks his head to one side and opens his mouth. She sees his little baby teeth—two on the bottom, one on top. They are as white as the marshmallow, as white as the moon.

"Where's the moon?" she asks.

He does nothing but open his mouth wider.

"Moon," she says. She points to the sky.

His mouth stays open, and he looks up, and she is washed in pleasure. She is teaching him this. Her word, her moon, her baby. "Moon," she says again. "Moon. Moon."

He points, opens his mouth, and although it seems to take forever, finally the 'm' comes deep from his belly and presses slowly through his lips.

She sits on her knees and holds his hands. "Mmmooooon," she says. It comes from her lips like a kiss, and he opens his mouth, licks at it, and kisses back. His word is clear—each consonant and vowel its own entity—and she is elated. She looks at her mother, who is propped on her elbow and smiling. "Where's the moon? Point to the moon," she says.

He is clicking his tongue now and has turned on all fours. She crawls beside him and asks again. "Moon," she says,

"Where's the moon?" His hair is golden, and she tickles her nose against the curls. "Moon," she says again. "Where is it?" And then he is saying it, and he is pointing, but he is not pointing at the sky, he is pointing at the bag of marshmallows. He is pointing and making baby sounds, and she thinks he is just being stubborn until her mother laughs.

"He thinks a marshmallow is called a moon," her mother says, and she is right because he is digging his tiny hand into the plastic bag and pulling out a fistful of marshmallows, and he is looking quizzically at them and saying it, saying moon, the word she taught him, and she pulls him and his marshmallows on top of her and laughs and laughs and laughs because she is loved and in love and nothing can touch this universe.

Now, the light seemed softer, sweeter, and Josie gently shut her eyes. Long ago everything had been good, and her mother had loved her. But then there was that awful day, and everything had changed. Her parents were going to Mexico for the weekend. She and Matthew were to stay with Aunt Steffi. They were to stay with Aunt Steffi, and Matthew had a cold, and her mother had packed him Vicks VapoRub. She remembered because she had found it in his packed bag and rubbed it all over each of her dolls' faces. They had colds, she told her parents, but they had not seen it that way and scolded her. Now they would have to stop at the store. Now they would be late for their plane. And they had made her stay in her room for a whole half hour. She remembered because she had pounded her party shoes against the floor. She remembered those shoes—fancy patent leather shoes with small red bows. She had pounded them, angrily at first and then in time to the music coming up through the floorboards. Dancing music. Party music. But wait. That couldn't have been that night. Why would there have been party music? She did remember a party, a party with tiny cakes with pink and white frosting, and fancy party shoes with small red bows and a matching polka-dotted dress. But that must have been another day. The day Matthew died, she had been punished, made to stay in her room for half an hour all alone before they left for Aunt Steffi's. She had been angry and pounded her party shoes against the floor. But then, had there been a party that night? Maybe. She remembered trying on a dress—red with white polka dots and a big silky sash. She had been sent to her room. And it was sunny. And there were fancy party shoes with small red bows and, downstairs, tiny cakes with pink and white frosting and happy music being piped throughout the house, and then she could see it, all in her head—every detail clear and bright, a confetti eruption, each piece falling dizzily into place.

There is sunlight everywhere. Sun on the yellow pinwheel in the window. Sun glaring off the easel and dried paints. Sun covering the plastic tiger and the elephant and the bear who is missing a leg. The sun is responsible for all this, the sun and the cat. The cat perches on the brick wall only when the sun is shining, and only when the sun is shining is it enticing to climb up with the cat and lie belly to sun. But this time, the sundial, which serves as a perfect ladder to the cat and the brick wall, tumbles when it's pushed off from, sending the cat, who has managed to be grasped, and the sundial, which should have been more securely fastened, and the mess of naked limbs, which are now covered with scratches, onto the ground in a crying mess. And now, because of the sun and because of the cat and because of the sundial and because of the discarded clothes hanging from the tomato bushes, the sunny bedroom is a prison.

There is nothing to do. Dresses have been tried on, balls have been bounced, crayons have had their wrappers peeled, and all there is left is to lie flat, flat, flat, on the bed like a moray eel, like a frog's lily pad. The top blanket is covered in yellow stars and yellow moons, but lying face down, eyes scrunched to blanket, only the strands of yellow that make up the stars can be seen. Each individual thread is visible, and it looks like tiny cats could walk tightrope style across each. One, two, three cats could walk, all in a row, all with four paws each, all prancing and dancing and making their cat ways across the blanket.

Downstairs it is very loud. There are people banging plastic chairs off trucks and clattering metal trays out of vans, and music coming in bits and spurts from the speakers that have been hung from the trees. It is a different world down there. Soon there will be tables full of tiny cakes with pink and white frosting, baskets heaped with chocolates wrapped in shiny blue and silver foil, bowls of thick whipped cream and bright red strawberries, and lots and lots of Shirley Temples speared with yellow umbrellas and more than one cherry. But now it is a noisy, fierce place, a jungle separated from the second story by a vast ocean of stairs.

Upstairs it is crystal quiet. The baby is asleep in his room, and no one is making a sound. It is so quiet that it may be possible to tiptoe around the upstairs in sock feet and not be heard or discovered by anyone—a top-secret explorer uncovering the barren tundra. It is the North Pole, or the South Pole, the one with penguins, the one where Santa does not live.

But tiptoeing outside the prison of a room must be done carefully and quietly. The blanket with the yellow moons makes a good parka, and once it is put on, it is easy to escape—one foot out of the prison, then two, look left, look right, then scurry like a great explorer down the hallway to the baby's room. It is easy. There is nothing to it. The baby's door is open, and perhaps the baby is awake now and wants to fly like an airplane around and around and around. This is a game that needs to be done when no one is looking; otherwise, there are gasps that the baby's shoulders will come unhinged and warnings of never to do that again unless a punishment is wanted. But the baby is so giggly and happy and holds tight, and it is worth the risk of getting caught to see the baby laugh like that. Still, it is important to stop spinning before someone falls to the floor and hits their head on a sharp corner. But this is easily done. It is easy to stop in time—to come gently careening to the floor in a brother-sister heap.

But then there is a noise. It comes from the stairs. It creeps slowly—heavy work boots on hard wood. It comes closer, and it is necessary to crouch behind the door in the baby's room and listen. The work boots fall one behind the other, moving forward, forward, forward, and although it is hard to remain silent, the blanket makes a good gag for heavy breathing. The work boots open the bathroom door and then, moments later, they are peeing. It is the loudest sound in the house, and it is very funny. It is hard to be quiet, but giggling into the blanket helps, as does thinking of sad things—like when the cat was almost chewed up by the neighbor's dog—and soon the work boots are scuffing back down the stairs, forgetting to wash their hands.

Behind the door, the baby's room looks like a huge dark cave. It is much darker than the prison room. The shades are pulled, and only a tiny stream of yellow sunlight creeps in. It lies like a skinny tree across the floor. The baby is fast asleep, and only soft breaths can be heard from the crib.

It is dangerous to wake the baby. Waking the baby is a sure way to be imprisoned in that too-yellow room for more than just a half hour, but there are ways to quietly approach the crib. By placing the yellow mooned parka on the slick wood floor and lying atop it like a sea lion on a rock, it is possible to slide silently under the baby's crib, which is like a little cave or a den for dogs. In this frozen tundra, a dog needs a den. There is digging to be done and gnawing of bones and scratching of hindquarters, and a den is the place to do these things. It is good to be a dog, and although it would be fun to have a doggy friend, it would be less fun to have the doggy friend shriek loud enough to bring the dogcatchers. It is hard to be quiet, but it is necessary, and after all, there are quiet things to do—fleas to scratch and corners to sniff—and these thoughts are being thought when the baby above begins to stir. The baby stirs ever so slowly, but this is just the beginning. When the baby wakes up it is a long process, but one that is impossible to stop.

There are two choices now—to run back to the prison or to stay and hope that, this one time, the baby will understand that this is still the beginning of the nap, that it's still sleep time, and that any peculiar noise is only a stray dog come to say good night. It is a hard decision. Pros and cons must be weighed, options examined, and time is beginning to run out when something happens. An arm is thrust between the crib slats. A single baby arm. It is short and fat, and it hangs in the air like a grownup's finger, stern and unforgiving. But just as quickly there is something else. There is a faint laugh, a tiny giggle. It drifts from the crib and makes the arm look different. It is not a grownup's finger. It is just a tiny arm, attached to a tiny hand, a paw really, and it looks so friendly that perhaps there is a third choice.

A den is a fine thing for a dog, but when there are babies to be played with, it is necessary to crawl out and then up to see the big-eyed baby face pressed against the crib. There is some eye rubbing and head tilting, and then the face smiles. It grins. It beams, and when it does, it looks like the moon, shiny and bright, just like the moons on the blanket.

See the blanket?

The baby grins.

See?

The baby giggles.

See?

The baby laughs because there are sunny yellow moons, but also because behind the moons there is another face—a sister face—and when the blanket comes up, the face goes away, and when the blanket goes down, the face comes back. Up and down, up and down. It is funny, and the baby wants to play, but it is hard to stick anything besides baby arms through the slats of the crib. Still, there is another way. It is possible for the baby to stay where he is and, instead, to put one foot on the bottom rail of the crib, both hands on top, and push and pull and pull and push, and land with a thud beside the gurgling, happy baby.

Then it is simple. Moons and faces, faces and moons. The blanket is raised in front of the baby's face. And then lowered. And then raised. And then lowered. It covers and uncovers, faster and faster, until the baby is laughing and giggling and making so much noise that the other sound, the sound from outside, is barely heard, but it is, and it is not the sound of work boots. It is the sound of pointy heels on slick wood.

The blanket is dropped.

The heels are at the prison bedroom where the door has been left opened. Soon, there is sure to be foot tapping and arm crossing and demands to come out from under the bed or within the closet, and after there have been threats and closet doors opened, there is sure to be a long-drawn-out calling of first-middle-last name and then the opening of the baby's door.

But there is not. The pointy heels say something about the half hour not being over yet, and they continue down the hallway. The heels get closer, and the baby pulls at the blanket and giggles. Soon the giggles will turn into laughs which will turn into shrieks which will bring the pointy heels.

A decision must be made, and the baby is tugging on the blanket.

Sh.

The baby giggles.

Sh.

The baby laughs.

Sh, and the pointy heels are at the bathroom. They will clip-clip their way into the baby's room, and even though the

baby is happy, there will be consequences. Parties might become off limits and desserts taken away.

The blanket is snatched away.

And then the baby fusses. The baby whimpers. The baby
whines. And although there is much begging—pleases, and
don'ts, and promises of cookies—it is useless. Out of the baby's
mouth comes a single birdlike shriek, and in less than the time
it took to fall from the cement wall to the hard ground, there is
a blur of yellow stars and moons, the baby is pressed down,
the little face covered, tiny threads of yellow blanket securely
plugged in the baby's mouth, which is now suctioning in, warm
and wet, like a newborn puppy, and an arm is pushing, pressing, fastening tightly into the mouth and nose like glue, no air,
no breath, pressing, holding, tighter, tighter, tighter until everything is going dizzy, dizzy, dizzy as if spinning in circles forever and ever and ever.

CHAPTER SIXTEEN

WHEN HER FATHER ASKED HER TO STAY FOR ANOTHER WEEK, SHE had not known what to say, and for the first time, she wished he could see her the way her mother had—see her insides illuminated like an X-ray, the small dark circle in her heart like a swallowed quarter. But he couldn't see. And he didn't need to, she told herself. It was her secret. Her marble. She would carry it the way she had all along, deeply and quietly. But she could feel it rumbling inside her, clanking against the tin can of her insides, threatening to expose itself, and she knew she needed to leave, needed to go back to North Carolina and see Tyler and Mary.

The night before she left, she forced herself to look at Matthew's room. She waited until her father went to sleep and then snuck down the hallway. The door was shut, and she stared at the knob for a long time before pushing it open. And then she simply stood, framed by the doorjamb, and looked. The room had been turned into a guest bedroom, painted a pretty sea green and filled with light pine furniture. She was taken aback. After Matthew died it had been a storage room of sorts—a stack of cardboard boxes in the middle, an old weight machine and extra television in one corner, a heavy oak chest of drawers in another. Now she could remember exactly where the crib had been, where the changing table butted up against the window, where the rocking chair that had once been hers sat. If what happened had not happened, the room was sure to have been filled with books and computer equipment and dirty laundry. Her brother would have grown up to be a real boy, a man actually, not "the baby," probably not even Matthew, but Matt. The idea was so startling she drew a quick breath.

She had never seen Matthew this way. He had always been the ghost baby, his little feet kicking her heart, his chubby fists grabbing for her mother, and she was the one who had trapped him there, stuck him forever in that moment. It had all happened so quickly. She remembered. Someone called from downstairs, and her mother answered and waited a moment, but then turned and walked away, and Josie, wanting to be extra careful, kept Matthew quiet even after he lay still, until she was sure they were alone. Then she took the blanket away and saw the vomit—milky white, marshmallow white—around his mouth. She called him softly, shook his little shoulder, and when he lay silent and unmoving even when she wiped his mouth and tickled him under the chin, she knew that something bad had happened. She remembered the way her chest felt full of wet sand, the way she knew—knew deeper than she had ever known anything—that this was very, very bad and that she should keep this secret, nestled deep inside her heart.

She stood there—trying to see where she had jumped from the crib, where she had tripped over the plastic truck, where she had dropped her blanket—and felt a deep and powerful sadness. She understood that if she had stuck him forever in

that moment, then she had also stuck herself. Josie slid down
the wall to the floor and cried. This was who she was. And now
she knew.

Still, it wasn't until she was standing in front of the Griffins' house that Josie realized that the rest of the world had not
changed. The house stood huge as always, its white double
doors still draped with the Halloween garland she and Tyler
had hung, and she walked down the Griffins' pathway, up the
steps, and knocked on the front door. When no one answered,
she knocked again. She had talked to Mary on the phone only
once from Santa Barbara, just long enough to say she would
pack her things and leave when she returned. Josie had hung
up quickly, and now she stood wondering if Mary would let
her in the house at all. She shoved her hands in her pockets.
She had brought the giraffe back for Tyler, and she was fingering its thin neck softly between her fingers when Mary opened
the door.

"Josie," she said. "You're back."

Josie stood very still and waited, but Mary just brushed
her hair out of her eyes and mumbled something about the
house being a mess.

"Well," Mary said, "come in."

Josie followed Mary into the living room and stood
awkwardly.

"You want some coffee?" Mary asked.

Josie shook her head. There was a long silence. Josie tried
to make out Tyler's voice or even the banging of toys, but the
house seemed completely still, and Josie wondered if Mary had
somehow sensed she was coming and taken the kids over to
the neighbor's.

"You okay?" Mary asked.

Josie was confused, and for a moment she thought Mary was asking if she was all right here, in the house.

"Oh . . . yeah," Josie said.

There was another long silence, and Josie was sure that, now that the formalities were out of the way, Mary would begin, but instead she stared at the ground. "You can . . . you can stay here awhile if you need to," Mary said.

"No." It came out of Josie's mouth so quickly, she didn't realize she had spoken, and spoken with such disgust, until Mary looked up at her and said, "Jesus Christ, Josie, I'm just trying to be considerate."

And then it was clear that Tyler had made what happened a secret, probably pushed the brush far under the bed among the dust balls and lost metal cars, and Josie realized that there were only two reasons he would have done this—to protect her or to protect himself—and either of the two options made her throat tighten and her legs grow weak.

"Is Tyler here?" Josie blurted.

Mary looked at her oddly. "No, he's playing next door."

"Oh," she said. Perhaps it was better this way. She would leave the giraffe on his pillow and hope he could at least sense her apology. She nodded her head and started to the bedroom, but stopped.

The first night Josie had slept at the house, one corner of her bedroom had been stuffed with cardboard boxes, and after everyone went to sleep, she had crawled out of bed and quietly peeked through each box. One was marked TYLER'S CLOTHES, but when she opened it, she found Mary's things—a few blouses, some maternity dresses, and a stack of sweaters. On top was a baby blue pullover, and Josie pulled it out, held it up to her chest, and caught a whiff of cigarette smoke and faint perfume. Her reaction was immediate and visceral. It was not her mother's perfume, but the sweet musky scent partnered with the smoky headiness made her heart swell, and she needed to press her palm firmly against her chest to force it back to normal. She shoved the sweater back into the box and pushed it all under the bed, but later that night, when she woke up needing to use the bathroom, she dug it back out again and held it to her mouth and nose, unsure who she was aching for.

Now, Josie spoke softly. "Mary," she said. She wanted to reach out to her, run her fingers through Mary's black halo of curls, kiss her softly on the mouth, and whisper something big and powerful. But what? And what would it change? Everything had happened as it should. Whether Josie knew it at the time or not, she had chosen—first Tyler, then Mary, then Devesh—chosen Tyler because he reminded her of herself, chosen Mary because she would make Josie ache, and chosen Devesh in hopes that he could take this ache away. Yes, the world was causal, but it was also messy, cryptic. It made a pattern you could decipher only after the fact, and now she was beginning to see—names and arrows and symbols in a fragile scrawl before her. This is who I am, she thought.

"I'm sorry," Josie said.

Mary looked at her, and Josie could see she was, even now, torn between affection and cruelty. "For what?" she said.

"For everything."

Mary picked up two stray socks, rolled them neatly into a pair, but Josie could see her hands shaking.

"I—" Josie started.

"Okay," Mary interrupted. She paused, then started again. "Look, Josie. It's ending this way. . . ." She paused, looked down. "But it doesn't undo how it was. I . . . I'm glad you were here. I'm just . . . glad."

Mary looked up, and Josie felt the whole of the declaration—an aching tenderness between them. "Me too," she said.

Mary nodded and bent to pick up a discarded pacifier.

"I'll go pack," Josie said. She made her way to her bedroom, sat on the bed, and looked at the boxes. She had spoken to Devesh before she left Santa Barbara, a strained short conversation, but he had insisted she move her things to his house. Permanently, he had said. A few months ago she would have been elated, her things in his house, and now she tried to grab hold of this feeling—everything she owned tucked up, supported and embraced. She could rest in his palm like a small, black river rock. But now the thought made her wince. This morning when she had dropped her suitcase off at Devesh's, she had thought it looked sad and out of place. She lay back on the bed and flipped through the mail Mary had left on the bed: her cell phone bill, a bunch of junk, and a postcard from Phillip—a picture of the new restaurant on the front, *Come visit; I promise no okra!* on the back. She dropped the card to the bed, closed her eyes, and heard the front door open.

"Can I eat at Clara's?" Tyler shouted.

Josie sat up.

"Yeah, fine," Mary said.

Then there was nothing, and Josie wondered if he had gone upstairs or just forgotten to shut the front door, but then she stood and saw him standing outside her room. He was wearing overalls and a white cotton T-shirt, and he held a long piece of green yarn. He pinched the ends and stretched it wide in front of himself. "This string is two feet eight inches," he said. "Birds can use it to build their homes."

She didn't know what to say, and she stood there until he brought his hands together and asked her where she was going.

"I'm moving . . . I'm not . . . I'm not going to live here anymore."

"Why?" he asked.

"Why?" She almost laughed. "Because it's time for me to move."

He was staring at the yarn in his hands, rolling it slowly between his palms like dough. "No," he said.

This was not the reception she had been expecting, and she realized that in her head, she had played this scene as if he were an adult. In it, he looked at her guardedly, and when she offered her apologies, he merely nodded and left the room. "Tyler," she tried again. She had practiced on the plane, saying it over and over in her head. "Tyler . . . I'm . . . I'm sorry," but it seemed almost laughable now. She felt the deep throb of the sadness she had been carrying radiate through her chest.

He didn't say anything, just stared intently into the green yarn in his hands, then pushed his palms together, squeezed the green invisible. He shook his hair out of his eyes, and for the first time, Josie could see how he resembled Mary—the same round chin and full lips—and she wanted to take him up in her arms and swear, insist, promise that he had done nothing wrong, that all that pain and violence she had almost shot into him was hers. She would kneel at his feet. She would beg his forgiveness. She would explain how what she had done was unforgivable, but maybe he could understand, maybe he could feel how much she loved him, how she often thought that if they had been six together, they might have been friends. They might have been like him and Katie. But the image of Katie buried in sand, Tyler on his knees commanding she lie still flickered on, and what followed was a too-vivid picture of that horrible day—his tiny body over her knee, his dinosaur underpants around his ankles, her limbs electrified with cruelty. An apology did not take it back, did not take anything back. She had done it, and even now, only a few minutes ago, she had imagined herself tiny and smooth, resting in Devesh's hand, small enough to be cradled, small enough to be pinched into submission. The image came so naturally, rolled itself into her head and made it throb. She did not want to be this person anymore. She knew who she was now, and no whipping or beating could release her, and if it couldn't release her, then what was it good for?

"Here," she said. She pulled the giraffe out of her pocket and held it in her palm.

Tyler glanced up at it, then at his palms, then back at the giraffe.

"It's yours," she said.

"The giraffe is the biggest ruminant and the tallest mammal. It lives south of the Sahara."

"Yes," she said.

She walked over to him. His head shone, and she wanted to push her fingers through all that blond hair, stroke his cheek, touch the tiny bones at his collar, but she opened his hand, placed the giraffe in the nest of green yarn, and then began to pack.

* * *

Mary said she could leave the boxes in the spare room for as
long as she needed, so she piled them in the corner, rode her
bike to Devesh's house, and opened the front door. It was dark,
but she could make out Devesh's cereal bowl still on the coffee
table, and an old newspaper scattered on the floor. She walked
down the hallway to the den, the study, and then back to the
kitchen. There wasn't a space he hadn't dragged her, tied her,
beat her. Every moment she had with him was soaked in darkness. This was who they were together. It twisted her heart,
and she suddenly wished he were here, trying to convince her
that yes, they could love each other the way normal people in
normal relationships loved each other. And yes, without the
striking of a whip, the knot that they had tied themselves into
would hold, would not unravel fiber by fiber.

She walked into the bedroom. The morning he left, he had
hidden the toys away in the chest, but he had missed the cuffs.
They were still attached to the rope but had fallen to the floor,
and now she could see the silver buckles glinting against the
black leather. They looked small and deflated and hardly suf-
ficient to keep her still, and the thick rope around the bedpost
looked like a shoestring. She bent to the floor and picked up
the cuffs. He had ordered them just for her, wrapped a tape
measure around her tiny wrists and then across her spread
palm, and made her remember the numbers. Six inches by six
inches, perfectly symmetrical.

Now, she held the cuffs in her hand, ran her thumbs along
the soft leather, then raised them to her nose and inhaled. The
sharp smell seeped through her. It grabbed and pulled. Her
body heated and gave, and the immediacy of her reaction so

shocked her, she pulled her hands quickly away and dropped the cuffs to the floor. She wanted it as much as ever, wanted to crawl on the floor and beg to be strapped, wanted to offer her body as reparation, wanted to be absolved by the whip. She took a step back.

"No," she said aloud, and the sharpness of her voice surprised her.

The phone rested next to the bed, and she dug the number out of her pocket and dialed slowly, pressing each digit with authority. It rang and rang, and when it put her through to voice mail, she hung up and dialed again. Finally, he answered.

"Hi," she said.

"Josie?" His voice was soft and faraway, and his words echoed on the line.

"Yes."

"What are you doing? Where are you? Are you okay?" She could hear him rustle the bed covers and sit up.

"I'm fine." The last time she had spoken to him, after insisting she move her things to his house, he had also begged her to fly to Chennai, made her write down his credit card number just in case she changed her mind. And she did, wrote it on the back of the scrap of paper that held his contact numbers. Now, she turned the paper over and over in her hand, looking at his precise blue writing—"parents," "hospital," "cell"—on one side, her scrawled penciled numbers on the other.

"Where are you?" he asked.

"Your house." She looked at the paper and said the numbers in her head, 011 91 9820138181 cell, 011 44 45552889 hospital.

"I can come home in a few days. I can be there soon."

"No," she said.

"Yes," he said, and the word came back doubled across the bad connection. "Damn it. Let me call right back."

Her stomach tightened, and she pressed her palm gently against her belly. "I can't . . . I can't do this anymore."

"Can't do what?"

She was silent.

"Josie, let me call you back," he said.

"No." She said it forcefully, and when it echoed back at her, she grew stronger. "I can't do this anymore. I can't see you."

"What are you talking about?" he said.

She was silent.

"Is this about the games? I told you, we won't do that anymore," he said. "It doesn't matter to me. I don't need to play like that." The words echoed across the line, and she imagined them tumbling behind each other, bumping across the thousands of miles of optic cable.

"I'm sorry," she said. She placed the phone down on the receiver, then picked it back up and called a cab.

CHAPTER SEVENTEEN

WHEN THE CAB CAME, JOSIE PUT HER SUITCASE INTO THE TRUNK, tied her bike to the roof, and told the driver to head toward Asheville. She didn't know where she wanted to go; she just knew she wanted to go away, and finally after driving for hours, she told the driver to pull off the highway at Hickory because she liked that the town's motto was "Come on in." The driver dropped her at the Goodnight Motel, and she paid him with almost all the cash Mary had given her as back pay. It was a small motel, a family place owned by a couple with three teenage sons. Josie liked the small sunny room and the paperback library in the lobby, and she stayed for two weeks, accepting the family's invitation to Thanksgiving dinner and letting the boys take her bike riding in the hills behind the motel. She rode under the canopy of bare tree branches and thought about everything in her life that had suddenly made sense. She thought about her mother, wondered if she had known what Josie had done or just sensed her guilt the way Devesh had sensed her need to be released from it, and she thought about herself, wondered how a little girl, barely strong enough to climb to the top of a sundial, had managed to suffocate a baby.

She slept and read, and watched Devesh's long Indian phone number appear on the screen of her cell phone again and again. She answered once, wanting to tell him something she thought might come to her when she heard his voice, but she was only able to ask where she should mail his key. He told her to throw it away, told her he had taken an emergency leave of absence and was staying in Chennai another six weeks if she was curious. She wanted to say that she wasn't curious, that she was doing fine, but she couldn't get her mouth around the words, and instead she simply said, "All right," and hung up the phone. After, she felt a stab of intense loss, and then the deep pulse of loneliness, and when it didn't go away after three days, she decided that, for the first time, what she wanted was not to click her heels together and be whisked away to some alternate reality, but to feel something familiar, something comforting and secure. So she called Phillip and then bought a bus ticket to Atlanta.

He welcomed her into his apartment, dragged the pullout couch into his small study so she could have a room of her own, and didn't press her for details on Devesh. She was grateful and she tried to settle into the unthreatening comfort of their normality. She liked Phillip's old apartment, liked the way the pipes whistled, liked the stray cats that slept on the porch, liked Atlanta. Everything was within walking distance. She could take Katie to the park, browse for books, and stop off for groceries all in the same trip.

Still, both Matthew and Devesh seemed to spin constantly in her mind. She imagined Matthew grown. He would call her "sis" and forget to phone on her birthday, and she would tease him that he went through girlfriends faster than their mother went through housekeepers. She made herself imagine, filling in the details, shading him like a coloring book. And she imagined Devesh—his palm firm and warm on her back, his voice soft and sweet in her head—b*aba*, he said, *aati kya Khandala?* It made her stomach catch, her breath struggle to stay steady. The pain lingered in her chest like a bee sting, real and unyielding, and so exactly three weeks into her stay, when Phillip pulled her in for a good-night hug and instead kissed her hesitantly, she didn't resist. She allowed him to lead her carefully to his bed, hoping he could at least tweeze whatever remained of Devesh from her heart.

That was a month ago, and with every passing day, Josie had indeed begun to feel the pinch inside her lessening. She had given up on her reading, knew by now she would need at least one extra semester to prepare for exams, and instead began taking Katie to school every morning and washing Phillip's chef whites at night. She asked if she could waitress at the restaurant, and Phillip, thinking she felt somehow obligated to him, refused until she simply started filling water glasses on her own. Eventually he taught her how to input orders into the computer and the proper way to pour wine. She served rolls, made small talk, explained the specials of the day. It was repetitious and monotonous and calming. She busied herself with Phillip's reservation books and Katie's spelling words, allowing the minutiae of their world to take over a little bit of hers.

Now, Josie sat on Katie's bed braiding her hair. "Pink or purple ribbons?" she asked.

"Pink." Katie wiggled beneath her.

"Stay still," Josie said, and playfully tugged her braid. "You're going to end up with lopsided pigtails."

"Can we go to the park today?" Katie asked.

"No, we have to go straight to the restaurant after I pick you up from school."

Katie sighed. "I hate the restaurant."

"No, you don't," Josie said. "You can string macaroni today, and I'll make you a Shirley Temple."

"Yay!" Katie squealed.

"All right, all right, but hold still."

Katie stopped squirming, and Josie tied a ribbon at the end of each braid. "There; you're done."

Katie spun around and cocked her head. She placed her small hand on Josie's knee. "Are you gonna stay forever?"

It was more of a plea than a question, and although Josie knew this, she couldn't help feeling as if she had been accused of something. She wanted this conventional definition of happiness, came here intent on feeling exactly what she was indeed feeling, but Katie's question poked at the stillness that had settled inside her, and she knew the answer without even needing to consider. "We'll see," she stammered, and placed the unused ribbons back in the box.

That night the restaurant was slow, and Phillip let the other servers go early. Josie managed the last table and folded napkins while Katie played in a booth.

"I need these for my ponies," Katie said, and reached for the napkins.

"Use the unfolded ones," Josie said and handed her a dozen.

Katie folded the napkins into small pillows and laid a pony on each. "They're sleeping."

"Like you should be," Josie said, and tickled her chin. Phillip had set up a cot in the office, and Josie and he had perfected transferring Katie from cot to car seat to bed without waking her. "Five more minutes, then bed,"

"No," Katie said.

"Yes."

"Daddy!" Katie yelled.

"Sh," Josie said. She could see Phillip scowling from across the room. "There are customers here."

"I want to show him my ponies," she said, and started to cry.

"Okay, but let's take them into the back." She picked up the napkins and Katie cried louder.

"You're ruining them."

Josie gestured to Phillip and he walked quickly over.

"Hush, honey," he said and pulled Katie to him, then saw the napkins. "Why'd you let her use those? I told her no yesterday."

"What does it matter?" Josie asked.

"They'll need to be rewashed now. It costs money."

"A few cents."

"Those few cents build up," he said, and turned to Katie. "Quiet now. It's time for bed."

"No!" Katie sobbed louder.

"Sh," he said sharply.

"She's tired, Phillip," Josie said. "It's hard for her to be here every night."

"Katie. Now," he demanded.

Instead, she curled up beside Josie, crying softly into her lap. "Just let her sleep here," Josie said.

"Christ," Phillip said. "Do what you want." He wiped his hands on his apron and stormed off.

Josie sighed. "Lie flat," she said to Katie. "Let me give this table their bill and then I'll tickle your back." She got up, ran the last table's credit card, gave them a doggie bag, and then locked the front door and slid back into the booth.

"Daddy's mad," Katie said, and rested her head on Josie's lap.

"He's just tired too." She rubbed Katie's back, traced letters for her to guess until she fell asleep. Katie was much smaller than Tyler and her hair darker, but the pressure of her head on Josie's lap, the way her mouth dropped open the moment she fell asleep, made her heart cramp.

She suddenly wanted a cigarette. She slid out from under Katie and snuck carefully out of the booth, through the kitchen, and into the alley behind the restaurant. The busboy had tied the trash bags tightly and piled them high in the Dumpster, but the sweet smell of rotten vegetables and cream sauces still saturated the air. She lit a cigarette she had bummed off a prep cook and inhaled. It felt familiar and comforting, and she inhaled and tried to imagine the smoke stroking her insides.

She leaned against the cold brick wall and looked up. Across the alley was another building, a converted granary with expensive loft space. She had once seen a young man hoist himself up the fire escape and climb to the fifth floor where he tapped on the apartment window for at least ten minutes. Someone had eventually come, but refused to let him in, and he yelled and pushed his forehead against the glass. Ultimately, he gave up and kicked his way down each landing.

Now she looked at the fire escape and traced his path down to the ground. At the bottom was a rusty ladder. It was tied to the first landing and one end of the rope was fastened tightly to the top rung while the other hung down a good four feet.

She dragged on her cigarette and looked down the alley. It was especially cold for January, and she could see steam rising from the manholes in big, billowy clouds. She exhaled the smoke and turned back to the fire escape. The rope dangled. It was blackened by soot and age, perfect for winding around wrists. You could suspend a girl like that, attach her firmly and spin her on her toes—first left, then right—so the leather of the whip caught each thigh with a fiery snap.

Josie closed her eyes and felt her body first warm, then melt, then seethe. She squeezed her thighs tightly together and inhaled, and when she did, her breath shot through her throat like a punch, pushing her head harshly against the brick. She felt the sting of concrete on her scalp, and she opened her eyes. Her heart raced. She dropped the cigarette and pressed her palms firmly against the wall.

She had not thought a single dirty thought since she had been at Phillip's, so what was this? Sex with Phillip was good. He stroked and kissed and licked so tenderly, and never once did she wish for his hand to come down hard against her backside, but here she was, imagining things that were supposed to be gone, things she had convinced herself she didn't need anymore.

Phillip opened the door, and she jumped. "Did I scare you?"

She tried to feel each individual brick against her back. "No," she said.

He put his hand on her shoulder and pulled her to him. His body was warm, and he smelled of frying oil and garlic, and she tried to soften into him.

"I'm sorry," he said.

Her heart was still racing, and she tried to slow her breathing. "Okay," she said. She pushed her lips against his chest. She wanted to take his T-shirt in her mouth, to bite down hard on something.

"I'm just tired tonight," he said.

She touched her tongue to the cotton and then took it between her teeth and counted.

Later that night, she lay in bed trying to read a magazine.

"Do you think we should start doing a catch of the day?" Phillip asked. He came out of the shower draped in a towel and knotted it at his waist.

She crawled to the edge of the bed and pressed her hands against his hips. "I think you should fuck me," she said.

He ran his hand through her hair. "Oh, honey, I'm so tired. I don't think I'd last more than a minute."

She put her forehead on the bed. "All right."

"I'm sorry." He dropped the towel and lay down beside her. His hair was still wet, and it tickled her cheek. "You're beautiful," he said. "And sexy."

"It's okay," she said.

He looked at her pitifully and then pulled her under the covers. "I guess I'm getting old," he said.

"No, no, it's okay." She lay on his chest, and he stroked her head until his hand rested on her pillow, and she knew he had fallen asleep.

She closed her eyes and tried to relax, but every muscle in her body was tensed. Once, when she had felt this way over something Mary had done, Devesh had told her to imagine a soft, warm current running from the base of her spine to the crown of her head. He had run his fingers up her body, stopping at her pelvis, her stomach, her heart, and told her to imagine tying the current into a knot. She had closed her eyes, pretended she was trying, but really imagined him tying her to the bed, hundreds of ropes crisscrossing her body.

Now, she tried to imagine something warm and soft tickling her tailbone. She focused on the knot, made a loop with the current, and pulled it gently through and up. It snaked through her spine, and her muscles seemed to pull gently away from the bones. She wound it through her bottom two vertebrae and then between her thighs. The heat pulsed and windmilled within her. She instinctively spread her legs and instantly she was back in the alley. This time it was very clearly she who was tied to the ladder, but now it was lowered to the ground, and she was bound hands and feet to the rungs. She opened her mouth and pressed her tongue against the cold metal of the ladder, and when she did, someone strong and rough pushed his fingers between her legs and then inside her. She gasped, and he reached around and pinched her nipple.

"Naughty girl." He spoke softly. "Slut."

She tried to turn to look at him, but when she did, he tangled his hand in her hair and held her head straight. "Stay," he said. He took a step back, and she opened her eyes. Her heart was racing and her mouth steamed with saliva. No, she thought; this is bad. Phillip lay next to her, gently breathing through his mouth, and she flushed first with guilt and then with the delicious haze of shame. She pulled the covers off slowly and crept to the bathroom. She locked the door, turned on the light, and looked at herself in the mirror. Her pupils looked enormous, and she could see her nipples hard beneath her thin T-shirt. She switched the light off and sat on the floor with her back against the tub. If she was going to do this, she needed it pitch black. She closed her eyes and pulled her panties around her ankles. She ran her hand down her belly, to her thighs, and between her legs.

The cuffs are still around her wrists and ankles, but now she is lashed so her back slopes against the ladder and her legs are spread. She looks down and sees the ground roll beneath her feet.

"Spread your legs," the man says.

She pulls against the ankle cuffs, but it is difficult to open her thighs any more than they are. She hesitates, and the man pulls her knees apart so that her back digs into the metal, and she feels like she may lose her balance.

From the corner of her eye, she sees him pull a belt slowly from his waist. She listens to the whisper of leather in his hands, hears the ankle cuffs clink against the metal of the ladder, and then there is just sensation, the heavy thud of the belt on her thighs, the deep pain that seeps from the surface of her skin down into her bones. She watches him do it, watches the faint red smudges against the white of her skin, the black tongue of the belt lapping at her thighs.

"You like it, don't you?" he says.

"Yes," she says.

He is tilting her head back, opening her mouth, and his tongue is hot and forceful in her mouth. She pulls against the restraints, and then he is inside her, making her gasp sharply, but the sound is suffocated. His mouth is tightly on hers. It swallows her, and yet she can also hear him speak.

"Greedy little slut," he says. "Tell me you want it. Tell me you want to be beaten and fucked," and she does. She wants it, and she can feel him, smell him, see him both inside and outside of herself when her body hiccups and trembles and then slams back to the bathroom floor.

In the morning, she woke up exhausted. She could hear Katie flipping through television cartoons, and then Phillip asking if she wanted more orange juice. Josie closed her eyes and pulled the covers over her head. What happened last night was bad. It had left her scared and shaken, and she had crawled back into bed and felt first unbearably guilty and then intensely angry.

"Josie." Phillip walked in and pulled the covers back. "You want some coffee?"

She shook her head, and he sat on the bed and rested his hand against her cheek. "You okay?"

He was wearing a blue sweatshirt with holes in the cuffs, and she snaked her thumbs through and against his wrists. "You need these sewn."

He took her hands in his. "You look tired. You want to sleep in? I'll take Katie to school."

"No." She sat up and looked at him. She looked at the space between his teeth, the scar that bisected his chin. He had always looked boyish to her, but with the sun streaming in through the window and illuminating his shoulders, he seemed especially so, and she had a sudden desire to tell him everything, to smack down any illusions of herself as his good girl. "I'll get up."

"No. Go back to sleep. Let me take her." He pressed her back to the bed. "I don't have to go in until two today," he said. "I'll come back, and maybe you'll let me make up for last night." He ran his fingertips along her neck and down to her breast, and she had to fight not to pull away.

"All right."

He kissed her and left, and she listened for the click of the door. She could feel her muscles tense again, each stretching taut and stiffening under her skin. She took a deep breath and closed her eyes. Well into the night, she had felt little ripples of pleasure flickering throughout her body. Her mind seemed to fall away, leaving just the pictures, and even now, she could feel them wanting to swell to the surface. All she had to do was let one tiny image in, and she would find herself flushed with need.

CHAPTER EIGHTEEN

TWO WEEKS LATER, JOSIE SAT AT THE KITCHEN TABLE, BLUE AND yellow construction paper strewn about her.

"What's this diorama for anyway," she called to Katie. She picked up the shoebox.

Katie ran in. "Open House. I found some ribbon."

"Honey, that's for your hair."

"So," Katie whined.

"You have plenty of supplies to choose from."

"I want to use it."

"No," she said sharply. Lately, she had been irritable and short-tempered. This morning she and Phillip had bickered again, this time about the heat in the apartment. She wanted it warmer, he cooler. It was ridiculous, but she fought vehemently, and in the end turned the thermostat up to ninety to show him what hot really was. Usually she apologized, but this morning she stormed out and sat in the coffee shop on the corner, drinking cup after cup of coffee until she was buzzing from so much caffeine she could feel her heart vibrate throughout her chest.

"Where's Daddy?" Katie asked.

"At the restaurant. Now choose something else to make the river."

"But it's Monday."

"Yes it is."

The restaurant was closed, but she was sure Phillip was there banging pots and pans around the kitchen. He was gone when she came home from the coffee shop, and when she picked Katie up from school this afternoon, they returned to a still empty apartment.

Now Josie was even more annoyed. She did not want to be making dioramas for second-grade book reports; she did not want to be awaiting his arrival; she did not want to be here at all. Still, it wasn't the here of the apartment, or even the glue sticks and animal stickers that she was recoiling from, it was the other stuff. At first she had thought perhaps it was just residual muck exorcising its way from her head, but it came back in an on-slaught. There wasn't a single day in the last two weeks that she hadn't felt the sharp tip of a fantasy chiseling its way to the surface. There were times she could ward it off, force herself to think of grocery lists and unreturned library books, but lately it was becoming more difficult. At night, she would end up locked in the bathroom imagining herself writhing under some anonymous whip, and in the morning she'd be afraid to look at Phillip, afraid he could read her, and afraid she would tell. But she hadn't told yet, and he didn't even seem to notice, and despite the fact that this was what she wanted, it also made her angry. How could he not see all that darkness seeping through her, corrosive and blistering? It made her snap at him and hate herself.

She heard the front door open and Katie ran to meet Phillip. Katie giggled, then shrieked, and she knew Phillip had scooped her up in his arms. She stood and walked down the hall.

"Hey," she said.

"Hey." He set Katie on the floor, and she gripped his leg.

"Again, Daddy," she said.

"Not right now. We can play later. Go color a picture for me."

"No," she said.

"You need to finish your diorama," Josie said. "Do that and you can use the hair ribbon."

"Really?" Katie asked.

"Yes."

Katie ran into the kitchen, and Josie looked down at the floor. Deep in the carpet was a perfectly round cigarette burn from the tenants before, and she covered and uncovered it with her big toe. She knew he was waiting for an apology from this morning, but offering him one seemed like bandaging a cut knee when she knew the whole leg would have to go.

"What's going on with you?" he finally asked.

"I don't know." It was an impulsive answer, and after she said it, she wished she could take it back. She did know, and to deny it was as silly as thinking that by leaving Devesh, she could also leave the familiar prickly place she had spent much of her life occupying.

"Well . . . something's going on, and if you don't tell me, we can't do anything about it."

"It's not you," she said.

"Good answer," he scoffed.

She looked at him and then at her toe again. What was she to tell him? He would be disgusted, or at least think her pathetic, or perhaps—worse yet—he would tell her he could try and do those things. The thought made her push her back hard into the

wall. Last week, during a pointless fight over whether the restaurant napkins should rest next to or on the plates, she pushed
him so relentlessly that he finally grabbed her roughly by the
wrists and told her to stop. She let out an impulsive cry, and he
pulled away, scalded. She had shocked him or he had shocked
himself. Either way, he was so shaken that he stood there
stunned, apologizing over and over. "Josie," he had said, "I'm
sorry; I would never . . . you know I wouldn't . . ." He stumbled
and stuttered, and she looked at him and wanted to slap his
concerned-looking face. She was disgusted by his tenderness,
then disgusted by her own reaction.

Now, the thought of Phillip taking her chin in one hand
and, with the other, slapping her swiftly across the face made
her cringe. She had melted to him precisely because he was
everything Devesh was not—soft and accommodating. He did
not make her want to get down on her knees and press her
forehead against the tops of his feet. Phillip was loving and
sweet, but he could not make her bow her head with a single
look, could not make her chest and stomach and lungs unfold
like lotus flowers. This thing, whatever it was, could not be
manufactured. It was either there or it was not. You did not
bring people back from the dead simply because you wanted
to, and you did not pull that hunger from your pocket like a
penny.

"There's something I have to tell you," she said, and
paused. It was cruel to make him wait for what she was sure
he knew was a goodbye speech, but she didn't know how to
put into words what she had never actually articulated. She took
a deep breath. "I want bad things," she stuttered. "I mean . . .
I want things you'll think are bad."

He looked at her quizzically. "Like what?"

"Like sexual things." She paused. "I want to be punished."

He was silent, waiting for more, but she said nothing. "Okay," he said.

"Do you know what that means?"

The light streaming in the bathroom window was fading, but she could see the discomfort in his shoulders, the way they twitched slowly toward each other. "Um," he stammered. "Like . . . spanked?"

"I want to be beaten," she blurted. The words seemed to somersault out of her mouth and consume the space between them, and he opened his mouth as if he were gasping for air, then shut it, then opened it again.

"Oh," he said. She knew he was trying to be impartial, but she saw the grimace flick across his face.

"Do you understand?" she asked.

"You mean . . . you mean like S and M."

She blushed at the letters. "Disciplined," she said. "With belts and whips and paddles."

She saw the words slice through him, and despite the fact that he was trying to put on a brave face, feign understanding, she knew he was repulsed. His body was suctioning in on itself, and she could see his chest concave. "Oh," he said.

"And there's other stuff," she said. "I like to be tied and cuffed and . . . and shamed." She felt the word grasp the back of her head, force her chin up, her eyes open.

"Shamed?"

"Made to say things . . . and do things." Her body weakened, her mind flooded.

"Okay," he said.

"No; it's not okay."

He ran his palms down the front of his jeans, scratched at the denim. "Well," he said. "Maybe we can get help . . . or something."

"No," she said quickly. For weeks she had felt like an addict, stealing pleasure as if it were illegal. It was maddening. She had created this life to remedy the last, and now she was backpedaling through spaces she had determinedly left behind. She refused to trade one guilt for another. "I can't do this anymore," she said. She was acutely aware of the irony of her words, how she had stared at that scrap of paper with Devesh's numbers and said the very same thing, but then she thought she could manufacture a life, thought she knew what the new Josie would want. But there was no new Josie. There was only the one that had always been, and this self held many selves, the little girl and the big girl and all the others in between, each snuggled inside the next like Russian nesting dolls.

"You don't even want to try?" he asked.

"I have to go," she said. "I'm sorry."

He shook his head, kicked at the molding with his boot. "Go where?"

She hadn't thought about this, but the answer now seemed clear.

CHAPTER NINETEEN

HER FATHER HAD HIRED A FULL-TIME COOK AND MAID, BUT JOSIE told her to take a few weeks off, and now Josie stood in the kitchen slicing tomatoes and scrambling egg whites and settling into the heady smell of sautéed onions and brewing coffee.

"Dad," she yelled. "Dad!"

"I'm here, I'm here," he said and kissed her on the cheek. "When did you become your mother?" he joked.

She socked him playfully on the arm. "Be nice."

He had lost a lot of weight, and his eyes looked hollow and sunken. Still, he was working again, and for the last weeks Josie had made him elaborate breakfasts and packed him full lunches, and he had started to kid her that she was going to make him fat.

"I have a dinner meeting tonight," he said. Josie poured him a cup of coffee. "What are you going to do?"

She shrugged. "See Natalie maybe."

"I can get you a job interview with the new regional director at the Four Seasons," he said.

He desperately wanted her to stay in Santa Barbara and, since she had come home, he had pestered her to meet with a slew of hotel bigwigs.

"Dad," she said. "No." She wasn't sure where she wanted
to be in the fall. Her program director had said she could take
up to a year off, so she had formally withdrawn for the spring
semester, but she wasn't ready to return yet. She had come
home to be with him, but there was that other reason as well.

"I'm not going to be an assistant to the assistant of the guy
who makes sure the McCormicks from Duluth have enough
mineral water in their room," she said

He raised one eyebrow at her. "You're funny," he said.

She brought the plates to the table. "Eat your eggs."

He ate and read the paper, and she watched him. She
couldn't remember a time the whole family had eaten together
at the kitchen table. They would have dinner in the dining room
with its stiff high-back chairs and towering china cabinet, or
she would eat alone in the kitchen, hurriedly scarfing down
breakfast before school. "You want more coffee?" she asked.

"No, no, I have to go." He stood and kissed her on the
head. "I'll be home around ten; call me on the cell if you need
anything."

She grabbed his hand. "Dad."

He looked at her.

"I"—she stumbled over the words—"wanted to talk to
you." She had already let a week go by. She had planned to sit
him down in the kitchen that first night, say it simply and
quickly and without hesitation. But this hadn't happened, and
every day that passed made it harder and harder.

"Okay." He stood, puzzled. "Should I sit down?"

"Yes . . . no." This was not the time to do it. He was running off. She had told Natalie she would call her at nine. And
he didn't need to know. But he did, or she needed to tell him,

she didn't know which, but it didn't matter anymore. She had made a decision. "I need to tell you something."

"Anything, sweetie," he said. He smiled and squeezed her hand. It felt warm and solid, and she pulled away. "It's about Matthew," she said.

His face fell, and she realized that the only way was just to say it, and she took a deep breath.

And then she told him, told him about that day, about sneaking out of her room and into Matthew's, the baby's funny face, the crib and the blanket, and how she had known even then that you could not undo what you had done, that you could not make it right, even if you had not meant it, even if you had just been a little girl, even if you had just been playing.

"No," her father said. "It's not possible. You were a child." He stared at his hands. "They said it had to be crib death. The doctors told us."

"No," she said.

He looked up. "Sometimes children think they're responsible for things like this. Maybe you thought . . ."

"No."

"You were little."

"No."

"You don't remember."

She was empty and spent, and if he did not believe her, if she had given him what she had spent her life protecting and still he could not see her, then perhaps she was invisible, perhaps she was not there at all. "I do remember," she said. And then the sobs came—slow and small and tender.

"Oh, God," he said. "Oh, Josie." His hands went instinctively to his mouth, and she saw his face contort, a lifetime of heartache rippling through him. He began to cry, silent tears streaking his cheeks, and she thought if there was something keeping track of her karmic sins, it would keep her stuck here, looking at what she had done, for a very long time.

She saw everything she had stolen from him—his son, his wife, his family.

His family.

The word rang hollow in her heart. They had lived, the three of them, in this house her father had bought for four. Her mother. Her father. And her. Each alone, each orbiting the others' grief like satellites.

She looked at him, saw the pain seep from him like sweat. "I can't . . ." he said. "I can't do this." His shoulders shook and his hands flexed, and he grabbed his briefcase and fled, leaving her alone in the house.

She sat—in her old bedroom, in Matthew's room, in her parents' room—numb and waiting for him to come home. She could be patient, had waited twenty-four years for what was to come, and when she finally heard the key in the lock the next morning, she stood slowly and walked down the stairs.

He was wearing the same clothes—his shirt now wrinkled and untucked—and when he looked up at her, she stopped. She could see the sadness soaked through him. His skin and bones and muscle and blood now heavy with the weight of what she had done, and Josie thought, This is where it ends; this is what I've waited for, but she felt ready.

He walked up one flight of stairs, to the landing where she stood, and reached for her. And what he did was pull her gently to him, press her head against his shoulder. "Oh, Josie," he said. "Oh, Jojo." And all it took was her little-girl name, blown like a glass ball, perfect and fragile and full of what might have been, to nudge the words gently from her belly: "I'm sorry," she said, "I'm sorry."

She could feel her heart unpack each apology, deal them out like playing cards—one for her mother, one for her father, one for her brother, and one for her.

CHAPTER TWENTY

THE NEXT WEEK HER FATHER STAYED HOME FROM WORK. HE HAD wanted to know the details, and she had told him, and when she couldn't remember any more, he had filled in the gaps, telling her how she had hid all of Matthew's toys under her bed, how her mother had slept on the floor of the baby's room for months, how he had made two million dollars the week after the funeral.

They took drives along the coast, walked the railroad tracks to the beach, and sat—long silences between them—until, eventually, her father's hand on hers felt real, and the marble in her heart began to wear slowly away, leaving something fragile but true between them.

The following week they went through the second floor of the house—boxing her mother's things, reorganizing her father's—finally arriving at the master bedroom. Her father had been sleeping in Josie's old room and Josie hadn't opened the door to her parents' room since her father came back. Now it loomed before them like a final frontier.

"I'll get your aunt to do it," her father said.

Josie shook her head. "I'll do it."

"You don't have to. Steffi said she'd do whatever we couldn't. I'll just call her—"

"Please," Josie interrupted. "I want to."

He stared at her.

"Go play some online poker. Lose some money," she said.

"You're not supposed to know about that." He laughed.

She shrugged and smiled, and he sighed and gave her a kiss on the forehead.

"Call me if you need me," he said.

She nodded and shut the door.

The room lay before her, the enormous king-sized bed spreading out like an island in front of her, newspapers and contracts covering the blue floral bedspread her mother had brought home from Paris. She was afraid of what she would find—a journal, perhaps, or private letters to her aunt—but she needed to do this. She would start with the bathroom, thinking her mother's hair spray and nail polish remover easier to dispose of and less likely to hold secrets. In the shower, she removed the color-enhancing shampoo, the lilac soap, the silver-handled razor her mother had taught her to shave her legs with on her thirteenth birthday. That day, Josie had watched her mother press the razor firmly against her own now teenage leg, watched as the blade made one clean, hairless stripe. Her mother then handed her the razor, told her to press gently, to pull in one steady stroke, and Josie did. She dragged the razor carefully, watched the stripe widen, and thrilled at the new leg that was emerging. She felt proud, exhilarated even, and she looked up to find her mother teary-eyed. "It's okay, baby," her mother said, and sat down on the edge of the tub. "You're doing great. Don't stop." Josie looked back at her white foamy leg and felt a lump rise in her own throat. She wanted to cuddle close to her mother, to feel her mother's tenderness as a real, live thing, but she focused on her leg and slowly removed every single hair, trying to make this warm closeness last as long as possible.

The memory pulled at her, and she held the razor a long time before placing it in a box and moving on to the bedroom. There, she went through her mother's dresser, breathing in the familiar cedar and fingering the dozens of stockings in varying shades of black and tan, the bra and panty sets fastened together with small cedar clips, the carefully rolled slips and camisoles. At her mother's nightstand, she found a tall stack of magazines and books—biographies of Pamela Harriman and Babe Paley and Slim Keith. She didn't realized her mother had been interested in these women, and she sat down and slowly thumbed the pages before boxing them atop old dog-eared issues of *Town and Country* and *Vogue* and *Vanity Fair*. She emptied the narrow nightstand drawer, bagged the matchbooks from hotels in Barcelona and Milan and Hong Kong, and neatened the pieces of scrap paper, each a To Do list: call Miriam re museum meeting, pick up sunglasses, return J's shoes to KC, check costs for benefit hall, Carmel week of 7th? She collected her mother's herbal supplements, the echinacea and melatonin and grape seed extract; her silk eye pillow; her boar's bristle hairbrush; her cucumber hand cream; her silver hairpins and brass cuticle scissors. But no secret diaries, no clandestine letters. Only traces of her mother, the remnants of a life more complex than just the disgust that Josie now realized was only one aspect of her mother, not the vastly complicated layers of a whole person, an entire universe. All of this had been eclipsed by rancor and guilt and pain, grown large and all-engulfing. Josie had never been able to see this, to see this Carol Maura Morgan, née Johnson, a little girl from Gambier, Ohio, who had grown up to become her mother, but neither had her mother been able to see her, to understand the complexity of a little girl who didn't even know herself.

Josie held a gardening book in her hand and flipped through the pages; page fifty-seven was earmarked and underlined. She read, "Though they have an ancient history, the popularity of roses as we know them today started with the Empress Josephine and her garden at Malmaison almost two hundred years ago. While Napoleon was off harrying the neighbors, Josephine was collecting and cultivating roses." Next to this, her mother had penciled in a few exclamation points. Josie smiled. Her mother had bought a rosebush for each of Josie's birthdays, pinks and whites and yellows clustering around the back of the house. Josie closed the book and went to the window. She could see the flowerless rose bushes, and she counted—one, two, three, four; all the way to twenty-eight. Even after Josie had left, her mother had continued planting, each birthday a celebration.

Josie could feel the tears threatening, but behind this feeling was something else, something comforting and almost sweet. Yes, all the bitterness and anger was there, the clear and constant undertone that the wrong child had been taken, but there had also been something else—a thorny kind of love and need that twisted through both her mother's heart and her own. It was there, in spite of everything that had happened or not happened. It was there and that was something.

Josie looked past the roses. The petunias that were left unplanted the night of the funeral now laced through the flower beds like long purple veins, and Josie wondered if her mother had instructed the gardener on where to plant the flowers before she died. Her mother had not liked the actual planting, but her eye for landscape was striking. She had designed the stone path and overhang of climbing wisteria, arranged the cherry trees so their blossoms fell and floated on the mossy koi pond, encircled the house with night-blooming jasmine and honeysuckle so, in the spring, every room of the house was flooded with their sweet smell.

Josie looked at the garden sprawling beneath her and suddenly wanted to be outside, in this space her mother had made. She tiptoed down the stairs, not wanting to disturb her father, and opened the sliding glass door in the kitchen. It was crisp, but the sun was shining, and she took off her sweater and felt heated both inside and out. She walked barefoot across the freshly cut grass until she reached a gardening shed at the edge of the property. She unlatched the double door and pushed it wide open. Inside was a large wooden counter. Above it ran rows of shelves, and beneath, six large drawers. Bags of soil rested against one wall, a lawn mower against another, and various garden tools hung from the ceiling. She walked to the counter and opened a large brown bag to reveal dozens of flower bulbs. Every year her mother would send for new and unusual flowers—blue Oriental poppies, black Easter lilies, orange two-budded gladiolas, lavender Zebra irises. They would arrive in the mail, and each year Josie would watch the dry brown bulbs go into the ground and wait with anticipation to see what would emerge.

Now, she took the bag and a small spade and walked to the flower beds at the front of the house. In between the petunias were clusters of white alyssum, but Josie knew that if she

lifted the tufts, she would find ample planting space. She knelt
on the grass edging, dug deep holes along the length of the bed,
and pushed a bulb into each. She dug and planted, creating
long rows of secreted flowers, until she was tired and dirty and
the bag was empty. She had not used gloves, and her hands
were filthy, but the dirt underneath her nails felt solid and real,
and she remembered something she had read about tribes in
South Africa: a family member often takes some of the earth
covering a grave, puts it in a bottle, and goes home, sure that
the deceased relative is coming home to look after the family.

Josie scooped up a handful of dirt, let it run back through
her fingers, then scooped again. Perhaps her mother was looking down on her, perhaps Devesh and Tyler were right. She
cradled the soil in her palm, then laid it down again. She patted
it softly. "Three days after death, hair and fingernails continue
to grow," Josie said, "but phone calls taper off." She smiled gently and sat back and looked at her work. Three months from now,
the shoots would appear, uncurling until each was a tall green
stalk, just grazing the vines that climbed the trellises against the
house. But before the bulbs would unfurl, the honeysuckle and
jasmine would bloom, and the air would be saturated with their
warm, sugary blossoms. Josie loved that smell. When she was
young, she would creep carefully through the flowers until she
could conceal herself in the tangled bushes that lined the house.
Once there, she would twirl the small white flowers under her
nose until she had breathed in all the scent. She had forgotten
about that. Somewhere among those bushes, she remembered,
there was a hollow of some kind, a hideout.

Now, she stood, wiped her hands on the back of her jeans,
and walked the perimeter of the house until she found it. It

was at the back, barely noticeable behind her roses. The bushes formed a barricade, but near the gas meter was a tiny path just wide enough for the gas man to sidestep along. Josie followed it several feet and sat down on the cool metal of the meter. In front of her, the bushes formed a deep green wall, and below, their thin trunks jutted from the ground like tridents. The space was small, but she could see how a child could manage to squeeze herself from the meter to the ground and then slide carefully under the bushes.

Now, she shifted slowly down herself. The spiky leaves of the jasmine pricked her arms, and she jerked up automatically and then laughed. Of course. That's why she had loved this place. She could be pricked and scratched to her heart's content. She could lie on her back, wrap her hands around the gas pipe, push against the thorny canopy, and daydream of orders and spankings. Josie grinned at her own ingenuity. If Devesh were here, she would beg him to cut a branch. They could play for days.

She smiled. They could play. Play.

She heard the word tinkle in her head like a thousand tiny bells. This thing they created, this dark and tender thing. It was punishment. It was ritual. But maybe it was more than that. Maybe, in some small way, it was a way to atone, and maybe this was okay, and maybe, just maybe, it was also play. The air seemed sucked from her lungs and she clutched at her chest. She could feel her heart pulled from her rib cage, and it was more painful than any beating. Oh, God, she missed him. She had never wanted anything so badly. And all their play. It was vaster than she ever thought. It was also adoration.

"Devesh," she said. His name was luminous in her mouth, and she said it over and over like a mantra.

CHAPTER TWENTY-ONE

She had thought she would be able to book a ticket online and leave two days later, but there were medicines to sort out—malaria pills and a tetanus booster—and her visa had taken two weeks to get, but with every passing day, she grew more and more sure. And her father was surprisingly supportive. "If you love him, Josie," he said, "you should go. Your mother would want you to go." She wasn't sure about this, but she allowed him this satisfaction. Her mother wouldn't have wanted her to go, but she would have known Josie would do it anyway, and this was somehow comforting. Her mother *did* know her, and the realization, for the first time, felt warm and gentle inside her.

And she felt inflated with love for Devesh, ravenous for even a piece of him—an inch of his skin, her name in his mouth. She had never felt so desperate, and yet in that desperation lurked a penetrating calm. She ached for him, but there was something staggering about the certainty of her want. It was pure and strong and good and unafraid, and she held it in her heart like a totem and knew she would need to show him.

When she landed in Chennai, there were endless lines, blurs of women cloaked in bright pink, green, and orange saris;

dark men handing over stacks of passports and worn luggage; wide-eyed children draped along the floor in tired piles. The place swirled and churned, and she felt bombarded by her senses. Bodies grazed and pushed and jostled, and the air—it seemed a living thing, surging into her like a live current. She felt as if she were wading through warm molasses, each step an achievement in itself.

She made her way through the arrival terminal, managed customs and immigration, found her luggage, but when she exited the airport, she felt the crush of this new world and desperately wished she had a guide to deliver her safely to her hotel. She knew the hotel address, and on the map it was only an inch from the airport, but now the airport seemed a continent, and all she wanted was to have Devesh rescue her. She could call him, tell him she was here, and to please come get her, but she did not want to come to him fragile and helpless.

At the curb was a line of motley-looking cabs. Young, mustached men rested on open doors, sat on hoods, and slept in driver's seats. She took a few tentative steps in their direction and was bombarded with cries of "Madam, Madam!" She chose a tall man in a formal white shirt. He lifted her suitcase into the trunk, and she slid into the backseat.

On the dash was a brightly colored statue of Lakshmi, two hands holding lotus flowers, the other two broken at the wrists.

"Where to, Madam?" he asked.

She had found and booked the hotel online, and she handed him a slip of paper with the name and address.

"Hotel Dakshin is not so nice," he said. "I'll take you to a much nicer place, closer to the water. Very nice."

"No. It's okay."

"Very nice, Madam. I take you there."

"No," she said. She could feel the threat of tears, and she clenched her teeth.

He shrugged.

"How much?" she said.

"Five hundred rupees."

She was too tired to barter, so she nodded and tried to focus on why she had come. If she thought of the trip as a trial, a test of sorts, perhaps she could be brave, stay calm. The driver pulled away from the curb and Josie looked out the window. They had driven for about twenty minutes when the lush green surrounding the airport began to change. In the taxi's head-lights, she could make out the mass of electrical lines that twisted and kinked throughout the towering palm trees. There were brightly colored billboards advertising movie starlets and laundry soap and fruit sodas, and Josie held her face close to the open window and tried to read the words as they sped by, but the road was narrow, and when the few trucks and cars that passed came frighteningly close to the taxi, the outside heat and exhaust and dust rushed in through the open window and into her nose and mouth. She could taste the place. It was tangible and animate, and she realized that the only other time she felt so absolutely cradled in space was when Devesh and she played. Then, too, she could literally feel the air press her temples, invade her lungs, squeeze her belly. She felt simultaneously compressed and expanded, and she was filled with something bright and hot and restless.

She opened her mouth and let the air rush deep within her. Before, India had been something foreign and faraway, one corner of Devesh she chose to peek at with a kind of curious apprehension, but now she wondered how she had ever thought she knew him. She had kept herself from him, but she had also kept him from her. The thought made her heart hurt. He would be right in not loving her. She had made a mess of them, and what was the point of hanging on to something this tangled and knotted? Perhaps he had let her go the last time they spoke, or, worse yet, perhaps he was seeing someone else. Her chest ached, and she leaned back against the seat and stared at the statue of Lakshmi until they reached the hotel.

When they arrived, she could smell the ocean before she could see it, and she was surprised at how, if she closed her eyes, she could think herself in Santa Barbara. She exited the cab and looked at the hotel. It was a sand-colored six-story building with rusty metal balconies and wide picture windows, and she craned her head and tried to see the beach beyond it.

"This way," the driver said. She followed him inside, and he handed her bags to a bellhop in full uniform.

"Madam," the driver said again.

"Oh, right." She paid him and walked slowly through the lobby. Everything seemed thick and dark, heavy wood furniture with maroon velvet upholstery, sprawling carpets in deep reds and blues and browns.

She made her way to the massive front desk. The man behind the counter wore a navy suit and striped tie.

"Good evening," he said.

"Hi," she said. "I'm checking in."

"Of course." He handed her some papers to sign and gave the bellboy the key.

"Have a pleasant stay," he said, "and if there's anything we can do it make your time with us more enjoyable, please don't hesitate to ask."

"Thank you." She almost laughed at the thought of this buttoned-up man trying to pleasantly mediate her impending reunion, but she bit her tongue and followed the bellhop to her room on the fifth floor. He unlocked the door, set the bag down on the luggage stand, and went to close the curtains.

"No," she said. "It's okay; you can leave them open." The moon was full, and from where she stood, she could see it glint silver across the ocean. Moon, she thought; moon. She walked to the window and opened the sliding door.

"No, no," the bellhop said.

She turned to look at him.

"Mosquitoes are bad at night."

"Oh," she said and closed the door, "right." She had read about this. Malaria was usually transmitted between dusk and dawn, but right now she could think of nothing worth more than standing above all that silver. It seemed to go on forever, and if she tilted her head upward, she could block out the strip of sand and clusters of palms and see only the moon mirrored double in the ocean.

"Anything else, Madam?"

"Oh . . . um." She dug in her pocket and handed him a fifty rupee bill, and he thanked her and left.

The clock beside the bed said four forty-five. She felt dirty with exhaustion, but she doubted she could sleep, so she stripped off her clothes and turned on the shower. Devesh had told her about Indian bathrooms—their buckets and hoses and whatnot—and she was glad that, at least for tonight, she did not have to figure out a whole new way to bathe. She was weary and dazed, and she made the water as hot as she could stand it and let it pound her skull and bead down her body until she felt clean.

She toweled herself off and dressed in fresh clothes. She knew she wouldn't be able to fall asleep, so she sat in a low armchair and looked out the window. It was beautiful, and she wished Devesh could see it before daylight, but the sun was beginning to shine a soft orange on the horizon.

She wasn't sure what she would do or say when she saw him. Perhaps he wouldn't press her for an explanation, would just let her exist, stand solely in that moment, independent of what had gone before. He had once asked her what it was about Westerners that they couldn't allow things to just be. There's not a reason for everything, he had said, some things just are, but she had not believed him. Actions produced reactions, but now the idea that everything had a reason seemed laughable. Some things had reasons, and some things just were. Some things controlled you, and some you could control. But most were an amalgamation, lacing inside you like a lattice, snaking and spiraling and weaving within each other until it was impossible to tell one from the other. This was who she was. This was what she had come here to tell him. This was what she would wrap her heart in and offer like a prayer.

At 9 A.M. sharp, she picked up the phone. Her palms were damp, and her breath shallow, and after she dialed the number, she had to hold the receiver with both hands to keep it steady. She had opened the sliding glass door, and she tried to focus on the sound of the ocean and the noisy gang of crows in the surrounding trees rather than the awful shrill ring of the phone.

"Hello," he said.

She had not heard his voice in a long time, and now he sounded so solidly Indian, she wasn't sure it was him.

"May I speak to Devesh, please?"

There was a long silence, and she could hear the Hindi radio whining love songs in the background.

"Josie?" he asked.

"Hi," she said.

"Hi." He was obviously surprised, and she tried to judge if it was the pleasant kind.

"How are you?" she asked. She hadn't practiced or even thought about what she would say on the phone, and she closed her eyes and tried to focus.

"I'm . . . I'm fine; well," he stammered.

She was silent, and she knew she needed to say something, but her tongue seemed glued to her teeth. The crows squawked louder, drivers leaned incessantly on their horns, and she wished they could all be quiet, just for a minute.

"It's very loud. Where are you?" he finally asked.

She hadn't realized she had been holding her breath, but it came out in a long exhale, and she felt her heart settle into place. "Here," she said. "India."

When the waiter sat her at a tiny table at the edge of the sand, she felt confined and restless, and she stepped over the low iron railing and onto the beach. She had fifteen minutes before he arrived, and she slipped her sandals off and walked toward the water. There was only a hint of waves in the translucent blue ocean, and she knew that even with the sand, warm and comforting under her feet, she was in a place both unfamiliar and uncertain. She sat down and ran her fingers through the sand. There were a few small fishing boats close to shore; in one, she could see two young boys throw their net into the ocean and then dive after it. She watched them go under then resurface, their dark heads sparkling in the sunlight. On shore, two barefoot girls called to them and laughed. The boys shouted back and the girls erupted in giggles. Josie watched the boys drape their arms casually over the boat's side, watched them rise up and down with the swell of the sea. It was hypnotic. She closed her eyes, put her head down, and felt a hand on her shoulder.

He touched her gently, and she barely felt it before she was looking up. His hair was longer and shone more than she remembered, and he wore a bright white shirt she had never seen. He was brilliant to look at, silhouetted against the vast sky, and she had to look down. She pressed her head gently against his legs, and he sank beside her and raked his fingers softly through her hair.

"Decided to drop by, did you?" he asked.

She laughed and tilted her head to look at him. He stroked her, and she was overwhelmingly grateful. He smiled softly and ran his thumb along her cheek. She knew she would tell him she loved him, knew she would tell him she understood that how or why they had arrived here didn't matter, that the cause only flickered in the background like an ember, and that what was important was that they were here together. She would say all this and more. But now she let the sun warm her face, let his fingers graze her skin, let the sound of the children laughing in the background tinkle over the ocean like tiny bells.

ACKNOWLEDGMENTS

For friendship, information, guidance, support, and inspiration, my thanks to: Deborah Abrams, Allan Abrams, Glenn Abrams, Tate Abrams, Christy Fletcher, Elisabeth Schmitz, Daisy Fried, Tara Gorvine, Rachel Maize, Maura Finkelstein, Maria Hummel, Melissa Chinchillo, Holly Miller, Daniel Mason, Dr. Anisha Abraham, Dr. Andrea Marmor, Dr. William Schecter, Dr. Martin Goodman, Daniel Blatt, Marc Gerald, Danny Cook, and Debra Sequeira. And to Vikram for his steadfast belief in me and this book, for his countless readings and rereadings, for his unwavering advice to "write the book you need to write," and for much much more.